No One in the World

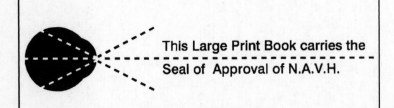

This Large Print Book carries the
Seal of Approval of N.A.V.H.

No One in the World

E. Lynn Harris and RM Johnson

THORNDIKE PRESS
A part of Gale, Cengage Learning

GALE
CENGAGE Learning™

Detroit • New York • San Francisco • New Haven, Conn • Waterville, Maine • London

GALE
CENGAGE Learning

Copyright © 2011 by The Estate of E. Lynn Harris and Marcus Arts LLC.
Thorndike Press, a part of Gale, Cengage Learning.

Thorndike Press® Large Print African-American.
The text of this Large Print edition is unabridged.
Other aspects of the book may vary from the original edition.
Set in 16 pt. Plantin.

LIBRARY OF CONGRESS CATALOGING-IN-PUBLICATION DATA

Harris, E. Lynn.
   No one in the world / by E. Lynn Harris, R.M. Johnson. —
Large print ed.
      p. cm. — (Thorndike Press large print african-american)
   ISBN-13: 978-1-4104-3770-9
   ISBN-10: 1-4104-3770-1
   1. African Americans—Fiction. 2. Twin brothers—Fiction. 3.
Large type books. I. Johnson, R. M. (Rodney Marcus) II. Title.
PS3560.O3834N6 2011b
813'.54—dc22
                                          2011015295

Published in 2011 by arrangement with Simon & Schuster, Inc.

Printed in the United States of America
1 2 3 4 5 6 7 15 14 13 12 11

RM JOHNSON
REMEMBERS E. LYNN HARRIS

I met E. Lynn Harris in 1998 at a book event. He wasn't the self-important man I assumed a brilliant, nationally bestselling author to be. He was humble, personable and funny and even offered to help me spread the word about my then soon-to-be released first novel, *The Harris Men*.

He fulfilled his promise. The book was a success, and I credit my longevity in this field to his help.

He was a great man. I loved him as a brother and looked up to him as a mentor, and he graciously considered me his mentee. We appeared at several book signings together around the country. He allowed me to benefit from his successful name through association, but I wasn't the only one. E. Lynn Harris helped dozens of up-and-coming authors by sponsoring their tours, inviting them to appear at his signings, or promoting their books as his favorite

5

reads. He was that kind of man, just as concerned about others' success as his own.

Lynn would often say, "We just need people to find out about you." So in 2004 he mentioned the idea of the two of us writing a novel about twin brothers. We played with that idea over the years, often meeting to take notes or discuss plot, but never completing any serious work until early 2008. Both of us living in Atlanta, Georgia, we met often, coming up with some really great characters, story lines and plot twists. We worked well together, as I knew we would, and created what I believe is a fantastic book, which reads both like a classic, drama-filled E. Lynn Harris novel and a suspenseful, fast-paced RM Johnson story. We were both so proud of what we created.

He always said how excited he was about going on the road and promoting our book together. Unfortunately, as we all know, our dear friend passed July 23, 2009.

There will never be another writer like him, another individual like him. He graced us with his talents, inspired many of the authors writing today and left us with his ingenious body of work. The book you're about to read was very dear to him. It was something we both thoroughly enjoyed writing and eagerly awaited to present to you all.

I would like to thank all those responsible in one way or another, for bringing this project to its deserved end. Many thanks go to Kerri Kolen, our tireless editor, and Andrew Stuart, my devoted literary agent. To Mrs. Etta Harris, E. Lynn's mother, thank you for bringing such a wonderful person into this world, and into our lives. He has touched so many of us, and we will never be the same. To all of E. Lynn's fans and to my own, to all the bookstore owners and operators, the publishing people and media people, the book club members and manuscript readers and, most of all, to our loving friends and family members, we could not have come this far without you all.

1

My opposing counsel was defending a sixteen-year-old boy accused of a double murder. My name is Cobi Aiden Winslow, and as I stood to give my closing argument, I told myself I would try to put this clown away for life.

"If it pleases the court, Your Honor," I said to the bearded, black-robed judge. "And the jury . . ." I said, nodding slightly to the haggard-looking twelve men and women who had sat through six days of testimony.

Before starting, I walked over to the boy being charged, stared him in the eyes till he looked away shamefully. DeAndré Marquis Moore was his name.

The police had found him a month ago, hiding in his girlfriend's garage. He had been gangbanging since he was eleven years old and had been picked up several times for truancy and an assortment of other misdemeanors, but nothing ever as serious as this.

The crime had happened on a beautiful Saturday evening. A thirty-two-year-old father and his seven-year-old son were walking down Jeffery Boulevard, when someone wearing a hooded jacket ran up behind them. The assailant pointed a gun at the back of the father's head and pulled the trigger, killing him in front of his son. He then turned the gun on the startled child and shot him twice, killing him as well.

There were eyewitnesses. Four separate individuals identified DeAndré in a lineup as the gunman.

DeAndré Moore's attorney was one of the best in Chicago, a man named Milton Crawford. He was a handsome white-haired gentleman who had once told me he was practicing law when I was still just a dirty thought in my father's head. I wasn't sure of his age, but he looked to be well into his sixties. Since I was thirty-three, Mr. Crawford was probably right.

His firm did pro bono work for the community, often defending violent cases involving the poor and disenfranchised like this one. Most of those cases were losers, but they kept the firm's name in the news and its phones ringing.

Milton Crawford argued that his client had acted in self-defense. Crawford stated that DeAndré had been deprived, destined to fail since birth. His father was absent, his mother a prostitute. DeAndré had cared for himself since he was seven years old, had no guidance, no love, no discipline. He was raised by the streets, taken in by a gang, and treated as a mascot till he became of age. At which point he had to commit a murder to become a member.

During Mr. Crawford's closing argument, he leaned on the jury box's railing. "He was told by one of the gang leaders, and I quote, 'If you don't do a killing, then we're going to do a killing on you.' My client was only trying to preserve his life by taking another," Mr. Crawford said.

It was the most ridiculous defense I had heard. All it did was make me angrier and more motivated to put this boy away.

It was my turn now, and as I stood over DeAndré, I shook my head in disgust before walking back toward the jury.

"Kevin Jones and Brandon Jones," I said. "Those are the names of the father and son that the defendant murdered in cold blood. Kevin has a wife, and two more children — little girls — at home. Kevin and Brandon have been forever taken from their family,

11

from this world by —" I shot a finger at De-André "— by him!" I paused to calm myself. "Who or what gave him the right? His circumstances? Yes, he was raised in the streets. He had no father. His mother gave him no attention. He had to fend for himself. But do those facts justify murder?" I paced away from the jury. "Do you know how many children grow up the same way? Does it give them the right to take lives? Does it give them the right to act outside the law? It does not. DeAndré was given life, and with that life he could've done whatever he wanted, despite his circumstances. I cannot and will not suffer fools who let the hand they've been dealt determine what they will do, and who they will be, and neither should you. DeAndré Moore was given a life, yet he chose to take two others. For that he must be punished," I said, walking back to the jury box. I took a moment to look each of the jurors in the eye one by one. "For DeAndré Moore, there is no other verdict but guilty."

2

Not long after lunch, the jury reached a decision. DeAndré Moore was found guilty. He was charged as an adult and sentenced to twenty-five years in a maximum-security prison.

As I drove my Audi S6 home, tension from the day still coursing through my body, I thought about how if it were up to me, I would've put him away for life.

I pulled into the circular drive of the historic brick mansion I lived in with my parents. Work had been hard, but considering what was going on here, I knew that today home would be harder.

Once inside, I went to my mother's bedroom to check on her. I stood outside her door and knocked gently. I didn't want to walk in on her if she was crying again.

"Cobi, is that you? C'mon in."

My mother was standing next to her bed in front of an open, half-packed suitcase, holding a lavender blouse up to her chest. "Do I need this?" She smiled, although her eyes were red, like she had been crying not long ago.

"Mother," I said, taking the garment, folding it, and laying it on top of the other neatly folded clothes. "Just take it. You never know."

"Was work good today?"

"It was work, like every day. These things that people do . . ." I lamented. "And some of them are practically children. I put a sixteen-year-old animal away today for twenty-five years."

"Don't call them that, Cobi. You don't know what they've been through. Some of them have no fathers. They grew up in foster homes," my mother said.

"It doesn't matter. It's —"

"Not everyone had it as nice as you growing up. What if that was you out there? What if you were forced to . . ." My mother reached for her box of Kleenex, snatched two, and pressed them to her nose. "You were lucky," she said, tears rolling from her eyes, her voice trailing off. "There was a chance . . ." my mother started to say but abruptly stopped herself.

"What was that you said, Ma?"

"Nothing, Cobi." She walked away from

me, blowing her nose into the tissue.

Last week, my mother received a call from Alabama. It was from Uncle Carl, my mother's brother in-law. She told me his voice was solemn as he regrettably told her that her sister, Rochelle, had died in her sleep. My mother told me she held the phone to her ear, staring into the space before her, gasping for words that wouldn't come.

"She went peacefully," my mother said Carl had said.

I loved Aunt Rochelle. She looked just like my mother. They shared the same cornflake-colored complexion, the same sandy brown hair, the same bright smile. The only difference was that Aunt Rochelle was shorter and funnier. When I was a child, whenever she saw me, she would tell a new joke. If I didn't think it was funny, she'd tickle me till I was in tears with laughter.

But I had not seen nor spoken to Aunt Rochelle in five years. She and my mother had fallen out. My mother had never told me why, and whenever I asked, she would simply say, "It's nothing you need to concern yourself with."

The funeral was to be held tomorrow. My parents intended to fly to Alabama sooner, spend time mourning with the family, but the business demanded that they stay for a meeting held earlier today.

There was trouble with the family business. Profits were down, our competition was gaining, and the future of the company's value was uncertain. Cyrus, my father, had even mentioned the idea of selling. The situation had to have been terribly bad for him to think of such a thing.

Our company, Winslow Products was started by my grandfather, in a single-boarder room he rented back in 1959. Through hard work, dedication, and anticipating the needs of Chicago's African American population, Charles Winslow grew Winslow Products into the most successful and recognized black hair care line in the country. I knew it would've killed my father to sell it.

I lowered the top of the suitcase and zipped it. "That's everything, right?"

My mother pulled another Kleenex from the box and pressed it to her nose, her back to me.

She was starting to cry again. I took a step toward her. She held out a hand, instructing me not to come any closer.

There was something gravely wrong, something my mother was not telling me. I knew she was mourning the loss of her sister, but this seemed like something more.

I stood three feet behind her, looking at our reflections in the mirror. I was tall, six foot, with an athletic build I maintained by going to the gym at least four times a week. My skin was not the color of cornflakes like my mother's and Aunt Rochelle's, but darker, like raisin bran flakes. My facial features were keen, my teeth straight, my nose broad, my eyes jet black beneath thick eyebrows, and my hair buzzed low, razor lined, where just a shadow could be seen.

Other than our difference in skin tone, I looked a great deal like my mother, a miracle, considering I had been adopted when I was three years old.

"Mother . . ." I said, my voice low.

She didn't answer. She pulled away the tissue, and I could see tears in her eyes again.

"Ma." I felt horrible. All I wanted to do was give her a hug, beg her to please tell me what else was wrong, because I knew it was something. My mother could never keep anything from me. It was she who, against my father's wishes, sat me down when I was eight years old and told me I was adopted.

My father was a quiet man — a man of few words. But when he spoke, everyone listened. He showed very little emotion. I don't remember a single time when he hugged me. He had told me he loved me before, but I could never feel the emotion in his confession. It always just sounded like something he thought he should say.

To tell the truth, I wouldn't have been surprised if my father didn't love me at all. We had a few issues, like any father and son. But I was sure, one day, we were going to work them out. I had actually told myself that when my parents returned home from Aunt Rochelle's funeral, I was going to sit Cyrus down, whether the man liked it or not, and have a good father-and-son talk with him.

Now my mother finally turned to me. "Sit," she said. "Your Aunt Rochelle — five years ago, we argued over some money. It was a thousand dollars or something. She said she gave it back to me. I said she didn't. This family is rich . . ." My mother chuckled sadly. "But I haven't spoken to my sister in all that time for a lousy thousand dollars. It was the principle of the matter, I kept telling myself. But now she's dead and . . ." My mother tightened her grip on my hands and wept loudly.

"Ma, don't —"

"I loved her. Your aunt . . . she was so wonderful."

"I know, and I know you loved her," I said, hugging my mother, feeling as though I was about to start crying myself. "She knows you did."

"But she's gone."

"She's with God, Ma. She's in a better place."

"I haven't spoken to her in years. I didn't say good-bye. And now she's gone," my mother said, pulling away from my embrace. "I don't want the same thing to happen to you."

I leaned away from her. "What are you talking about?"

She pulled more Kleenex from the box on the nightstand, dried her face, and looked deeply into my eyes. "Your father didn't think you should ever know this, but I don't want you to go through life without ever . . . without . . ."

"Mother, what are you talking about?"

"I begged your father. It wasn't right to separate you. I wanted to take you both."

"Mother, please. What are you saying to me?"

"Forgive me, Cobi, for what we've done," my mother said, smearing tears from her eyes with the tissue. "But when we adopted you, there was someone else. Cobi . . . you have a twin brother."

3

I marched down the long halls of my parents' mansion, my heels clicking loudly against the black-and-white tiles, the sound echoing up to the high ceilings.

My mother told me not to bring this to my father. "This is between us," my mother said, trying to hold me in her room. "He never wanted you to know."

In front of the door to his study, I raised my fist and prepared to knock but grabbed the knob instead and pushed through the door unannounced.

My father, the great Cyrus Winslow, president and CEO of Winslow Products, looked up from his computer monitor. His reading glasses sat low on his nose.

"Why didn't you knock?"

My father was a big man with broad shoulders. His skin was the color of peanut butter. His dark, wavy hair receded from his lined forehead. His face was clean shaven, and although very distinguished looking, he appeared much younger than his seventy years.

"Mother told me," I said, infuriated.

"Told you what?"

"About my brother. I have a twin brother and you never told me!"

"Don't you raise your voice in my house," my father said, taking off his glasses, tossing them aside on his desk.

"I'll do whatever the hell I want," I said, no longer caring if he chose not to speak to me for days because he disapproved of me, like he had so many times in the past. "You kept this from me. Why would you do that?" I was on the verge of tears.

My father stood, all six foot three inches of him. He walked around the big oak desk. "Sit down."

"I don't want to sit."

The room was mostly dark, except for the lamp burning dimly on his desk. The ceilings were high. The hardwood floor was covered with an expensive Persian rug. The room smelled of the old leather-bound books stacked on the shelves lining his office walls. I stood before him, my arms crossed over my chest.

"Your mother and I had already adopted your sister," my father said, leaning on the edge of his antique desk. "We wanted a little boy. We chose you."

"But there were two of us."

"Like I said, we chose you."

"Why not both of us?" I said, my voice high pitched. "Or neither?"

My father scoffed. "Is that what you really would've wanted? Do you know how most people live? Do you know what's out there? We've given you everything. A top-tier education, the freedom to pursue a career as an attorney. You have a twenty-million-dollar trust, and you're about to receive shares of this company on your next birthday, and you question me? Do you know the kind of life you would be living right now if we hadn't adopted you? You could've been the scum you're putting behind bars every day."

"I've worked hard to get to where I am today, to achieve what I have. It wasn't just about what you provided me."

"If that's what you want to tell yourself, son." My father walked back around his desk. "Leave my study and come back when you're able to discuss this sensibly."

"If you couldn't take both of us, why didn't you just leave me there, too? I know it's what you wish you could've done."

"We are not going to talk about that,

Cobi," my father said.

A tear ran down my face as I thought about that spring afternoon, back in high school when my father discovered me and a very handsome football player from school with the body of a junior Olympic athlete, kissing and petting in the darkness of the garage behind my house.

I had been one of the most popular boys in my school at the time. I did my best every day to play the role. But like every teen, I had a secret. Liking boys was mine, and although I constantly tried to deny myself, the urge was always too strong.

In the middle of our kissing and necking, the garage door was abruptly thrown open, sunlight invading the dank space. The silhouette of my father darkened the doorway. He stared at us with our shirts off, our pants halfway down our thighs for what seemed like forever. Then he simply turned and walked away.

The talk did not happen till a day later. The conversation lasted for only ten minutes, but there was a single message — my father would not tolerate a gay son. I was told never to let him see evidence of that abomination again.

I yelled, cried, screamed that I could not help who I was, that I should not have to

23

hide myself, not from my own family. My father stared at me like I was a freak, reminded me of the warning, and then ended the conversation. He never brought it up again.

"After that day, you stopped loving me," I said.

"That's not true!"

"You were ashamed of me. Still are. I'm the secret that would've killed your precious business."

"You're the one who wanted to pursue law. You didn't want to enter the business," my father said.

"Because I knew you saw me differently. You didn't trust me anymore."

My father lowered himself into his chair, exhausted. He looked every bit of his seventy years now. "Son, I'm sorry that you feel this way, that you feel I treated you badly. I may have my ways, but know that I love you. I do love you."

I looked hard at him, examining every line in his face, searching for the truth. All I could see was the same man I had seen for most of my life. The man I always felt cared little for me. Another tear fell. I angrily wiped it away and then said, "Well, I don't believe you when you say that, Dad. And to tell you truth, I never have. If you want, I'll drive you and mother to the airport. But when you come back, I'll be gone. This way you'll never have to see your abomination of a son again."

4

I had to get out of the house if only for a little while before it was time to take my parents to the airport. I made a phone call, drove downtown, then pulled along the curb of the state building and waited with my hazards blinking.

It was spring, my favorite season in Chicago, and the May evening was a warm one.

My sunroof was open, the windows down as a slow Mary J. Blige song played softly while I stared down at my hands.

My passenger door opened and shut. When I looked up, I saw Tyler Hayden Stevens sitting in the car beside me. An Illinois state senator, he was six foot one, 205 pounds, and his skin was the color of beach-baked sand. His jawline was strong, and although many men thought they were out of style, Tyler wore a thick, perfectly shaped mustache. He looked like a black Tom Selleck in his prime or a young Stedman Graham. He showed a smile of straight white teeth, but when he saw the sadness on my face, the smile disappeared. "Baby, what's wrong?"

"Stuff with my father again."

Tyler looked out the back window for oncoming cars. "Let's get out of this traffic and go somewhere we can talk about it."

We finished talking in the dark parking structure under the state building.

"So you have a twin brother. That's great news," Tyler said. "What are you going to do?"

"I don't know."

"You going to look for him?"

"I need to find him," I said, turning away from Tyler, an angry frown on my face.

"Are you okay?"

"I haven't had an open relationship since I've come back from school to live there, all because I know what my father would say, how he would look at me. Over five years of sneaking around. I'm tired of clandestine meetings."

"Then why stay?"

"I told him I was moving out, but it's my home. I love seeing my mother every day, and even though he has his ways, I like the fact that he's there, too. You know what family means to me. But if I did get my own place, would that change things between us? Would we come out, announce to all our friends and the world that we're seeing each other?"

"That's nobody's business."

"Then would you move in with me?"

Tyler looked uncomfortable when he said, "You know I'm not in the position to make that happen. Not now."

"Yeah, I know," I said, disappointed. "So I'll stay at home in the meantime and work things out with my father. We fixed things before. We'll fix them again."

5

An hour later, I stood at the front door hugging my mother as my father waited in the back of the large Mercedes S600, the uniformed driver standing by the passenger side, holding open the back door. My father had decided he didn't want me taking them to the airport after all.

"We'll straighten all this out when we return, all right," my mother said, holding my cheeks in her hands.

I hugged her once more, wishing I could go with her but knowing my trial schedule wouldn't allow it.

When the driver opened the door, I caught a glimpse of my father. I looked at him with an expression on my face pleading for us to talk further. He looked away.

At 1:24 a.m. I woke up, startled out of my sleep by a ringing phone. I rolled over in bed, clumsily answering the call.

My eyes were barely open, my voice was groggy. "Hello."

It was my sister. She was crying, hysterically. I could barely understand her through her tears when she gave me the news.

At 5:13 a.m. I stood, my arm tightly around Sissy's shoulder, the two of us waiting in the emergency room of the Indiana hospital where survivors of the Delta 767 plane crash had been taken.

One hundred sixty passengers were already confirmed dead, but Sissy and I had not yet heard whether our parents were among those listed.

Sissy told me she had worked late, like she always did, over at Winslow Products headquarters in downtown Chicago.

She said she didn't walk in the door of her house till almost eleven. After having a drink and winding down, she sat on the living room sofa and clicked on CNN. The news of our parents' plane going down on an Indiana farm not long after takeoff was all over the news. She phoned me moments later.

Now Sissy and I stood in the emergency room, waiting for a close friend of our family, Roger Welkin, to walk back through the door.

He was a police detective, knew important people working for the National Transportation Safety Bureau, and could find out whether our parents had survived the crash.

When I saw Mr. Welkin enter the room, I could not read the man's blank face. But when he approached Sissy and me and politely asked if we would follow him to the back of the room, where we could sit and talk, I knew.

The funeral was held one week later at Trinity United Church of Christ, on the South Side of Chicago. It was the same church President Obama and his family had attended when they lived here.

Scores of cars moved slowly into the parking lots around the church, while countless stretch limos with darkened glass sidled up to the curbs, letting out Chicago celebrities and VIPs.

To say the event was well attended was an understatement. Because my father had such high standing in the community, everyone from Kanye West and Jesse Jackson, to Al Sharpton and former mayor Daley attended, as well as members of the Johnson family, publishers of *Ebony* and *Jet*.

As everyone entered, they gave me looks of sympathy, shook my hand, and hugged me and my sister.

I watched the sea of people coming to mourn my parents and was happy when I saw Tyler. He walked over to me, shook my hand, leaned in to me, and whispered, "You're going to get through this. I'm here for you."

Because my parents' remains were never found, there were no coffins or urns, only two large portraits of my mother and father and a snapshot taken years ago that we had blown up. It was a picture of them at a hair care conference in Atlanta. They had never looked happier in their lives.

Sissy and I sat in the first pew, holding hands. I felt hers trembling in mine, heard her sobbing, though I knew she did everything in her power for me or anyone else not to notice. My father had raised her to be strong, to never show weakness, and although she made an earnest attempt, the grief was too much for her to bear.

The reverend, a bearded, distinguished-looking man who had known my father for thirty years, had been speaking for only a moment, but the words of love and loss must have cut deeply into my sister's soul. Helpless, she cried louder. She pressed her handkerchief harder against her face, but she could not muffle her pain.

Shaking her head, she turned to me with tear-flooded eyes and said, "I'm sorry. I can't." Sissy stood and hurried away. I reached out for her and considered following, but felt like I'd be abandoning my parents. I couldn't do that. So I sat there, feeling the tears crawling down my cheeks.

I had cursed my father, told him I had never believed he loved me, because he had kept me from my brother. He made me walk through this life by myself, when I had a twin all along. But the loneliness I had then was nothing compared to how alone I felt now that I had lost my mother and father.

6

Three days later, Sissy Winslow sat at her office desk, clutching the framed picture of her late mother and father.

She hated to think of where she would've been now if her parents had not adopted her. She had never made an attempt to find her biological mother or father, because the day they had given her up was the day they had stopped being her true parents. She owed the Winslows everything.

"One day you're going to take over this company," Cyrus had told her when she was just fourteen years old.

Yes, she was a straight-A student, read and studied because she thought it was fun, not because she had to. She considered Madam C. J. Walker, Congresswoman Maxine Waters, and Oprah Winfrey her role models, but she had always thought her older brother, Cobi, would take over the company when it was time.

It was only when her brother told her about what had happened in the garage that Sissy understood why her father chose to groom her to take over Winslow Products.

She hurt for Cobi but accepted the obligation of becoming future CEO with an excitement she never before had felt.

Sissy was often found at her father's side while he worked in his study, absorbing all that he taught her. Many days after school, a driver would take her to the corporate office, where she spoke to employees and spent hours gathering a wealth of information.

Sissy had grown to love Winslow Products. Not just because it was what her father and grandfather devoted their lives to, but because of its high standing in the African American community and its charitable contributions to organizations such as the NAACP and the Sickle Cell Foundation as well as many historically black colleges and universities, such as Howard University, Spelman College, and Florida A&M, where Winslow Products recruited many of their outstanding employees.

Sissy was always honored to know that one day she would head this wonderful corporation. She just wished the time hadn't come so soon or under such life-shattering circumstances.

A knock came at her door.

"Come in," Sissy said, smearing tears from her cheeks and rolling her chair to face away from the door.

Sissy's secretary peeked in. "The board is assembled and ready for you, Ms. Winslow."

Sissy stood at the head of a long conference table, wearing a business suit that was perfectly tailored to her athletic body. It was the color of a ripe peach. She was an attractive woman with large, bright eyes, full lips, and a button nose. Her hair was sandy brown, straightened, and cut shoulder length.

She stood tall and looked around the table at the twelve board members, who were also shareholders of Winslow Products. They were older, distinguished-looking men and women, their hands folded before them, attentive looks on their faces.

This meeting was being held to discuss the dismal state of the company and to install Sissy as the new president and CEO of Winslow Products.

To offset his business's losses, Cyrus Winslow had sold off a great deal of the company's shares, making it vulnerable for other companies to buy a majority stake.

Procter & Gamble was who they were most worried about. P&G had bought Johnson Hair Care Products, Winslow's competition, in 2003, made a mess of it, then sold it in 2009 to some small investors.

"We're concerned. We don't want that happening to us," Mr. Donaldson, the senior board member said. He was a thin man in his sixties with a short Afro of gray hair.

"Winslow Corporation was started by my grandfather and continued by my father," Sissy said. "They both loved this company, made it their life's work, and I vow to do the same. I will do everything in my power to avoid a takeover and to make Winslow stronger and more profitable than it's ever been."

At the meeting's end, when it was time for her to be formally installed as CEO, Mr. Donaldson stood and said, "We know it was your father's wishes for you to lead Winslow Products, but a vote was taken earlier, and we feel as though your appointment should be on an interim basis, which will be made permanent once you deliver us from this crisis."

Sissy stood frozen. She could not believe what she heard. "For over fifteen years my father planned on me heading this company.

Now you're saying there is a chance you will hire someone else? Who?"

"We have no one in mind," Mrs. Williams, a regal-looking woman with beautiful styled, short gray hair said. "But there are individuals we can consider."

"So you expect me to fail?" Sissy said, trying her best to suppress her anger.

"No, Ms. Winslow," Mrs. Williams said. "There is nothing further from the truth. But if we feel you aren't capable of doing what's required, we will do everything in our power to find someone who can. We believe that's what your father would've wanted, too."

7

Not a week after the funeral, Sissy and I sat in a small office with our family attorney, Mr. Rochester.

The slender, balding man pushed his glasses up on his nose as he continued to read from my father's will.

As our parents' only children, everything would be left to us. The mansion in Chicago, and the three homes in DC, New York, and California were now ours.

There was a trust fund of $20 million, plus valuable shares of company stock that I was to inherit on my thirty-fourth birthday, which was just forty days away. It was the same fund Sissy would inherit when she turned thirty-four in two years.

All this we had always known, but not until that moment was I informed of the single stipulation.

Mr. Rochester looked over his glasses at me, cleared his throat, and then continued reading. "In order for you to take possession of your inheritance, you, Cobi Aiden Winslow, must be lawfully married to a woman, by your thirty-fourth birthday, for a period of at least two years. On the date of your wedding, you will receive one hundred percent of your shares and twenty-five percent of your monetary inheritance. Another twenty-five percent will be given to you on your one-year anniversary, and the remainder will be given on the second-year anniversary."

I shot up from my chair.

Sissy grabbed my hand tight. "What is this? There must be some mistake," she said.

"I can't believe him," I said. "He could never accept me when he was alive, now he's trying to force me to be who he wants from the grave. Fine. If he wants to hold on to his money that badly, I don't need it. He can keep it."

"No, Cobi, Daddy wants you to have it, otherwise he wouldn't have left it in the will," Sissy said, still holding my hand. She turned to Mr. Rochester. "I'm sure there's some way around this."

"I'm afraid there isn't," Mr. Rochester said.

"Like I said, I don't care," I spat at Mr. Rochester. I walked out the door and paced down the hallway. I heard the door open and close. A moment later, Sissy was standing beside me.

My father adopted a son because he wanted someone to take over the family business when he stepped down. He told me as much, and I remember him always talking about it, what I needed to know for when that fateful day finally came. But the day in the garage came first, and all the grooming stopped then. Sissy then became the person who would succeed him. Funny thing is, she should've been the one from the beginning.

She was a whiz with numbers and had a mind like a supercomputer. She earned both an MBA and a law degree from the University of Chicago, where she graduated top of her class. She approached the most daunting situations with optimism and the tactical mind of a five-star general.

"We're going to get your trust, Cobi," Sissy said, taking me by the shoulders.

"Whatever you say. It's not like I earned it. If Dad didn't want me to —"

"Cobi, stop it! He wanted you to have it, so you're entitled."

"Okay. So what do we do now?"

"We think about whatever we have to do to get it. And I mean whatever. It's that important."

"No. It's not that important. I make enough money to —"

"This is not just about you, Cobi," Sissy said. She lowered her voice. "Do you want the company to stay in our family?"

"Of course, I do. It always has and it always will."

"What if we lose it? You know the company hasn't been doing very well. There have been other companies interested in the success we've had in the past, in the millions of people who buy our products."

"I know, but I thought we were getting that under control. We are getting —"

"We could lose it," Sissy said, narrowing her eyes at me, tightening her grip on my shoulders. "Do you hear me? If things aren't played perfectly, we could lose Winslow Products. So that money, it might not be a lifesaver for you, but those shares, Cobi, we have to get those shares, because they might play a major role in whether or not we keep Winslow Products. Do you understand?"

I looked sadly at my sister. "Yes, I understand."

8

The next day, during my lunch break, I sat in front of a desk at the True Home Adoption Agency. I was waiting on Ms. Aims, the large, well made-up woman with a beautiful smile. I had spoken to her moments ago, and she had gone to look up some information for me.

I told her I had come with the intention of finding my brother. I also felt compelled to tell her about the recent death of my parents and how much I missed them.

"That was your family?" Ms. Aims said. "The hair products people?"

"Yes."

"I'm so sorry for your loss. Your father was a great man."

"Thank you. I know," I said. "Do you think you'll be able to help me find my brother?"

"I truly hope so. Do you know his name?" Ms. Aims said, her eyes smiling sympathetically behind her stylish eyeglass frames.

"I don't. But I have this," I said, digging my adoption certificate out of my briefcase and presenting it to her.

She read it, looked up at me. "This was your name before it was changed?"

"Yes. Everette Reed." I felt strangely outside myself.

"Have you seen or spoken to your brother since you were separated?"

"I haven't."

"Okay," Ms. Aims said, standing from her desk. "All the information I should need is on this certificate. I'll be right back."

Ten minutes later, Ms. Aims returned with a manila folder. She sat down behind her desk with a smile and opened the file.

"Did you find something?" I asked, hopeful.

"Your brother's name is Eric, Eric Reed."

"Eric. Okay," I said softly, feeling a smile appear on my face. "Where is he?"

Ms. Aims chuckled. "I wish it were that simple, Mr. Winslow. But we don't keep track of the children after they leave us. So there's no way we would know where he is now."

"Can you at least tell me the name of the family that adopted him?"

"Legally, I wouldn't be able to release that

information to you if he had been adopted, but . . . he wasn't."

"What do you mean, he wasn't adopted? Where did he go?"

"If a child is not adopted by his or her tenth birthday here at True Home, they automatically go into the foster care system," Ms. Aims said, the smile no longer on her face.

"Foster care," I said, feeling badly, knowing that when I was Eric's age, complaining about my father never being home, my brother was living with strangers in foster care. "Can you please give me any information you have on the foster care system and the contact numbers of anyone who might have an idea of where my brother might be."

"Yes, of course, Mr. Winslow," Ms. Aims said.

After work, I stood in one of the foster care offices downtown, looking for answers regarding my brother.

"I'm sorry, sir, but we don't have that information to give you," a thin, overworked woman wearing a slightly wrinkled dress said.

"This is very important," I said, feeling as though I was on the verge of losing my patience. "You don't have it to give to me, or you *won't* give it to me?"

"We purge all records of individuals who have been out of our system for ten years. I'm sorry, sir."

I stood there staring at her, anger boiling in me. I calmed down enough to say, "Is there *any* information you can give me? Anything at all?"

"I'm sorry," the woman said, looking at me with concern, as if expecting me to go off, run around, and start flipping tables over. "All I can do is suggest you write the Social Security Administration, or go on-line, and maybe check the phone book for all the Eric Reeds you can find."

That evening, I came home and parked behind Sissy's BMW 750, which meant she was visiting. I had spent much of the day trying to get information about where my brother Eric might have been and wound up with nothing. Seeing my sister would make me feel better.

I walked in the front door of the eight-bedroom mansion I had lived in all my life (and now owned). It was built in 1912. The ceilings were twenty-four feet high, the walls were a warm, medium brown wood, and the floors were a beautiful deep cherry color.

Every room was decorated with expensive

leather and upholstered antique furniture, with ornate carvings. An iron chandelier hung high in the living room.

After I closed the door, I was met by Stella, our housekeeper of twenty-five years. She was a woman in her early sixties, with flawless skin and graying hair that she always brushed and pinned back. She was like a second mother to me.

"Evening, Mr. Winslow," Stella said, taking my briefcase as she always did. "How was your day?"

"Horrible. I hope yours was better."

"Despite our challenges, every day is a blessing, more beautiful than the last."

I looked at Stella a moment, hugged her, and kissed her on the cheek. "You've always had a way of putting things in perspective."

"Thank you."

"I just wished it worked this time," I said, walking toward the stairs. "Where is my sister?"

"I'll give you one guess."

"My father's study," I said, climbing the first stair of the long, curved stairway.

"Shall I bring your dinner up to you, or will you take it down here?" Stella asked.

"I'll come back for it. Thank you, Stella."

At the door to my father's study, I knocked.

"Come in," I heard my sister say.

I entered to find Sissy, with her back to me, watching the wall-mounted flat-screen that displayed financial news.

"The new president has taken office," I said, loosening my tie.

Sissy turned, her arms crossed over her chest. "Interim president," Sissy said, sounding offended.

"Don't worry," I said. "I'm sure it's just a matter of time. The position will be yours. They know it belongs to no one else."

"Thank you, but that is based solely on my performance in this situation. I spoke to one of our brokers again today, and Procter & Gamble has bought more of our shares."

"What?" I said. "Is there really a chance of them taking us over?"

Sissy said in her most calming voice, "Don't worry about it. I'm taking care of it. You know that."

Rattled, I walked over to the bar to pour myself a quick shot of Scotch. I lowered myself into one of the two leather chairs in front of my father's desk. I took a sip of my drink. "So exactly how are you taking care of it?"

"We need your shares to help ensure that no one can come in and take over Winslow."

"Doesn't the will say I have to get married? How are we —"

"We get you married."

"Yeah, right," I laughed.

Sissy's face was stone. "I'm not joking. There is no other way. You marry, or the shares will be given to me in two years on my thirty-fourth birthday. By then, it might be too late. Winslow Corporation might already belong to someone else. Is that what you want?"

"Of course not."

"Then you'll simply have to marry to save the company."

"Fine. What guy do you have in mind?" I said, trying to lighten the mood.

"This is serious, Cobi. I've been thinking about women high in Chicago society, and although I haven't approached any of them yet —"

"Sissy, I was joking," I said, standing. "This is my life, my future we're talking about. I'm not just going to give it up to —"

"To save Daddy's company? To save our way of life? Everything he worked so hard for over the years?" Sissy walked over, stood right in front of me. "If this company is taken from us, no, we probably won't go hungry, but do you really want that to happen? To lose Winslow the moment Daddy dies, when he and Granddaddy managed to keep it going for fifty years?" Sissy was two inches shorter than me, but with her heels on, she was staring me directly in the eyes.

"What has he ever done for me?" I said under my breath, still burning about him withholding the knowledge of my brother. "Other than condemn me for being gay."

"What did you say?" Sissy said, shock in her voice.

I didn't respond, just turned away from her.

"No!" Sissy said, stepping in front of me. "You know what he's done? He worked till his death, trying to maintain a company that provided for his wife and children. Children that he adopted, not because he had to, but because he wanted to. I'm sorry he didn't accept your way of life. And whether you believe it or not, he did love you and provide for you, as he did me. Now if that's not good enough for you, and you don't want to help me try to save this company, then tell me now, and I'll find another method."

Sissy had a point. I was being selfish, letting my anger potentially decide the future of the company. Would I feel as though I gained some form of retribution from my father by allowing us to lose it? Would it be worth my sister losing her job, as well as all the other Winslow employees? And what about all the great things the company did in our community? All that would just disappear because I was still angry with my deceased father.

"This is something I have to think about. Will you at least allow me time to do that?"

"Yes. But we're on a deadline, remember. You turn thirty-four in less than a month."

Feeling burdened, I downed the rest of my Scotch. "Is there anything else?"

"Actually, Cobi, there is."

"What is it?" I said, not liking the grave tone of my sister's voice.

"A young man visited me today. He said he was doing a college internship at the DA's office. Do you know a twenty-year-old by the name of Kendrick Dunstan Wilshire?"

I felt myself becoming lightheaded. I reached for something to hold on to, then answered, "Yes, I know who you're talking about." The moment he'd walked into my office at the beginning of his semester, I knew he was trouble.

He was handsome, tall, well built, had green eyes, and played college football. Immediately, I was attracted to him, but I was smart enough to leave that jailbait alone. There were already enough city and state officials in the news caught up in some kind of sexual scandal.

But Kendrick kept placing himself close to me whenever he could. He kept saying how much he envied me, how he wanted to have a law career just like mine.

One late evening, when we were in the office alone, Kendrick asked if I liked men. I told him no. He looked at me with those green eyes, ran a moist tongue over those pink lips, and seductively asked if I could possibly like him.

I reminded him that I said I didn't like men and told him our relationship was strictly mentor-mentee, and it would have to stay that way.

Obviously used to getting whatever he wanted, Kendrick lunged in and kissed me, full force on the lips. I pushed my palms into his chest, backing him off.

"Why did you do that?" Kendrick asked.

"Because I don't play with boys. And if I did, it wouldn't be with the ones that work under me," I said. "Now get your things. You're done for the day." The next day I got rid of him. "I never saw him again," I told Sissy.

"Well, he's threatening to go to whoever's willing to listen, including your boss, saying you harassed him for sex, and when he didn't give in, you terminated his internship."

I shook my head, feeling myself anger. "He's going to do that unless we do what? I know there's more to this than him just feeling wronged, because he wasn't."

"I know he wasn't, Cobi. He's asking for money."

"No. Hell no!" I said. "Let him tell the press, the AG, the mayor for all I care, but we aren't giving him a red cent. I've done nothing wrong."

"Cobi," Sissy said. "I'll handle this, okay? And no, I have no intention of paying this clown because he delivers an idle threat. At least until I hear all he has to say."

"This is my reputation, Sissy. Once one mofo takes advantage of me, the floodgates open, then every cute boy I pass on the street is saying I felt him up, wanting a payoff. You can't let that happen."

"Like I said, I want to talk to this Kendrick Dunstan Wilshire first. But I promise you, I'll stop this."

9

I sat in my office at work, thinking about how it was now just twenty-five days till my birthday. Sissy's idea to save the company still rang in my head. Part of it made sense, but did I really want to enter into a relationship, a marriage no less, based on lies? I would be lying to myself, to everyone that knew me, not to mention the poor woman, whoever she may be. What about what I wanted? I had always told myself that when I did get married, or devote myself to a life partner, it would be with a man I truly loved. Marrying a woman I didn't even know wasn't quite what I had in mind.

And then there was the situation with Kendrick Wilshire, that dirty little lying scoundrel.

I cleared my head of that for the moment, trusting that Sissy would take care of it. I reached into the bottom drawer of my desk and pulled out the huge book of white pages.

Over the past fourteen days, I had already drawn lines through half a dozen Eric Reeds confirming that none of them was my brother, but there were still at least another dozen to call in this city alone. I didn't want to think of how many there were left in the rest of the country.

Pressing a finger to the next phone listing, I picked up my office phone and dialed the number. I got a recording informing me that the number was no longer in service. I drew a line through that name and dialed the next number.

"Hello," I said, after a woman picked up the phone. "May I speak with Eric Reed, please," I said, hoping his name hadn't been changed as mine had been.

"Who's calling?"

"My name is" — I stopped myself. "My name is Everette Reed," I said, using my pre-adoption name.

"May I ask why you're calling, Mr. Reed?"

I swallowed hard. "I have a brother named Eric, but I haven't seen him in thirty years. I'm trying to find him, and —"

"My husband doesn't have a brother."

"There's a chance he wouldn't have

known about me. Can I please speak to him?"

"I'm sorry, Mr. Reed, but Eric has been dead a year now. Car accident," the woman said, her voice low.

"I'm so sorry," I said. "I really don't mean to bother you, but can I please ask you a few more questions? Just so I'll know."

"Yes."

"Eric was my twin. I'll be turning thirty-four in three weeks."

"My Eric was forty," the woman said.

"Oh," I said, feeling as though my brother would be lost forever.

"I hope you find him, Mr. Reed. Good-bye."

After work, I was exhausted. I went home, took a nap on my living room sofa, and awakened half an hour later to the ringing of my home phone.

I had been dreaming about my childhood again, something that seemed to happen now each and every time I closed my eyes.

In the dream, I was sixteen. It was not long after my father had found me and the boy, Steve, in the garage. Since that day, it seemed my father had very little to say to me. He gave me instructions when he needed to, like "Make sure you're packed for tomorrow's trip," but simple, everyday conversation between a father and son was no longer there.

Because all I wanted was the love of my father, I did what he told me to do. I had stopped seeing Steve and did the same with all the other boys I called friends at school. I had little interest in girls, and besides my sister, I was basically alone.

I could not be who I really was, and despite how much I tried to be what my father wanted, he would never accept me as that person either. I was damned either way.

The dream shifted to a memory of me pushing through my parents' door, and gently shaking my mother till she awakened.

"Baby, what's wrong?" she asked.

I stood there in the dark room, tears rolling down my cheeks. "I . . . I . . ." I wasn't able to speak.

My mother hurried out of bed, wrapped her arms around me. My father didn't wake, didn't budge. She walked me down the hallway to my bedroom. Sympathy in her eyes, she begged, "Tell me what's wrong. Please."

"I don't . . . I don't know if I can do it anymore," I said, sniffing. "Nobody understands. Nobody cares."

"Don't know if you can do what, Cobi?

Nobody understands what?"

"Me, Ma. Me! And I don't know if I can live."

My mother leaned away from me as if wondering who this strange boy was. Then she noticed what I had in my fist. Her eyes focused on the orange plastic bottle with the childproof cap. She snatched it from my grasp. "Cobi, what are you doing with these?"

They were her sleeping pills.

I didn't answer, just kept crying. She scanned my room and saw the tall glass, filled halfway with water. She quickly put two and two together. Her eyes ballooned. "No! You didn't!"

I hadn't. But five minutes earlier I had been on the verge.

I was scared and lonely and felt as though no one really understood me. But my mother had always been open and honest with me. I thought the least I could do was tell her what I was considering before I actually went through with it.

She shook me out of my thoughts. "Did you take any of these? Answer me!"

"No, Ma. I didn't," I cried.

She threw the bottle of pills across the room and yanked me close to her.

Fully awake now, I sat up and picked up the phone. "Hello?"

"I'm at the gate. Buzz me in," a deep, throaty voice said.

"What are you doing here?" I asked.

"I was in the neighborhood. I tried calling your cell a few times before coming over. You didn't answer. Were you asleep? Is this a bad time? I can come back."

"No, no, I wasn't sleeping." I lied. Wiping sleep out of my eyes, I triggered the gate out front.

When I opened the door, Tyler stood before me, wearing a gray pinstriped suit. He hugged me.

Tyler and I met a year ago at a One Hundred Black Men social downtown. I was standing near the bar, holding a beer, when he walked up. "Cobi Winslow, right? State's attorney and heir to the Winslow hair care fortune. My name is Tyler Hayden Stevens," he said, extending a hand. "State senator from Illinois."

I looked down at his hand, saw the Rolex Milgauss peeking out from under his cuff and then the platinum wedding band on his finger.

"Pleasure to meet you," I said. "And to what do I owe this pleasure?"

"I was watching you since you walked in the place. Just thought I'd come over and say hi."

"Are you a stalker? On the way home, should I be worried that I'll look into my rearview and see you following me?"

"Only if you want me to," Tyler said with that dapper smile. "Say that you want me to."

"You're married," I said.

"I am."

"Wouldn't that be a problem?"

"Only if you made it one. Will you make it one?"

I blushed a little. "Not at first. But I need to let you know up front, I'm going to want more than what you're looking for."

"What do you think I'm looking for?"

"Wild, sweaty, no-strings-attached-sex with a handsome man."

"Yup," Tyler said, showing a beautiful smile again. "That's what I'm looking for."

I closed my front door and walked back into my living room.

"How are you?" Tyler asked.

"I'm managing, but it's rough, you know. I still expect Mom to step into the room and ask me if I'm hungry or walk in on Dad up in his study."

"I'm sorry about that."

"Me, too."

"Have you found out any more about your brother?" he asked, mercifully changing the subject.

"I mailed a letter off to the Social Security Administration yesterday, like the lady said."

"You're going to get through this." Tyler had a seat on the sofa. "And like I said, you know I'm here for you."

"Are you?"

"Cobi," Tyler shook his head as though he didn't want to start with this discussion. "I told you —"

"I've been having nightmares. If I wake up at two in the morning and wanted to call you, or come over, could I?"

"You know you can't. I have a wife and children. You know that."

"Yes, I do. You have a wife and children. You don't have time for this, for me."

"Don't say that."

"We've been doing this a year. I told you when we first met, this wasn't what I was looking for," I said.

"I know."

"When my father was alive, I had an excuse for not seeing you as often as I wanted. But now he's gone and . . . I want

61

someone who can be here for me."

"I'll do better."

"Will you?"

"I will. I promise."

"I need for you to be telling me the truth, for you to be serious about this."

"I am, and I will," Tyler said, pulling me to him. "I'm so sorry about everything that's happened."

"It's not your fault."

"I know. I just missed you."

"I missed you, too. But I need for you to keep your promise and —"

Tyler leaned in to kiss me softly on the lips. He was about to pull away, but I wrapped my arms around him, kept him there, only then realizing just how much I missed him.

After our kiss, Tyler said, "It's been too long. I want you."

I laughed sadly. "If you knew how much I wanted you too . . . but I'm worn out. It would be a waste of two minutes."

"Don't worry. I'll do all the work," Tyler said, pressing his hand into my chest, and pushing me back onto the sofa. "You need to take it easy anyway," he said, lowering himself to his knees, spreading my thighs, and moving between them. "All I want you to do is relax, okay?"

"Okay," I said, laying my head back, closing my eyes, and taking this time to forget about all that plagued me.

10

Two days later, halfway through reading the sports section, I heard the front door open. My sister called out. "Anyone home?"

"In the family room, Sis."

She walked in wearing a suit and carrying her briefcase. She set the case down at the door, walked over, and lowered herself onto the sofa next to me. I could tell by the blank, sad stare on her face that she had bad news.

"We have to pay off Kendrick Wilshire, Cobi."

I shot up from the sofa, waving my hands hysterically. "No! No!" I shook my head. "I told you no! I did nothing wrong, and for us to lie down and take this from that little lying, manipulative mofo — it's not going to happen."

"Okay, Cobi," Sissy said, her voice very low and calm. "What do you think will happen if we don't pay him?"

I paused for a moment, having not thought that far into the potential, dark future. "I'll file charges against him for blackmail."

"Okay, I'll play," Sissy said. "So do you have proof that you didn't sexually harass him?"

"Does he have proof that I did?"

"Does he need it? Or will the accusation be enough to have people suspecting that you're gay, something that you have not admitted. But worse, it will have people questioning whether you are an at-work sexual predator. Then what happens to your future plans to one day be attorney general?"

My sister stood and took me by my elbow. "I know this stinks, and if karma is really real, that little fucker will pay dearly at some point in his pathetic life. But for now, let's just save ourselves the anguish of it all and pay the fool the fifty thousand dollars he's asking for. I'll have a confidentiality agreement drawn up protecting you from any more of his bullshit."

"Fine," I said, agreeing but still not wanting to. "But he comes to us, and I'm the one handing him the check. Understand?"

"As you wish," Sissy said.

Two days later, Kendrick Dunstan Wilshire

walked on crutches into my sister's office at Winslow corporate, wearing a jacket and tie, like he was about to be picked for the NFL draft. That would never happen, because he was wearing a knee-to-toe cast protecting, as I had read on ESPN.com, a career-ending injury. I guess Sissy was right, and karma was not only real but swift.

Beside him stood his attorney, a woman named Lilith Banner. Coincidentally, she had been a year below me in law school; she now worked for a small firm out of Orland Park.

She had a copy of the confidentiality agreement we had sent to her office. She acted as though she didn't know me, and I played along.

Lilith set the contract on Sissy's desk.

Kendrick hobbled over on his crutches.

Lilith pulled a pen from her suit jacket pocket, gave it to Kendrick, and instructed him where to sign.

He glanced up at me with what I once thought were eyes the color of a beautiful green sea but now looked like the color of infant diarrhea. He signed the page, gave the pen back to Lilith, and rose up smiling.

"Mr. Winslow," Lilith said.

I walked over while Kendrick stumbled his crippled butt out of the way and signed the contract as well.

"Excellent," Sissy said, in an overly cheery voice. She grabbed the cashier's check that had been made out to Kendrick for 50K and gave it to me.

I stepped up to Kendrick, leaving not a foot between us. He beamed, obviously excited about his payday. I gave him the check, then held out my hand.

He took it, and we shook.

"Sorry about your injury," I said. "You would've gone high in the draft, maybe even number one."

"It's okay," Kendrick said, confident. "I've still got the legal profession."

With a vengeful smile, I said, "I hope you don't intend to practice here or anywhere else in the country. I put the word out about you. Have a nice time trying to find a job."

11

Over the past three weeks I had devoted almost all of my attention to finding Eric. I had been checking the mailbox every day for any information from the Social Security Administration. Nothing. I had been on the Internet, night and day, searching for any clues. I had even been actively searching obituaries.

It seemed like a hopeless cause.

Last night I told my sister what I had been doing. She was appalled.

"You don't even know this man. What if he's crazy, or worse? What if he's poor?" my sister said, pacing back and forth in front of me. "You're part of Winslow Products. What do you think it would look like for you to have a homeless brother, living on the streets?"

"Who said he was homeless? He could've accomplished what I have. He could be a physician, the head doctor at some hospital somewhere. Maybe a teacher or something."

"Cobi, just drop it. Please. We have other much more important things to take care of, like finding you a wife."

"How's that going?" I said, still not certain if what Sissy was suggesting was the right way to go.

"I found someone in serious financial need. I hear she's not quite as cultured as many of the society women I know, but she might have to do. You know Priya Parks, formally Priya Parks-Frazier. Married to —"

"Winston Wallace Frazier, the investor that swindled all that money?"

"Yes. The one they call the black Bernie Madoff. She's the one."

"But I thought they were very well off."

"They were, till the feds came and took all of their money and threw Frazier in prison. The poor woman is lucky she didn't go, too. Now she's broke and looking for someone to save her. The meeting is tomorrow. Let's hope that someone is you, Cobi."

The next day, I was trying to appear as though I was not staring at Priya Parks as she sat in my living room across from Sissy.

Priya was much more attractive than the pictures I had seen of her in the newspapers and tabloids. Her hair was long and parted down the middle. She had a small mouth, big eyes, and wore a diamond stud in her nose. She wore a dark dress, as if just coming from a funeral. She sat with her hands clasped in her lap, listening to my sister.

"No one can know that this marriage has been arranged. You will be free to divorce only after two years, and you must live here at the Winslow Chicago residence for the duration of your marriage," Sissy said. "Any questions?"

Priya Parks glanced over at me. I quickly looked down at my hands. This was the most ridiculous idea I had ever heard.

"You said there would be financial compensation?" Priya asked.

"Yes," Sissy said. "Two hundred and fifty thousand dollars annually. Plus room and board. All your expenses will be taken care of, to include a car if you need one, so the full five hundred thousand will be yours to do with as you please."

Priya chuckled a little as she sat up in her chair. "I thought I heard something about his inheritance being twenty million dollars. I'm sorry, miss, but you're going to have to do a little better than that."

I wanted to laugh at how shocked my sister looked.

"Really, Ms. Frazier, all you'll be doing is

lying around here collecting a check."

"No, sweetheart. There won't be much lying around, considering your brother over there is gay. And didn't you say something about me not being able to see other men?"

"No, you can't see other men," Sissy said. "How would that look if you got caught?"

"How would it look if you caught me jackin' off on a vibrator every night. A woman has her needs, and the dick is one of mine," Priya said with a snap of her fingers. She stood, grabbed her purse, and straightened her dress. She walked over to me and held out her hand. "I'm sorry that I can't be the one, Mr. Winslow."

I was smiling, almost laughing. "Me, too. But I appreciate you coming out. Is there anything you need for your time and trouble?"

"No. I'm fine. But thank you."

Still holding on to Priya's hand, I added, "I trust this will remain between those in this room."

"After what I went through with my husband, having my business put out in the streets for all to hear, I would never think of doing that to another human being. Your secret is safe with me, honey."

I walked Priya Parks to her car. When I stepped back in the house, Sissy was standing in the middle of the room, her arms folded, looking betrayed.

"I guess that gets me off the hook."

"Don't even think about it. We have approximately three weeks left till your birthday. You're getting married by then," Sissy said, grabbing her keys off the end table. She headed toward the door, but stopped and turned around. "There's another person I've been considering. I promise I'll thoroughly vet her."

12

It was early. The sun was out, and it was going to be a beautiful day.

But for Austen Melrose Greer, it was already starting horribly.

Austen had jet-black hair brushed back in a ponytail and beautiful, flawless Hershey Kiss–colored skin. Her eyes were almond shaped, and her lips were the shade of rose petals.

Austen pulled the key out of her car's ignition and exhaled deeply as she sat behind the steering wheel. She had loved this car. It was a 2008 Jaguar XJ8. It was silver with dark gray interior. She had bought the car in late 2007. It had just hit the dealership, and the housing business had still been great to her.

As a Realtor, she had heard grumblings about awful things to come in the market, but like so many of her friends in the business, she ignored those warnings. At the time, Austen was still selling downtown Chicago properties as fast as she could list them.

But not three months into 2008, things started to change drastically. There was talk, then evidence of a recession. People stopped buying houses, then houses started to go into foreclosure. Folks started losing their jobs, the value of properties dropped, and the stock market did things Austen never thought possible.

By the time 2009 rolled in, Austen had lost almost all of her savings and hadn't sold a property in over six months. With each month that passed, it became harder and harder to scrape together the money to pay the mortgage on her very expensive Michigan Avenue condominium located in the heart of the Gold Coast.

Austen flipped open the armrest between the seats of the Jaguar and set the key inside it. She leaned over, checked the glove compartment to make sure she hadn't left anything, then climbed out and closed the door.

She stood in the Jewel grocery store parking lot, as mothers dragged their kids by the hands, and pushed their carts past her.

Austen felt like crying as she turned and walked away from the vehicle.

After climbing in a cab, she dug her cell phone out of her purse and dialed the 800 number of the finance company she was giving her car back to.

"Yes, this is Austen Greer," Austen said. "The car is in the Jewel Foods parking lot on North Clark." The cab driver glanced up at her. She cut him an evil look, then went back to her conversation. "But if you don't pick it up by closing, I'm sure it'll be towed."

Austen disconnected the call and settled back into her seat for the remainder of the ride home.

When she walked through the heavy wood-and-glass doors of the aging but beautifully kept condo building, the uniformed attendant stood from behind the counter. "Ms. Greer, this man is here to see you," the attendant said, gesturing to a blond man wearing shorts, topsiders, and a baseball cap.

Austen hooked a finger over the top of her glasses, pulled them down a bit. She looked the man over suspiciously.

"Hi," the man said, extending a hand. "I'm Ken. I came to look at the —"

"This way, Ken," Austen said, cutting the man off before he could put her business out for the entire building to hear.

On the elevator ride up to the twenty-third floor, Austen kept her eyes down.

The elevator doors slid open with the *ding* of the bell.

"This way," Austen said, stepping out first.

Austen pushed open the heavy wooden door of her 2,000-square-foot condo. She walked in first, Ken following behind. Her heels clicked loudly across the immaculate hardwood floors and echoed through the huge space; it was practically empty.

There was a beautiful Asian antique dining room set in the dining room, and a burnt orange antique leather sofa with claw feet in the living room.

"So that's it, huh?" Ken said, walking over to the sofa, his fists on his hips.

"That's it," Austen said, hating the fact that she had to sell it.

Austen had once been so successful that she would fly all over the country looking for furniture to decorate her new condo. When she found the perfect piece, no matter the cost, she'd buy it and have it shipped home.

The sofa was a piece she had found in San Francisco and just had to have. It was in flawless condition. She happily paid $12,000 dollars for it, and now had it sitting on Craigslist for a quarter of that.

"I like it," Ken said, his arms crossed. "I want it."

Austen was both relieved and disappointed. Once the sofa was gone, all that would be left was the dining room set and her bed.

Ken sunk his hands into his pockets. "Will you take fifteen hundred?"

Austen almost choked and thought about smacking the baseball cap off the man's head. "If I'm not mistaken, it's listed on Craigslist for three thousand."

"Okay, how about two thousand."

Austen stared at the man through her dark glasses. "That antique is in perfect condition."

Ken smiled. "I know. That's why I'm offering two grand."

Her teeth clenched, her hands in fists, her long nails digging into the flesh of her palms, Austen walked briskly to her front door and yanked it open. "Get out."

"Ms. Greer, I don't mean to offend you, but times are tough for everyone. I know the value of what you're selling, and I also know you want to sell it or you wouldn't have it listed. I'm here right now with two thousand dollars cash. If you let me, I'll give you this and send someone back to pick up the couch tonight. If you let me."

Austen thought about her situation. No one else had called about the sofa. Over the last week, she had relisted it four times. She wasn't penniless, but she was damn close. She needed the money. She looked over her glasses at Ken. "Twenty-five hundred," Austen said.

Ken smiled. "Deal."

13

Today had been a rough day for me. By the time I pulled the Mercedes into the drive at home, I felt as though I couldn't deal with another single thing.

I had driven up to Joliet State Prison earlier to meet with another attorney and his client. The client, a man named Roger Finch, was in prison on charges of attempted murder. Last week a policeman had been shot. There was a sketch of the suspect splashed across every news channel, and this Roger Finch said he recognized the guy. Finch said he knew the man's phone number, who his friends were, and where he lived. He would be willing to part with that information in exchange for a shot at a reduced sentence. I heard the man out and told him I would have to get back to him.

I was in a hurry to get out of there. That place was depressing and so disproportionately occupied with black men. Every time I walked through those corridors, I became more depressed. I know many, maybe even most of them, were guilty of their crimes and had been justly convicted. But I also knew that the legal system was biased against black men, resulting in them often being falsely imprisoned, or when they were found guilty, getting longer, harsher sentences, or being sent away for crimes white men would get probation for. Not to mention the situation they would find themselves in when they finally got out — jobless, often uneducated, and branded as convicts — it was almost hopeless. No wonder so many went back.

Finally climbing out of my car, I felt dirty and exhausted. All I wanted to do was step into a steaming shower. I caught sight of my mailbox not twenty feet from where I stood. I should check it, I thought. Maybe the letter from the Social Security Administration had been delivered.

I walked toward the mailbox. When I opened it, there was a single letter lying inside. I pulled it out, read the envelope, and it was indeed the letter I had been waiting for.

Finally, a breakthrough.

I went inside, took a shower, and slipped on some khakis, a T-shirt, and my house robe. I went downstairs, poured myself a cold glass of white wine in anticipation of opening the letter and finding the address where my brother was currently living, or at least some information that would make him much easier to find.

I carried my wine and the letter into the dining room, set the letter on the table, and stared at it.

I felt my heart speeding in my chest and urged myself to calm down. I could not. This would be the closest I had come to actually meeting my brother. I wanted it to be a special occasion of sorts.

I took a celebratory sip of my wine, inhaled, exhaled, then tore the letter open. It took me only a moment to find what I was looking for. I read it, set the letter down, then smiled, then forced myself to laugh. I took a giant gulp of my wine before I angrily slung the glass across the room where it shattered against the wall.

I looked down at the letter and again read the line.

Unable to provide requested information.

I crumpled the page into a ball as I yelled into the empty house, "I fucking give up!"

I stood there infuriated, my chest heaving.

I took another deep breath and told myself
if my brother didn't want to be found, or if
the universe was in some way preventing it
from happening, maybe it wasn't meant to
be.

14

Eric Reed lay in his prison cell bunk moments before lights out. His cellmate, in the rack above him, was already snoring. Eric was staring up at the tattered old photo that he had stuck into the springs of that overhead bunk. The picture was of his little girl, Maya. She was two years old then — the most beautiful little brown baby in the world. She had thick black hair, big brown eyes, and the fattest dimpled cheeks.

Eric hadn't seen his daughter, or the mother of the child, in a little more than two years.

As Eric lay in that bunk, wearing jailhouse trousers and a wife beater undershirt, he remembered the days when he was free.

He had dated Jess, a gorgeous, shapely, loving sister for twenty-four months.

Eric loved her and had been honest with her about his upbringing in foster care and his run-ins with the law. Jess said none of that mattered. She felt he was a good man, and as long as he was good to her and stayed out of trouble, she would stick by him.

There were nights when he lay in bed beside Jess after making love, and he couldn't understand why she had chosen to stay with him, why she loved him. He told himself he wasn't good enough for her. He knew that any day she could leave him for someone better.

Eric worked when he could find day labor, pouring what cash he made onto the coffee table at the end of the day when he walked into the small one-bedroom apartment they shared. There were a couple of days when the ten- and twenty-dollar bills totaled close to a hundred dollars. Most days he barely made twenty or thirty, but Jess would smile and tell him what he gave was much appreciated and would help a lot. Eric knew she couldn't even buy a decent pair of shoes with that money.

Eventually, Jess picked up on Eric's insecurities. She started going out of her way to tell him how much she loved him. She had even bought him flowers on two occasions. None of it worked. One night, before bed, Jess walked over to Eric, her hands behind her back.

"I have something to ask you."

"What?" Eric said.

"I want you to say yes."

"Ask me first."

"Will you say yes?"

"Just ask."

Jess raised her hand from behind her back, opened it. In her palm was a plain, dull gold wedding band. "Will you marry me, Eric Reed?"

Eric had nothing. He was no one. He took Jess's hand in his and softly closed her fingers back around the ring. "You know I love you, right?" he said.

"And I love you, too. That's why I'm asking you to marry me."

"That's why I gotta say no. Just for right now, until I can be the man I need to be for you. Will you understand that for me?"

"Only if you stop acting like we don't belong together and believe me when I tell you I need you with me."

Eric smiled. "Yeah, okay."

A week later, after coming in from standing on the corner all day, hoping for work and not getting it, Eric found Jess sitting in the living room, a smile on her face.

"What?" Eric said, smiling too, after closing the door.

"Come here."

He walked to Jess, sat down beside her. She took his hand, kissed Eric's lips.

"What?" Eric asked again.

"I'm pregnant," Jess said softly. Eric could feel her practically trembling with excitement. "I had a doctor's appointment. I'm one month!" She threw her arms around Eric's neck.

"That's great news, Jess," Eric said, hugging her back. He didn't mean it. The money Jess made as a supervisor at Target was enough to take care of the two of them, allowing the little bit he gave her to seem like a meaningful contribution. But once a baby and a number of new expenses came, Jess would see just how little Eric was doing for them. It would make even plainer the fact that she had to find a better man than him.

Every day up until the baby's birth, Eric wished the pregnancy away. Then Maya was born. It turned out to be the happiest day of Eric's life. He stood in the delivery room, wearing a white gown, holding his baby for the first time and smiling through his joyful tears.

For the first time, Eric felt good about not having a job and being home, allowing them to save on child care. The first eight months, he cared for Maya full time, feeding her, changing her, bathing her. He grew very close to the little girl. Many days he would just hold her, marvel at how beautiful she was. He never knew he was capable of helping to create someone so perfect. He loved that little girl so much. At times, it made him wonder how his mother could've put him up for adoption and just walk away.

"I'll never leave you, baby," Eric said that night, leaning over and kissing his sleeping child on the cheek. "I'll always be here for you."

Soon, the bills began to stack. Eric would see the frustration on Jess's face when it came time to try to pay them all. Utilities were soon to be cut off, and Jess had been hinting to Eric for a number of months that he would have to find employment.

While Jess was at work during the day, Eric would cart Maya with him down the street to the public library and search online for job opportunities. Jobs he was qualified for were almost nonexistent, and with his criminal record of theft convictions, he quickly realized he had no chance at anything legal.

The next day, Eric got in touch with two friends of his, a guy named Luck and a chubby guy who insisted on being called Skinny Steve. In the past, the three of them ran small crime jobs together. They never amounted to huge money, but Eric was hoping they'd be on to bigger things by now.

The next night, when the guys got together, Skinny Steve said to Luck and Eric that he knew a guy who ran a chop shop.

"He'll give us five hundred to two thousand dollars a car, depending on what kind of rides we bring him."

"That ain't shit," Luck said, wearing a do-rag tied over his head.

"It's better than what we got now," Skinny Steve said. "And we can make as much as we want. Just keep on bringing in cars."

"Steve's right," Eric said. He was already counting the money in his head, thinking about what it could provide for Jess and Maya.

On the night of Eric's first job, he told himself things were going to work out just fine. That was until, while speeding down Stony Island Avenue in the Ford Expedition he had just stolen, he saw the blue lights of a Chicago police car flash in his rearview mirror.

Luck and Skinny Steve were in Luck's beat-up Mustang, trailing Eric. They quickly made a left on Seventy-ninth Street when they saw the cops on Eric's tail.

Standing in front of the judge, Eric could

hear Jess bawling as he was sentenced to four years in prison.

The first year Eric was in, Jess and Maya came often. It was the only thing that made prison tolerable. They were his link to the outside, something to look forward to.

On his year anniversary of being incarcerated, Jess came to visit Eric alone.

In the visitors' room, she really looked nice. She wore a lavender skirt and a floral print shirt. Her hair was freshly done. It was shiny, straightened, and hung to her shoulders. She looked good, but she looked sad.

"You okay?" Eric said.

"Yeah."

"I got a surprise for you."

"What is it, Eric?"

"I know I got two more years up in here, but I was thinking. I'm ready to say yes to your marriage proposal."

Jess didn't do a backflip like Eric had been expecting. She didn't shriek with surprise or throw herself into his arms. None of that. She just smiled a little, as if someone she didn't know had told her she looked nice that day.

Eric didn't know what was wrong. "Is that a yes?"

Jess nodded. "Yes," she said.

Three days later when Eric tried calling her phone, Jess didn't pick up. That was the case for the next two weeks. On her regular visiting day, she didn't show. The next time Eric tried calling Jess, her voicemail didn't even pick up. The phone just rang.

Eric stood there, the phone in his hand, looking stupid and feeling betrayed.

Now, lying in his cot, looking up at his child's picture, he told himself, *yes, it's been a little over two years since I've seen my child or my baby's mother.* He had no idea what happened to them. Did Jess stop loving him? Did she and his child die in some horrible car accident? He had looked her name up on the Internet and searched Facebook trying to find her, but she just disappeared.

Earlier that afternoon, Eric sat in the cafeteria, hunched over a metal tray of chili-mac. The old tattooed man Eric sometimes ate lunch with was spooning some of his chili-mac onto a slice of white bread.

"You find your girl and your baby?" the old man asked. Eric didn't know what his real name was, but inside everybody called him V.C.

"Not yet," Eric said, picking at his food. "But I'm still lookin'."

V.C. set down the half sandwich he made.

"You better not stop."

Eric heard what the man said but wasn't paying him much mind. He was too lost in his own thoughts.

"Look at me, boy," V.C. commanded.

Eric looked V.C. in the face. The whites of his eyes had yellowed. Several teeth were missing from his mouth, and a scraggly beard grew spotty from his gaunt face. "You told me how much you loved that woman and that child but didn't feel you deserved them. You ever think if you told yourself different, your mind woulda been so on proving that, you woulda done everything to keep from being locked up?"

"No."

"You ever think that without you, your little girl might have a fucked-up life like you got and might end up in here one day, too?"

Eric concentrated more on the old man, then said, "Yeah, I think about that all the time."

"I had a son once," V.C. said, staring into his memory. "He was eleven years old. I hadn't seen him since he was six, but I had two months to go on a five-year sentence, and I promised myself when I got out, I was gonna be the best goddamned father I knew how to be. But his mama would write me,

91

tell me he was runnin' them streets. I told her to keep him in the house, but the boy was wild and he'd get out there. Every night I prayed that he'd be okay till I got out. I would tell him that I loved him, teach him that all he needed was in here," V.C. said, pressing his fingertips to his heart. "But two weeks before I was released, his mama called, told me he had been shot and killed and left on the street. Garbage man found him the next morning on his route."

V.C. wiped a tear from his face. "It was all . . ." he tried to speak, but his voice cracked with emotion. He cleared his voice and said again, "It was all my fault. He was trying to be like his old man, and look where it got him." V.C. reached across the table, clamped Eric's forearm with a dirty wrinkled hand, and held tight. "You be a man, find that little girl, and be a father to her again. You hear what I'm sayin'?"

"I hear you," Eric said, his voice soft.

In his bunk, Eric told himself he didn't need V.C. to tell him what to do. He had realized it sometime ago, but the pain in that man's eyes, the regret that dragged him down was something Eric couldn't get out of his head.

He would be getting out of prison on parole in just three days. He would find Jess

one way or another and tell her he wanted
his family back.

15

Austen sat at her dining room table. She was working from home today, but not by choice. She had no clients to take out to show properties. She had no closings scheduled, which meant no money coming in.

Across the table were printed listings of homes that had been drastically reduced but still no one wanted to buy. There were envelopes that contained unpaid bills that Austen saw every day but ignored. And then there was one envelope that she had been avoiding for two days but knew she had to address today. She hadn't been able to make a mortgage payment in over six months, and something dreadful told her that within that envelope may have been news she didn't want to know.

In an attempt to avoid having to deal with that bad news, Austen was on the phone, calling numbers off a list of people she had taken out once or twice to look at houses.

"Hello, Mr. Hadley," Austen said, smiling, because she'd been taught if she smiled on her end of the phone, the sound of happiness would be conveyed to the caller. She didn't know if that was true or not, but she needed every advantage she could gain right now. "This is Austen Greer. We went out two weeks ago, looking at properties."

"Yes, I remember," Mr. Hadley said.

"You told me to call you back in a couple of weeks. So here I am, calling you back." She smiled.

Silence.

"So are you still in the market?" Austen asked. "I was thinking we could meet downtown, and I could walk you through some more places that have just been listed."

"I have a busy day today, Austen."

"Oh, no problem. I can always email the listings to you, and you can get back to me. What is your email address?" Austen asked, grabbing a pen.

"Austen, I don't think I'll be doing that."

"A couple of weeks ago you seemed very interested in —"

"I was," Mr. Hadley said. "Actually, I just closed on something two days ago. I'm sorry."

Austen was speechless. Two weeks ago, she had driven this man all around the city for more than six hours. She had even taken him out a week before that for almost the same amount of time.

Austen was crushed. "Excuse me, Mr. Hadley," Austen said, trying to maintain her composure. "But you told me that we would be working together, that I would be your agent."

"I know Austen, but my wife found someone that she preferred, so we —"

"But you *told* me we'd be working together. Your wife finds someone else, and what does that mean? Aren't you supposed to make the decisions?"

"Excuse me?" Mr. Hadley said.

"Do you know what that commission would've meant to me?" Austen said, feeling herself starting to lose it. She didn't care. The client had defected. The money was gone. "I'm about to lose my home. I give you valuable hours I could've spent with someone serious, and you screw me like I work for free. Mr. Hadley, you are nothing but a —"

Click!

"Hello," Austen said into the phone. There was no answer. "Hello!" She slammed the phone into its cradle and turned away from the table, wanting to cry.

She focused on the Bank of America let-

96

ter and grabbed it. She tore it open to see it was exactly what she had feared. It informed her that in five days her condo would be foreclosed on, then auctioned off on the steps of the courthouse.

16

Eric sat on his bunk, unable to believe what he was looking down at. Just last night, he was thinking about Jess, wanting to hear from her, and like magic, this morning she had contacted him through the letter he was holding now from a lawyer she had hired.

He would've never guessed it would've been a petition from Jess, trying to strip him of all his fatherly rights, but that's what the letter said.

"Can she actually do this shit, man?" Eric said, waving the document in front of his cellmate, Blac.

"Yeah, man. I knew a dude it happened to. And once it's done, it's permanent."

Eric's cellmate was an extremely well-built man, with very dark skin the color of crude oil and a perfectly shaped shaven head. He wore sagging prison trousers, a tank top, and an unbuttoned blue prison shirt.

"Why she doing this now? I been in here

three years, and now when I got two days left, she does this," Eric said, standing from his bunk. "I gotta find her, talk her out of this."

"She call you recently?"

"No."

"Is her address in that letter?"

"No."

"Then I'm thinking she don't wanna be found."

Eric turned to Blac. "She don't have a choice. I'm gonna go to the library right now, do some damn research on this letter, try and find something that'll lead me to her, and when I get out, she and I are gonna straighten this out."

"You know I get out two days after you. If you need any help out there, just let me know," Blac said. "She might have a boyfriend who don't care how much you want your daughter back. A boyfriend that might have to be dealt with while you take care of your business."

"You'd help me with that?" Eric said.

"You my boy. You know I always got your back."

17

The day had not really even begun yet. I had made it to the prison and was being escorted by a corrections officer through the halls toward the counsel room, where I would speak again to Roger Finch. Turned out my boss was interested in what he had to say.

Other officers, as well as the occasional inmate, walked past me through the corridor. This prison had an open-cell policy for the nonviolent offenders. They could move around a few select areas: the commissary, the gym, the library, the rec room, and the church.

Walking toward me I saw a colleague of mine who I had not seen in almost a year.

Raymond Tyler Jr. was a tall, hazel-eyed, handsome man with a reputation as one of the best and most compassionate attorneys in the country. Although I only saw him annually, at the National Bar Association conferences, I considered him a mentor and called him for consultation whenever I had a tough legal matter.

"Raymond Tyler," I said happily, shaking his hand.

"Cobi Winslow," he said. "Rich kid. What are you doing in the big house? Finally caught you for embezzling money from your family's business, heh?"

"Not quite. Making a deal on a cop shooting case. How about you? Didn't expect to see you here."

"I relocated to Chicago. I'm a defense attorney now, so this prison is my second home."

"Poor guy."

"You must not know how well defense pays."

"You know that's not what I meant," I said.

"Well," Raymond said, slapping me on the shoulder and releasing my hand. "Time to make the doughnuts. It was really good seeing you. Maybe we'll bump into each other again sometime."

"Hopefully," I said, smiling.

I said good-bye and started down the hall but stopped and turned, watching as Raymond walked away, thinking that maybe I should've asked him out for a drink. It would've taken my mind off of everything that was going on. But then I figured I had enough on my plate. Why drag him in to experience my drama.

When I turned back around, I was almost knocked off my feet. My briefcase flew out of my hand, banged to the ground, and belched all of my confidential papers into the air. I immediately dropped to one knee to gather them up.

As I quickly swept the papers together, I saw another pair of hands helping and heard a man's voice apologizing for steamrolling me.

"It's okay," I said, my head down, my eyes focusing on stuffing the documents back into my briefcase. "Next time, just watch where you're going."

"I'm really sorry," the man said again.

Finally looking up to see the man's face, I froze, lost balance, then toppled backward onto my rear. Looking up at the man, I couldn't believe what I saw. The man staring back shocked and wide-eyed was the spitting image of me.

He slowly reached out to grab my hand and help me up.

I stared at his hand for a long moment before taking it. This man, who could be no one but my brother, pulled me to my feet.

The corrections officer did a double take, then shook off the disbelief that momentarily appeared on his face and said, "I'm sorry, sir." He turned angry eyes on my brother. "Get back to your cell and watch where you're going next time."

"No," I said, my voice softer than I wanted it to be. "He's fine." My brother and I stared at each other for a long moment, as if we were the only two men in the corridor or in the prison.

I finally spoke. "What is your name?" In my heart, I already knew the answer.

"Eric Reed," my brother said. "Who are you?"

I extended my hand to him. "Everette Reed, but please, call me Cobi. I'll explain later." I smiled.

18

After my meeting with Roger Finch, I sat slumped in the chair across the table from where Roger had sat. Holding my head in my hands, I felt conflicted. I had given up looking for Eric but now had found him. Unfortunately, just as my sister predicted, he was not the man I thought he would be.

I looked up at the cell door. The guard was still posted there. I could walk out, forget I ever saw Eric, and never come back. I didn't have to ask why Eric was here. I already knew. Something told me he was the same man I'd prosecuted a hundred times in the past. He was DeAndré Moore. Roger Finch. I had no time or love for men like that.

I stood, grabbed my briefcase, and walked toward the cell room door.

The corrections officer said, "Is there anyone else you need to see, sir?"

"No," I said, without giving it any thought.

I walked ten feet or so, hearing his steps echo mine. I stopped. Eric was just like all those men I knew so well, but there was one difference. He was my brother. I turned to the CO. "On second thought, there is one more I need to see."

When I finished telling him all that happened to me over the last thirty years, Eric gave me a very strange look, one I didn't think I could imitate, even though we had the same face. "Why didn't the family that adopted you take me, too?"

"They said they only wanted one son."

"Oh," he said, frowning, looking away from me.

"What's wrong?"

"I knew about you," Eric said softly.

"What?" I said, shocked. "How?"

"My mother — our mother — wrote me a letter when I was eight, explaining why she gave us up, apologizing, stuff like that."

"Why did she do it?" I asked, yanking the seat out from under the table, and sitting so I could look directly into my brother's eyes.

He stared back at me and said simply, "We were too much for her. She was young, stuff going on, you know."

I didn't know. I felt jealous, envious. We had both been given up, and even though I had been adopted by a wealthy family, even though I was raised by a mother and a father, it felt as though he knew our natural mother much more than I did.

"Why are you in here, Eric?"

He scratched the back of his neck. "It hasn't been easy for me."

And there it was. My brother was indeed one of those guys. "What hasn't been easy?"

"You know . . . life."

"Were you ever adopted?" I asked.

Eric shook his head. "One foster home to another. Shitty way to be raised, you know."

"One day, I want you to tell me why you're here. Can you do that?"

"You a big-time lawyer. Access my records. Find out for yourself."

"I don't want to. I want you to feel comfortable enough to tell me. Why don't you try now?"

"No."

I looked away, up at the ceiling. "Okay, how much time do you have left?"

Eric's face brightened a little. "I'm out in two days."

"Really?" I said. "What are you going to do? Where are you going to go?"

"Don't know," Eric said. "Halfway house, I guess." He looked at me as if waiting for an invitation.

I could not help but think what Sissy would say. She'd lose it. There was no question. I looked up at Eric and said, "Why don't you stay with me?"

19

Eric walked back into his cell as if in a daze.

Blac was lying in his top bunk, deeply engrossed in his handheld videogame device. Eric stood in the middle of the cell. He didn't say a word. Blac paused his game, swung his feet over the side of his bunk, and sat up.

"What's up?" Blac asked.

"You'd never guess what just happened to me."

"We in prison, playa. Try me. The same thing might have happened to me yesterday."

"I just met my brother."

"You ain't got no brother."

"I do. I just never told you about him. We're twins."

"Naw," Blac said, jumping down from the bunk. "Naw! Two of you? I don't believe it."

"I just bumped into him in the hallway."

"Well, I guess it's cool you saw your

brother, but it sucks that he's a convict just like you."

"He ain't no convict. He's a lawyer. And he's rich. Dude's name is Cobi Winslow. You know, the people that make the hair stuff."

"You mean Winslow Pomade, in the little metal can?"

"Yeah, those Winslows."

"Hell, naw! When I used to grow my hair, that's all I'd use. Winslow Pomade, do-rag, brush it all day with the soft bristle brush, waves like crazy. That's what's up, yo. He's paid like that?" Blac said, seeming not to believe the news.

"That's what he told me."

"Damn, he gonna break you off with some money? Give you like a million dollars or something?"

"I ain't playing it like that. He's already doing enough by letting me live with him for a while."

"He's gonna let you live at his crib?"

"Yeah."

"You still ought to ask him for some money. And if you don't want it, give it to me. I could always use some cash."

Eric laughed. Blac wasn't smiling. "I'm serious."

"No. Blac, why is it always about money

with you? He's on the outside, and he's a lawyer. I told him about Jess, about her trying to take my daughter away. He's gonna try to find her address for me and give it to me when he picks me up day after tomorrow. I ain't messing that up by begging for money."

"Okay, man," Blac sighed. "Your life is about to change."

"C'mon, yours is, too," Eric said, slapping Blac on the shoulder. "We both getting out of here, and we gonna still be tight when we do."

20

Austen sat in the booth of a diner down the street from where she lived. In the seat across from her sat a very handsome man named Emmet. He was well built, looked younger than his forty-five years, and had a cute smile when he decided to show it.

Emmet owned a successful construction business and always made a point of telling Austen how well he was doing. Since Emmet came to swap out Austen's bathroom faucet last year, he had been trying to pull her into a relationship.

Yes, she had slept with him a few times. The sex was good enough to keep her sexual needs met, but when he asked for more, to become exclusive, Austen dodged his advances.

If she gave in, she knew he would one day ask her to move into his modest home, then one day, maybe even present her with a diamond engagement ring. If Austen were to accept, that's when she believed her life would change, when she would give up ownership of her mind, her will, her freedom to do things without clearing it with him first.

Austen was very familiar with men like Emmet. Her father was a man like Emmet, and as a child, Austen had watched him claim ownership of her mother.

Since becoming an adult, Austen always looked out for the men who wanted to "take care" of her. She knew exactly what that meant, and she was not interested. No way, no how!

Over the last month, Austen had distanced herself from Emmet, but she had not anticipated just how hard things were going to get for her. She actually had thought on a couple of occasions that maybe she shouldn't have pushed Emmet away so quickly. That maybe now she could've benefited from a man like him, willing to take her in, pay for everything, while she worked to rebuild her company.

She even thought of calling him back, maybe apologizing, and hoping he hadn't found anyone to replace her just yet. But losing her house or not, Austen didn't know if she was ready to give over control of her life.

Then to her surprise, this morning her cell phone rang. She saw that it was Emmet calling and quickly picked up.

Sitting across from him now, Austen watched him pick at his fries. He had something pressing on his mind, Austen could tell, and she was bracing herself for the moment when he finally found the courage to come out with it. She didn't have to wait long.

"I love you," Emmet said.

Austen stopped sipping from her glass of water. "Really."

"Over the last month, I realized that," Emmet said. "And I asked you out today to tell you that we should be together. I think things might be kinda hard for you right now, and us getting together might make it easier."

He was putting on his cape, trying to be Captain Save-a-Ho. He was asking for permission to rescue her. If she could just put aside her beliefs that every man wanting marriage wanted to control her, she could use this opportunity to save herself from impending doom. But Austen wasn't sure she could do that. "And when would you want us to get married?"

"As soon as possible. I can take time off

whenever," Emmet said, starting to get excited. "You know I got my own business, so I make my own rules."

"I know that, Emmet."

"We can take two weeks and go anywhere you want to go."

"That's nice, but I couldn't be away from work that long."

"Work? You wouldn't have to work no more if we got married."

"Yeah, but I would."

"But I wouldn't want you to. I wanna have kids, and like I said, I got my own —"

"I know you got your own business, Emmet. I've known it since the first day I met you," Austen said, aggravated. "Remember, I hired you. But just so I get this straight, you'd want me to have kids."

"Yeah."

"Stop working."

"Yeah."

"And what would I do for money?"

"I'd give you an allowance. A little something every week so you could buy yourself something nice. I wouldn't have a problem with that." Emmet smiled.

"Is that how your parents did things? Daddy gave Mommy five dollars a week?"

Emmet nodded. "But it was a little more than that."

"Well, that's how my father did my mother, too. He treated her like a child. Worse, like his pet dog. He told her what she could do and when, and when she misbehaved, he beat her. Is that how you want things to be between us, Emmet?" Austen said, loud enough to draw the attention of the other diners.

"Austen, look. I just wanna take care of you, because I know times gotta be hard and —"

Austen laughed. "Oh, you don't know the half. My car was repossessed, I sold all my furniture for cash, and my house has been foreclosed on. But I'll find a way to make it without your weekly allowance," Austen said, standing from her seat, grabbing her purse.

"Good-bye, Emmet. And please, don't contact me again."

21

At Winslow Corporate headquarters, I took the elevator up to the twentieth floor, hardly able to contain myself. I had finally found my brother. I was so happy. But then again, I was also conflicted. Eric wasn't what I expected. But that made little difference to me now. I had been reunited with someone from my true family, and that's all I cared about. The other stuff, I'd concern myself with later.

The elevator doors slid open. I walked out, and practically skipped down the hall toward Sissy's office.

Her secretary, Trina, a young woman with big eyes and blue mascara, stood when she saw me. "Good evening, Mr. Winslow, is Ms. Winslow expecting —"

"No," I said, happily blowing past Trina.

Sissy was standing behind her desk, wearing a tweed skirt suit, the jacket of which was hung over the back of her leather desk chair. She wore very stylish eyeglass frames; the microphone of a telephone headset was positioned an inch from her full lips. When she saw me, she held up a single finger, gesturing for me to wait.

"No, that's not good enough," Sissy said. "If they can't get the shipment there on time, then find another distributor. Good-bye." Sissy pulled the headset off and tossed it to the desk.

"Hey, Sis," I said, walking over to give her a kiss on the cheek.

"To what do I owe this pleasant surprise?"

Smiling, I said, "Sissy, we have an addition to our family."

"Don't tell me. My gay brother has knocked up some hoochie, and she's suing for child support."

"Yeah, you wish."

"Then what?"

"The best news you could ever imagine. You ready?"

Her arms crossed, Sissy said sarcastically, "I'm tingling."

"I found him! I found our brother. Can you believe it?"

"Really," Sissy said, sounding sincerely excited. "Where?"

"It was kind of right under my nose, but I never thought to look there. This morning,

I was up at the prison, and —"

"Cobi, no," Sissy said, taking a concerned step toward me. "Tell me he works there. Please, tell me he works there. He's the warden, right?"

"I was at Joliet this morning," I said, ignoring Sissy, "and this guy bumped into me, and when I looked up —"

"He's a corrections officer? He can be the damn janitor, but —"

"— when I looked up —"

"Enough with the freaking narrative, Cobi," Sissy demanded. "Is the guy a convict or not?"

I paused a moment. "Yes. He's an inmate there, Sissy."

"Okay," Sissy said, going into strategy mode. She paced a line before me. "So you found — what's his name?"

"Eric," I said.

"You found Eric. You're going to visit him in prison for the next ten years, and no one ever has to hear about it. I understand. That's admirable. And as long as word doesn't get out, the family business will be fine."

"No, Sissy. Eric's getting out in two days, and I invited him to move in with me."

Sissy started choking. I ran to her and patted her on the back till she stopped.

"Invited him to live in the mansion to do what — rob you of everything? Cobi, that's not happening."

"The other three houses are yours, the mansion is mine. I'll have whomever I like."

"Cobi, please. Understand, nothing good can come from this. At the very least, he won't be the man you think he is. And if this leaks and the public gets a hold of it, then —"

"Then what, Sissy?" I said, raising my voice. "Does this make our products any less valuable than they are? Accepting my brother — our brother —"

"That ain't no brother of mine."

"Will accepting our brother into my home change the people we are, what we and Winslow Products stand for?"

"No, Cobi."

"Then what's the problem?"

"Perception is everything. Public opinion is everything. People get off on this elite family crap. Think Kennedys, think Clintons, and the Obamas now. Remember Roger Clinton? Wasn't a good look. What if little Sasha Obama was a pyromaniac? Or Malia, a juvenile alcoholic? How do you think that would play? If we welcome a convicted felon into our home, into our family, we no longer maintain that elite status. Our public perception will suffer, our sales may suffer, and in a time like this, we cannot afford to lose the sale of a single can of Winslow Pomade. Do you hear what I'm saying to you?"

I stood there, angrily absorbing everything my sister said. There were things I wanted to say back to her, but I held my tongue, fearing I'd regret those words. Instead, I waited another couple of seconds till I calmed down and said, "I know, the circumstances aren't perfect. He's not who I expected him to be either. We'll deal with that. But I came here to share this wonderful news, not to ask for your permission. Everything will be fine. And if all goes well, Eric, our brother, will be moving into *my* house in two days." I forced a smile. "Come by and say hello. I'm sure he'd like to meet you."

22

It'd been half an hour since lights out, and Blac lay in his bunk, his arms crossed under his head, staring upward. He was so excited he could not sleep. He might actually survive after his prison release. Up until his last conversation with Eric, Blac didn't know if that would be the case.

Blac was finishing a four-year prison sentence for drug possession with intent to distribute. Off his last prison bid, he had been out only four months, but he couldn't find any kind of work that would give him decent money. The woman he lived with, Theresa, was giving him all kinds of static about contributing financially, so Blac had to make some money. If that meant risking going back to prison, so be it. Since Blac could remember, jail had always been a possibility. It ran in the family.

Blac's grandfather was sentenced to life in prison for murdering a white man. When

Blac was ten, his father tried to rob a guy on the street. The guy happened to be an off-duty police officer. He drew quicker than Blac's father and shot his dad dead. That left Blac with his mother, who was just getting into heroin. The reality of her husband's death only got her into it faster. By the time Blac was twelve, his mother had spent more time on the floors of abandoned drug houses, and performing sexual acts for drugs in alleys, than she did at home.

Blac practically raised himself from that point on, and did a poor job of it. By the time he was sixteen, he had been in and out of juvie so frequently they should've given him a key.

He did time at eighteen for aggravated assault, at twenty-three for breaking and entering, at twenty-six for armed robbery and possession of a controlled substance, and now in four days, he would be released from his last violation, the possession and distribution rap. It was a good thing nobody ever found out it was him that shot that white man on the North Side ten years ago, or he probably would've been in jail for life.

Since he could remember, Blac's life had been one big fucked-up ball of hate, anger, hopelessness, and disappointment. But before he was thrown in prison the last time, he thought things would change. As always, he needed money. He had managed to get hooked up with an up-and-coming drug dealer named Cutty.

Cutty was short, five foot six on tippy toes. He had short, buzzed black hair, chocolate-milk-colored skin, and a lazy eye that made him always look like he was speaking to someone he wasn't. He was in his midthirties, but with not a strand of hair on his face, he looked like he hadn't even gone through puberty.

Cutty was mean. It was rumored that he had been the one who killed Booky Bear, the dealer in control of the territory Cutty now ran.

Rumor had it that Cutty walked up to Booky in an alley while he was screwing a prostitute in the backseat of his car and stuck the 9mm to the back of Booky's head, firing two shots into his skull.

Blood painted the screaming woman's face. Cutty told her to shut her mouth once, and when she wouldn't, he emptied the rest of the magazine in her. At least that's how rumor had it.

Back then, Cutty was trying to make a name for himself, and those were the worst kind of criminals — the ones with something to prove. At the same time he was looking for people to distribute his product deeper into the community.

Blac was down. He would start his own little operation, taking a cut of the drugs he sold for Cutty, but Blac had no startup cash.

"I don't normally do consignment," Cutty said one day, puffing on a burned-down nub of a cigar. "But considering you ain't got no cash, it's the only way you can get product. You down for that?"

"Hell, yeah," Blac said, overly excited.

"Consignment ain't no punk, just so you know," Cutty said. "You don't get my money, plus my profit back to me in ten days, somebody gonna end up dead, and it won't be me." Cutty was smiling. The three men standing around him were not.

"Okay," Blac said.

"No. I really need for you to understand this shit. Bones," Cutty said, snapping his fingers at one of the men.

The man who stepped forward was tall, thin, and muscular. He walked over to Blac, pulled a Glock from the front of his jeans, and pressed the tip of the barrel flush to Blac's temple. Blac immediately started to tremble.

"Bones here is a killer, like all my men. If I gave the word, he'd put a bullet in your head and wouldn't blink when your blood hit his face. You hear me?"

Blac nodded, trying not to mess himself, he was so nervous.

Cutty waved a hand, and Bones shoved the gun back into his jeans and backed off.

That afternoon, Blac drove away in Theresa's car with $150,000 worth of crack cocaine in his trunk. Blac hadn't known that Theresa's brake lights weren't working. The cops who had been following behind him for four blocks finally flashed their lights, hit the siren, and pulled Blac over.

Because he was nervous as hell, acting more like he had a dead body stashed in the trunk instead of $150K worth of crack, the cops asked Blac to step out and they searched his vehicle.

Before being sentenced, Blac could've struck a deal — told the cops where the drugs came from — and they would've reduced his sentence considerably. But Blac wasn't a snitch.

A week into his incarceration, Blac was doing laundry with a few other guys. After pulling his clothes out of the dryer, he looked up to find himself suddenly alone. A moment later, three hulking, tattooed men with evil expressions walked into the room and stood around him.

Yes, Blac thought. This was when he'd die

for losing Cutty's drugs.

He set his laundry basket down and tried to accept his fate. "Cutty sent ya'll, huh."

"Yup," one of the men said. He had a diagonal line of scar tissue dissecting his face.

"Okay. Let's get this shit over wit'," Blac said.

"Cutty sent us to thank you for not rattin' him out. He suspended your deadline while you locked up," the man said. "And while you in, you ain't got nothing to worry about from these fools in here. Cutty got your back, 'cause you work for him now."

"Really?" Blac said, grateful. "Okay, right."

"But like I said, Cutty suspending your deadline. He ain't wiping that shit away. You lost one hundred fifty thousand dollars' worth of his product. Snitch or not, you still owe him. So you get out, that ten-day clock gonna start ticking again, and you gonna need to get him back his money, or same outcome applies," the man said, holding his hand as though he were pointing a gun. "You gonna end up dead."

As Blac lay in the dark on the bunk above Eric's, he was thankful for the man sleeping beneath him. Eric said this newfound brother of his, Cobi, was filthy loaded. Blac didn't know how he would capitalize on that situation, but he was a criminal, a swindler, a manipulating thief. His father was before him, his grandfather before that, and the line could've continued even as far back as slave days. Blac knew Eric and his rich brother Cobi were just about his best and last hope of staying alive.

23

Austen stood by the door of her condo, her arms folded across her chest, as a couple of burly men in brown uniforms moved out the last two dining room chairs.

She had posted pictures of the antique table and chairs for sale at $3,000 on Craigslist.

Ten minutes later, the phone calls started pouring in.

The first to arrive was a young couple, a tall, thin, boyish-faced doctor and his pregnant wife. The two walked in and their faces lit up when they saw the table and chairs.

"It's beautiful," Austen heard the woman say to her husband as she lovingly rubbed her round belly.

"Yeah, it is," he said, then turned to Austen. "Three thousand, right?"

"Yes. And the price is firm," Austen said.

Austen shut the door, then pulled the thin

wad of thirty crisp one-hundred-dollar bills from her jeans pocket and fingered them as she walked through the living room and dining room. She stopped all of a sudden in the empty space, feeling a chill. She looked up from the money in her hands to see that the room was as completely bare as the day she bought the place.

All she had now was her bedroom furniture and the small flat-screen that sat on the chest of drawers. How long before she would have to sell that? Where would she sleep after that? On the floor? Would she even have a floor underneath her to consider, or would the bank have taken her place by then?

Austen felt a single tear crawl down her face. She swatted at it angrily with the back of the hand holding the money, feeling as if allowing herself to cry would be admitting that she was defeated. She was up to her neck in it this time, but there had to be a way out.

Austen took a step toward the bedroom when a knock came at her door.

She opened the door, expecting the young couple to tell her they had forgotten something.

Who Austen saw standing in her doorway was a tall, beautiful woman, wearing a sharp, tailor-made business suit. Beside her stood an even taller, well-built man, wearing a chauffeur's uniform and dark glasses.

"Austen Greer," the woman said. "My name is Sissy Winslow. May I come in? I have an important proposition for you."

24

Loosening the gold diamond-print tie around my neck, I stared down at the criminal file of the young man I would be prosecuting. His name was Ra'Mond Williams. He was twenty-three years old. In his house was found $100,000 of marijuana.

He was charged with possession with intent to distribute. He had no prior offenses, but still, I would make it my business to ensure he served time in jail. If the warden wanted me to walk him to his cell myself, turn the key, and toss it down a sewer drain, I could do it and have no problems closing my eyes at night.

What I knew would keep me up about this case was the fact that the house where the drugs were found was not Ra'Mond's, but his grandmother's. Ra'Mond's mother was in prison herself, had been for some time. Ra'Mond's grandmother allowed the young man to live in her house, the house her late

131

husband had paid off while working on the railroads. Not until police officers wearing armored vests, riot gear, and carrying high-powered weapons busted through her door did she know that her grandson was using her home for drug storage.

Ra'Mond's grandmother had lived in that house for fifty years, but now it was scheduled to be seized by the city of Chicago.

I dragged a hand down my face and flipped the file closed. I was disgusted.

I wondered if I was placing myself in a similar situation welcoming a brother I did not know into my home. I had been up all night battling those thoughts, as well as the warnings Sissy gave me, which played over and over in my head. But I told myself I had done the right thing. He was my brother, and he needed a place to stay, to get back on his feet. It was what I wanted to do.

A knock came at the door.

"Come in," I said, knowing who it was and wishing I had not interrupted his day by asking him to come over.

Tyler stepped through the door, looking as handsome as ever, wearing a million-dollar smile. Knowing me better than I always thought he did, he immediately walked across the room with concerned eyes and stood beside me.

"Baby, you okay? You look exhausted." He leaned down and gave me a kiss on the lips. I know he meant for it to be longer, but I pulled away.

"I'm fine. Just tired is all. Didn't sleep much last night."

Tyler walked back around to the front of my desk and had a seat in the guest chair. "Tell me what's bothering you."

I looked in his eyes and saw how sincere his request was. It was one of the reasons I loved this man. "This was supposed to be a happy occasion when I told you this."

"Told me what?"

"I mean, I put so much effort into —"

A wide smile brightened Tyler's face. "You found your brother?"

"In prison," I said, deflated. "Locked up for a crime he won't tell me about."

"You spoke to him."

"Yes."

"And?"

"He gets paroled tomorrow."

Tyler sighed, a perplexed look on his face. "How are you going to play it? I mean, Cobi, you have options. You don't owe —"

"He needs a place."

"Cobi, what did you promise him?"

"I told him he could stay with me."

"Sissy tore you a new one, huh?"

I couldn't help but smile a little. "Of course. I mean, he's in prison for a reason. I'm picking him up tomorrow and taking him to my house. I'm actually supposed to go there later today to see him and give him some information he asked me for. Am I crazy?"

Tyler smiled that comforting smile that always made me feel more relaxed. He stood and opened his arms. "Come here."

I walked around my desk and into his embrace.

"In answer to your question, hell yes, you're crazy. But you're also caring, and thoughtful, and charitable, and if I were him, I would thank God that I had a brother like you. I'm sure you have nothing to worry about, and everything will be fine."

"Famous last words," I said.

"Famous last words." Tyler smiled.

I wrapped my arms around him, smoothed my hands over the back muscles under his suit jacket. "I need to see you tonight."

"I can't. Taking the wife and girls to Cirque du Soleil."

I leaned out of the hug without taking my arms from around him. "Tyler, what are we doing?"

"Don't," he said.

"Don't what?"

"This discussion. You have great news, you found your brother. You have that to deal with. And I have enough work to keep me locked up round the clock, so let's not go back into the 'What are we doing?' discussion, okay? Can we just leave that alone for a while?"

25

Eric stood in the prison's recreation room, leaning on his pool cue, waiting for Blac to take his shot at the eight ball.

Normally, Eric would've whupped Blac and left him with at least five balls on the table, but today Eric had things on his mind.

Wearing a white wife beater that contrasted sharply with his dark skin, Blac leaned over the table, sized up his shot, then looked up at Eric. "This yo' ass. Eight ball, corner pocket."

"Make the shot, then talk," Eric said.

Blac held his pose stretched over the table, then stood straight and glanced down at his watch.

"Dude, what are you doin'?" Eric said, agitated. "You takin' the shot or what?"

"Didn't you say your brother was supposed to come here like an hour and half ago?"

"Yeah. So what? You takin' the shot or not?"

Blac laid his stick on the table. "So, what's up? Did he call and say he wasn't coming?"

"No. But what does that have to do with you? Why you so concerned about whether or not this man show up?"

"I'm concerned because I'm your boy, and the other day you was all tiptoein' on air, singing and dancing about how you got a brother and how you gonna live with him."

"I wasn't doin' all that."

"You need to find out what's going on."

"Maybe he realized he made a mistake by callin' on me, by tellin' me all that stuff and asking me to live at his place. And to tell you the truth, hell, I don't blame him." Eric turned, ready to walk out.

Blac rushed over, grabbed him by the arm. "So you just givin' up on that?"

"Blac, what the hell you want me to do? Call him? I ain't got his number. Go by his house? I don't even know where that fool live. It's over, okay." Eric turned again and headed toward the rec room door.

Blac called out to him. "Yo. Just tell yourself he gonna be outside that gate tomorrow, waiting for you in a stretch Mercedes or somethin'. You gotta do that. The power of positive thinking and all that stuff, right?"

"Right," Eric said, as he continued out the door.

26

Austen lay in her king-size cherrywood, four-poster bed, wearing nothing but a short T-shirt hiked up to expose her flat, smooth belly. The Egyptian cotton sheet lay just below her hips. Her right hand was beneath it, the tips of her two fingers pressing on that very sensitive place between her thighs.

She threw out her left hand toward the nightstand and blindly fumbled for the vibrator.

The last time she pleasured herself was two nights ago, and it had been pretty much every other night for the last month. It was all the stress she was feeling from watching her life and all that she had worked so hard for spiral down the drain.

But tonight, she was super stressed because of that woman who had the nerve to knock on her door earlier today.

"I don't know who you are," Austen said,

after hearing the woman tell Austen her name was Sissy Winslow. "What do you want?"

"Like I said, I have a proposition for you. May I come in, or will you have me conduct this business in the corridor?"

Austen wasn't certain of what to do, she thought, looking this woman up and down. If she was a crook, she was a very successful one, because the clothes and jewelry she wore, Austen was sure, cost as much as some folks' houses.

"I assure you, if you aren't interested in what I have to say, I'll leave. May I come in?"

Austen stepped aside and pulled the door all the way open.

"Wait out here, Harold," Sissy said to the man beside her.

"Yes, Miss Winslow."

Sissy Winslow stepped into the bare condo. Austen closed the door behind her.

"Beautiful place you have here," Sissy said, walking casually through the large, open living room with the high ceilings, over to the glass wall of windows.

Austen watched her, glaring down at the woman's pumps, with their blood-red soles.

The woman stopped in front of the windows. "Breathtaking," she said. "Northeast view. Lake Michigan, and you can even see Evanston from here. It would be a shame to lose it, huh?"

"What did you say?" Austen was startled to hear those words come from the woman's mouth.

Sissy turned to face Austen. "That is why these rooms are bare, right? You're selling off all your furniture to pay the mortgage."

"I don't know what you're talking about. I'm buying all new furniture for —"

"Miss Greer, we need to be honest with each other if we're going to work together."

"Lady, I don't know who you are and what you're selling, but ain't nobody said nothing about us working together."

"I'm Sissy Winslow," Sissy said, walking back over to Austen, her hand extended, as though she had not already introduced herself. "President and CEO of Winslow Hair Care Products, and what I'm selling you is your life back. Would you like me to tell you more, or would you rather I leave?"

As Austen lay in bed, she found that she was no longer in the mood to pleasure herself. It had been spoiled by that arrogant woman who recited Austen's life story like she had written it.

She set the vibrator down on the night-stand and grabbed the folder Miss Winslow had given her. Inside were clippings from newspapers and magazines, with headlines that read, "Cobi Aiden Winslow to clerk for Illinois State Supreme Court Justice" and "Cobi Winslow Named Editor of *The Harvard Law Review*" and "Mr. Winslow Joins Cook County State's Attorney's Office."

There were pictures. *This Cobi guy is handsome,* Austen thought as she browsed the pages again. But she still couldn't believe what this Sissy Winslow was asking of her.

"I should've kicked you the hell out of my place the second after I heard what you were offering."

"But you didn't, because you need it. Isn't that correct?"

"Get out," Austen said. "I'm not some high-priced prostitute." She walked toward the door, preparing to put Sissy out.

"I don't understand the correlation," Sissy said. "There would be no sex. As I said, my brother is gay."

"The answer is still no," Austen said, grabbing the doorknob and pulling the door open.

"Stop."

Austen halted, her hand still on the knob.

"I've done my research, as you can tell, and I like you. I think you'll be good for

Cobi. I'm prepared to sweeten the —"

"Not interested, Miss Winslow."

"You've been in this beautiful home for four years now," Sissy said, looking around as if in awe of its elegance. "The bank plans to foreclose on it in four days. In all honesty, it's no longer even yours. Do what I ask you and we'll buy it for you."

Austen slowly pulled her hand away from the doorknob, considering the benefits of all that Miss Winslow was offering. "I don't know."

"That's better than no. It's progress," Sissy said, turning toward the door. "Take a day, think about it, then call me and arrange for a meeting with me and my brother." Sissy held out a gold-colored business card. "You have one day, Miss Greer, or the offer is off the table."

As she lay in bed, the newspaper and magazine clippings spread out before her, she had no idea of what decision she'd make. With a frustrated swoop of her arm, Austen brushed the clippings and the folder to the carpet below, reached over, and clicked off the lamp.

27

"One leather wallet," the corrections officer, a broad-shouldered, shaved-head man said, passing Eric his wallet into an opening in the mesh fencing that separated him from the inventory room. The wallet had been taken away from Eric when he was arrested three years ago.

"One wristwatch."

Eric picked up the watch and fastened it around his wrist. It had stopped working.

"You're done," the corrections officer said. "Go that way for fingerprinting."

In the clothes that he had been arrested in, Eric walked down a long corridor with dirty walls toward the fingerprinting room.

A large woman wearing a white lab coat took Eric's forefinger and pressed it into a pad saturated with ink, then rolled it over a piece of cardboard.

"Ya'll fingerprinted me when I came in here three years ago," Eric said. "Why we got to do this again?"

The big woman performed the same action with another of Eric's fingers, looked up at him through thick glasses, and said, "Because we need to make sure we're releasing the same man we locked up."

"How am I not gonna be the same man?"

The woman opened her mouth to answer the question, when Eric said, "Just finish. I'll do whatever to get out of here."

But as Eric wiped his fingers free of ink with the moist napkin she gave him, he wondered what good getting out of there would really do him.

He knew it would never happen, but he could barely sleep last night for hoping that Jess would show up, or at least call to say that she had reconsidered that petition to take his parental rights away. He dreamt she would tell him she was happy he was getting out, and she and Maya would be there to receive him, or at home when he showed up. No call came.

After fingerprinting, Eric was directed to continue down the same corridor. It was the one he was brought into three years ago, cuffed and shackled after he had been convicted.

Back then, he knew exactly what his immediate future would hold. Now, walking down this same hallway in the opposite direction, he had no clue what the next hour would bring.

The evening sun was brighter than Eric had expected when another muscle-bound corrections officer walked Eric outside and toward the front gate of Joliet State Prison.

Eric walked in silence, his laundry bag over his shoulder, his empty wallet in his back pocket, his broken watch on his wrist.

When he and the officer approached the front gate, it was as Eric expected — no one there on the other side to meet him. The street was quiet. Not a single car passing by.

Eric turned to the CO, saw himself in the big man's mirrored sunglasses. He looked for something to say, but all he could come up with was, " 'Preciate it."

"No problem," the officer said. "We'll be seeing you back here real soon, I'm sure." He cracked a sarcastic smile, then raised an arm high in the air, triggering the locks on the gate.

The mechanical gate lurched, then rolled slowly open to one side, and Eric stepped out.

No money in his pocket, no destination planned, Eric turned right and started walking.

After two minutes, he stopped. It made no sense to walk any further, not knowing where he was going. That moment it all hit him. He was alone. And even though he had always been that way, from the day his mother dropped him off at that adoption agency, at least there was someone, or some entity — the government, at the very least — who felt responsible for him. After that, there had been girlfriends, or friends he could rely on, but now there was no one.

Eric felt his knees tremble. What would he do? What was he going to do? No answer came to mind. Just when he thought about lowering himself to the ground and simply giving up, Eric heard a car horn honk behind him.

He turned, startled to see a large, black Mercedes idling at the corner.

Eric couldn't believe it. It was just like Blac said. There behind the wheel, the spitting image of himself, sat his brother Cobi.

Eric walked over to the passenger door. When the window finished powering down, he leaned into the cabin of the car.

"You honking at me?" Eric said, afraid to smile just yet.

"Yeah," Cobi said. He was wearing a suit and tie, like an Eric from an opposite universe. "Sorry I'm late. That Dan Ryan traffic can be a mofo."

28

After ringing the doorbell, Austen stood on the porch of her mother's house — the house she had grown up in.

When the door opened, Austen's mother, a short woman with skin the color of toasted wheat, opened her arms for a hug. She wore a flower print housecoat over her blouse and slacks.

Austen gave her mother a hug. "How you been, Mommy?"

"I could've been kidnapped and held for ransom, for all you know, since you never come to see me," Angela said, kissing Austen's cheek.

"I was here just last week, Mommy."

"I can never see my baby enough," Angela said, play pinching Austen's cheek. "I was making some tea. We can take it out back on the deck. It's a nice evening."

Outside, Austen's mother sipped from one of her old porcelain teacups, the matching saucer balanced on her lap. She stared up at the sky as if she didn't have a care in the world. Setting her cup back on the saucer, Angela said, "Not that I don't love to see my daughter every opportunity I get, but what brings you here? I wasn't expecting to see you for another few days."

"Oh, I just wanted to tell you that the mortgage has been paid."

"You didn't have to come all the way over here for that. You could've called, like you normally do when you pay it."

Years ago, Austen's mother's house had been paid for. When Austen needed money to rebuild her late father's business and was unable to get a bank loan, her mother gladly offered to refinance the mortgage on the house.

Austen vehemently objected.

Angela said, "With the money, do you think you'll be able to make your father's business better than it was?"

"Yes."

"Will the business provide a good living for you?"

"Most definitely."

"Then we're getting you that money."

Austen was able to keep only two of the promises. The business was successful, and it did provide well for her, but soon Austen would not be able to pay back the money. That meant that the mortgage on her mother's home would go unpaid, and her mother, who was retired and only drew Social Security, would lose her home. Austen could not let that happen.

"Austen, are you okay?" Angela said, pulling Austen out of her thoughts.

"Yeah, Mommy, I'm good."

"No. There's something wrong. This whole recession and housing thing . . . you okay with money? You don't need —"

"No, no. Everything is fine," Austen lied. "Actually business is much better than you would think. I really came by to give you some news."

"What news, baby?"

Austen sighed and tried her best to pass her smile off as a sincere one. "I'm getting married, Mommy."

29

I took Eric to one of my favorite steak-houses in Chicago and ordered the ten-ounce filet, with sautéed spinach and garlic mashed potatoes.

When the tall, dreamy-eyed waiter turned to Eric and said, "And you, sir?" Eric seemed uncertain. He stared at the menu as though it was a tough school exam, and then ordered a cheeseburger and fries.

"Hold on," I said to the waiter, turning to Eric. "Are you sure that's what you want? Why don't you get a steak, or lobster, or both?"

Eric gave another puzzled look at the menu, then back up at me. "That would be okay?"

"Sure. Order whatever you want. This is your first meal out of pri —" I caught and corrected myself, afraid of embarrassing Eric in front of the waiter. "Your first meal back in town."

Eric smiled a little at my mistake. "I . . . I don't know what's good. Can you order for me?"

"I was hoping you'd say that." I happily looked up to the waiter. "He'll have the ten-ounce filet, medium well, the lobster tail, the potatoes au gratin, and grilled asparagus." I turned to Eric. "Would you like beer or wine?"

"Beer."

"And a Stella, please."

The waiter took our menus and disappeared.

"Wow, you really know your food," Eric said.

"One of my favorite things, along with Broadway shows, great music, and good wine."

We were silent for a moment; both of us, I imagine, were looking for something to say. I looked up at him, and as with every other time, I was mildly startled to see a spitting image of me. It was truly eerie just how much we looked alike.

The waiter brought us bread and butter, which mercifully gave me fuel for conversation.

"This is some of the best warm bread you'll ever taste," I said, sliding it over to Eric.

He took a couple of pieces and started to butter one. He held it up to his mouth, about to take a bite, but before he did, he said, "It wasn't the traffic that made you late, was it? You weren't sure you still wanted to pick me up. Same reason you didn't come yesterday."

Before my mother had passed, she always said I was very intuitive. "You're a mind reader," she would always tell me. I obviously shared that gift with my twin brother. I pondered whether I wanted to be truthful with him.

"No, Eric. It really was the traffic. You saw all the cars on the way out here. That's what I was stuck in." I lied, not sure why. "And yesterday I had trial. Couldn't get away."

"So, were you able to get that info I asked you for?"

"I had to pull some strings, but yes, I did. That was for the mother of your daughter, right?"

"Yeah," Eric said, looking as though he didn't like having to confirm who the number was for.

"I guess there would be nothing wrong with you calling her."

"Wouldn't matter if it was. I need to find out why she's tryin' to take my rights away. So do you have it or what?" Eric said.

"I do. But I'm going to need something in return."

"What?"

"I asked you before why you were in prison. You said you'd tell me later. I need that to be now."

"Why is that important?"

"Because we're brothers, and if we're going to try —"

"Try?"

"If we're going to do this, we can't be keeping secrets."

Eric looked down at the piece of bread on his plate, then back at me. "No." He picked up the bread and his knife and sloppily smeared butter on it. "I'll find the information myself," he said, while chewing. "That's that. Now can we just move on?"

"This is no longer about the phone number and address. After we're done here, I'll be taking you to my house . . . my home, and I hate to say it, but I need —"

"To know what I was locked up for, before you go letting some ex-con, who could've been locked up for murder or something, into your crib. Don't worry, Cobi, I won't steal your mother's silverware."

"Don't talk about my mother," I said, defensive all of a sudden.

Eric looked at the frown on my face, then

155

down at my left hand. I had a tight fist around my butter knife, as though I were going to do something criminal with it.

"I'm sorry," Eric said. "But you're making a big deal out of nothing. It ain't nothin' crazy."

"Then tell me," I said, getting tired of this back and forth. "Or not. But know, if that's the way you want to play it, we'll be going our separate ways when we're finished eating."

"You just like all the rest of them: got a little money, look down your nose at folks when they don't do exactly what you say. Well, fuck you!" Eric got up, turned to leave, and then turned back to grab a handful of the sliced loaf before walking out.

I watched him make his way toward the door, then exit, and I felt bad for what I had done.

"Is everything all right, Mr. Winslow?" the manager, a graying man in a dark suit asked.

"Yes," I said, still looking at the door.

"Shall I call the police?"

Taking offense, I said, "Why? Why would you do that?"

"I'm sorry, Mr. Winslow, forgive me," the manager apologized, and then left me.

Had I made a mistake? I had been looking for my brother for almost a month, then after finding him, I drove him away after only a few days.

I stood up from my chair, prepared to go after him, but a moment later I sat back down. If he could not be honest with me, there was no way I could invite him into my home and expect things to work. This had to be done on terms that I was comfortable with, and honesty was a priority.

I lowered my eyes, still not feeling any better about forcing my brother away, when I felt the chair opposite me move.

I looked up and was surprised to see that Eric was taking his seat again. "You really need to know?"

"Yeah, I really do."

"I stole a car. That's what I did. Okay?"

"Okay," I said, picking up my fork, prepared to eat again, but I stopped. "Why was it so hard for you to tell me that?"

"You have everything given to you. From what I see, there ain't nothing that you don't got, or can't get if you wanted it. That little information you just got from me, all you had to do was punch a few buttons on a computer, and you could've known it. But I had to give it to you. All my life people been in my business, the foster care system, the city, the courts. I just wanted not to be forced to give up what's my personal business for once."

I realized I'd made a huge mistake. "I'm sorry, Eric."

"Don't worry about it," he said, looking away. "I'm used to it."

30

"After you," Cobi said, unlocking the huge wood-and-glass door to the mansion.

Eric stood at the threshold, intimidated. This place seemed like somewhere he should've never been.

Eric walked into the foyer and waited for Cobi to close the door and walk him the rest of the way into the house. He looked down at the beautiful, waxed hardwood floors beneath him, the old paintings, from the original artists long passed, hung in giant wooden frames on the walls. He saw furniture that looked as though it may have cost more than Eric would make in his lifetime.

"So, what do you think?" Cobi said, resting his briefcase on the floor beside the leather sofa.

"This is your house? Where you live?" Eric said, as though he had a hard time believing what he was seeing.

"I know, a little over the time top, huh. It was rumored to have once been owned by a prince who would visit on occasion from England. But I don't know if that's true or not. Want me to take you on a tour of the rest of the place?"

"Yeah, man," Eric said. "Sure, let's see the rest of it."

What Eric saw was a first floor with a restaurant-style kitchen with professional-grade, stainless steel appliances. He saw the indoor swimming pool, the bathrooms done in black granite and marble, the media room that sat thirty people and looked like a real movie theater. He saw the library, the den, and the recreation room that housed a red felt pool table with a surface larger than any bed Eric had ever slept on.

Outside were five acres of gated, sloping, manicured lawn, shrubs, and bushes that looked meticulously tended to. There were even trees towering a hundred feet high on one end of the property.

Cobi walked Eric over to the six-car garage, then hit a button on his keychain that rolled up the door.

"That was my mother's car," Cobi said, pointing to a beautifully preserved, vintage silver 1970 Jaguar. "And that one's mine," he said, nodding toward the Audi. "But I just keep it parked back here, since I'm driving my father's now."

"Your father. The same guy that adopted you but not me? Where is he? I'd like to meet his ass," Eric said, resentment in his voice.

"He's dead, as is my mother," Cobi said, looking unblinkingly at Eric. "Plane crash about a month ago."

"I'm sorry," Eric said. "Were they —"

"That's all you need to know about them. Come on, I'll show you the rest of the house."

Cobi led Eric up the long, curving staircase to the second floor.

"My bedroom is the last room at the end of that hall," Cobi said, pointing down the black-and-white tiled corridor. Cobi walked a few more steps and stopped between a pair of doors, spaced ten feet apart. "One of the bedrooms up here was my parents', one is my father's study, one was converted into a sitting parlor for my mother, and the other is a designated guest bedroom, which leaves these two free. You have your choice of either."

Eric turned to Cobi. "One of these?"

"Yeah, whichever one you choose," Cobi said. "They're both around the same size, just decorated differently. Go ahead, step in."

Eric walked into the first to find an enormous bedroom furnished with a California king-size bed, the blades of a copper ceiling fan rotating lazily above it. There was a dresser and chest of drawers, a forty-two-inch flat-screen TV, and a leather sofa, loveseat, and table in a separate sitting section of the room.

"Okay," Cobi said. "Let's check out the other one."

"I don't need to," Eric said. "This one is perfect."

"Are you sure, because —"

"Dude, I'm coming from a jail cell. The closet is probably bigger than where I lived."

"Well, when you go to hang up something, you'll find that you're probably right."

"Won't need to hang nothing up," Eric said, spreading his arms out. " 'Cause all I got is the clothes on my back."

Cobi looked sadly at his brother but didn't respond to what Eric said. "Is there anything else, before I leave you alone to get settled in?"

"Yeah. That information I asked you for. You never gave it to me."

Cobi reached into his jacket pocket and pulled out a folded sheet of paper. He passed it to Eric.

"Thanks. You got a phone here I can use?"

"On the nightstand, by the bed."

Eric turned back to Cobi, fishing for words. "I'm sorry if I seem ungrateful for what you're doing or resentful for all this stuff you got."

Cobi smiled. "I understand. I might feel the same way if things were the other way around." Cobi walked toward the bedroom door. Before he stepped out, he said, "I hope things work out with your phone call."

Worry on his face, Eric said, "Me, too."

31

After five full minutes of staring at the phone, Eric picked it up, dialed the number from the paper Cobi gave him, and held his breath. As the phone rang, he stared down at the petition, the legal document to strip him of his parental rights. There had to have been some mistake.

"Hello?" A woman's voice said.

Eric froze at the sound.

"Can I speak to Jess Freeman?" Eric asked, his voice trembling slightly.

"This is Jessica Freeman. Who is this?"

Eric paused. "It's . . . it's Eric."

The silence lasted so long that Eric thought he had been hung up on. "Jess, you there?"

"How did you get this number?" Jess said, her voice only a whisper. Eric pictured her hunched over the phone, her hand cupped over the receiver like she had something to hide.

"I'm out. I'm out of prison."

"How did you get this number?"

"I got this thing, this petition from the lawyer. Why are you doing this, Jess?"

Silence again.

"Jess?"

"Read it again. It's self-explanatory. I'm sorry, Eric. I have to go."

"No, Jess. Wait! I need to —"

The line went dead.

Eric held the phone to his ear a moment longer.

He pushed the redial button, waiting while the phone rang. It was picked up by voice-mail.

"Jess, I don't know why you hung up on me. I need to talk to you. I want to see you and Maya. Please. Call me back." He thought to give her the number but realized he didn't know what it was. "Call me back at the number on your Caller ID, okay?"

He placed the phone back in its cradle. What was going on? What was Jess doing, and why in the hell wouldn't she at least tell him? Did she no longer love him? Even if that was the case, why would she try to steal his baby from him?

Eric dropped his head in his hands. After a moment, he looked up, looked around the room. Why was he even here? Did he expect the man down the hall to save him? Eric knew Cobi lied about the traffic being the reason he was late. Eric had always relied on his intuition, and it told him by the look on his so-called brother's face that the man had doubts about him. He was probably in his bedroom right now, regretting inviting Eric in and trying to find the most polite way to tell him that in the morning he would have to leave. Eric decided he would save him the trouble.

He walked over and pressed his ear to the door and heard no one moving around outside.

He carefully opened it, stuck his head out, and looked both ways down the hall.

Downstairs, there were lights on. The dim light above the stove, the lamp burning in the living room window, and an overhead hallway light that allowed Eric to see as he searched the first floor.

He stopped by a plaque hanging on the wall by the front door, a half a dozen small hooks protruding from it. This was where Cobi had hung his ring of keys when they walked into the house earlier.

There were three sets hanging there. Eric walked up very close to the plaque, fingered the sets till he noticed the Audi key with four interlocked silver rings on it.

He gently lifted the set and headed for the back door.

32

Eric made a turn onto a dark, winding road, wishing he had paid more attention to the directions on the way here.

As the Audi's xenon bulbs cut through the dark space ahead, Eric leaned close to the windshield, the glow of the car's illuminated red instruments painting his face as he squinted to see where he was going.

Before leaving the house, Eric stopped in the family room, where the entertainment center was. He stood in front of the sixty-inch flat-screen mounted on the wall above the fireplace and sized it up. It would be too big to fit in the car and too time consuming to take down. He snatched the DVD player, the Bose Surround Sound system, and cable box instead.

As he drove, Eric knew the plan wasn't fully developed, but it was in action. He would pawn the electronics he stole for spending money, and then he'd take the car to a chop shop.

But what if the shop he knew of was no longer there? He knew he'd only get a few grand for the car, and then he'd have no transportation. Maybe he should keep it. But then exactly where would he go? To Jess's?

She sounded like she didn't want to see him. But if he pulled up in a big, expensive new car, he was sure that would be a different story.

Eric cut the wheel, made a right, and thought the surroundings were starting to look familiar. He relaxed a bit, feeling more confident about the decision he had just made.

All of sudden, the car lost power. Not just the engine, as if he had run out of gas, but the entire car. The lights shut off, the cabin went dark, the car shut down and eventually rolled to a slow stop as Eric steered it toward the side of the road.

"Fuck!" Eric said, hammering the wheel with the side of his fist. He yanked the hood release from under the dash, threw open the door, and sprang out of the car. He raised the hood and stared down at the engine with only the light of the moon to see.

He fidgeted around in there, pulling on

belts and hoses, till he heard the sound of an approaching car.

He hunkered down behind the hood, then scurried around the side of the car, not wanting to be seen.

Bright lights lit up the Audi and the space around it. Eric heard the sound of tires crunching gravel as the approaching car pulled up slowly behind his.

A moment later, still crouching, Eric heard a door open.

"Eric, you over there?"

It was Cobi.

"If you're over there, come out. I didn't call the police."

He thought a moment of just turning and running, but he finally stood and slowly walked out, his hands raised over his shoulders.

"Put your damn hands down. I'm not the cops," Cobi said, anger in his face.

Eric lowered his hands. "I think I messed up your car."

"No, you didn't. I called the antitheft service and had it shut down." Cobi dug his cell phone out of his pocket. He was wearing pajamas, slippers and a trench coat. "I'll have it turned back on, and you're going to drive it back home."

At the house, Eric silently followed behind

Cobi like a child awaiting punishment. They ended up in the kitchen.

Cobi opened the fridge door. "I'm having milk. Do you want something?"

"I'm good," Eric said, his head down, brooding on one of the kitchen chairs.

His back to Eric, Cobi poured himself a half glass of milk, took a sip, set it on the counter, and then rested his hands there. From behind, Eric saw Cobi take a deep breath, then heard him exhale. Finally, he turned around, indignation on his face. "Exactly what the hell were you thinking?"

"I wasn't."

"No. No!" Cobi said, taking two steps toward Eric. "Play stupid, but I know you're not. You had a plan."

"Fine. The plan was to take the car and some of your shit, and I hadn't thought about anything past that."

"Bullshit! That's not good enough, Eric," Cobi yelled. "I find you, take you in as my family, welcome you into my home, and this is what you do? How could you?"

"What the fuck did you expect!" Eric shouted, standing from his chair. "Think about where you found me — prison. I'm a criminal. A fucking car thief. Then you trust me with your big cars and all the shit you got?"

"So I can't trust you? Is that what you're saying to me?"

"Why are you doin' this?"

"Because you're my brother."

"That don't mean shit. You don't know me from any fool on the street. I'm asking you again. Why you doin' this?"

Cobi took a moment before answering. "I was adopted by good people, but I never knew my family — my real family. You had hard times. It's probably what got you in trouble to begin with. But I know you can do better. I want you to do better. I'm going to help you, because now that I found my family, I don't want to lose you."

Eric dragged a hand down his face. "What if I can't live up to your standards? Just because we look alike don't mean we are alike."

"So that's why you did it? You stole from me on the first night you're here, because you'd rather kill our chances now than put forth the effort it takes to make this work."

"I don't know if I can be who you expecting me to be."

"What if I hadn't known it was you who took the car? What if I had called the police, and they tracked you down? You would be in custody right now. You would've violated your parole and you would be going back to prison. Is that what you wanted?" Cobi said, walking up to Eric.

Eric turned from Cobi's harsh stare.

"I said, is that what you wanted to do!" Cobi shouted.

"No!" Eric yelled back.

The two men stood, eye to eye, each looking like a mirrored reflection of the other, until finally Cobi stepped away. "I can't make you do something you don't want to do, or be someone you don't think you're capable of being." Cobi walked to the kitchen table, grabbed the keys to the Audi, walked back, and placed them in Eric's hand. "You want it, the car is yours. I'll go upstairs and get the title for you. Then the choice will be yours. You can get in the car, drive off right now. Keep it, sell it, whatever you want, but don't ever, in your life, think of contacting me again. Or you can stay and we can work on getting to know each other, being a family. We'll both make mistakes. I'm okay with that. But if you ever steal from me again, I'll be the one prosecuting your case and personally sending you back to prison. The choice is yours."

Eric looked down at the keys in his hand, then at the path to the back door. He gave the decision long, hard thought, then said, "Okay. I guess I wanna try."

"Can't be any guessing," Cobi said.

"All right, I want to try."

"Good."

33

Austen sat on a stool, beside her friend of ten years.

They sat in Julia's West Loop condo, drinking coffee, the balcony doors open, enjoying the late-morning sun.

Julia owned a hair salon called Exposure, just three blocks from where she lived. She considered herself the best weave artist in all of Chicago. Her motto was, "I'll take you from bald to Beyoncé in just two hours."

Julia had an eight-year-old daughter, Jasmine, who she had already dropped off at school when Austen had called and said she needed to have "a life-and-death conversation."

Austen had just disclosed the details of the dilemma she was facing. Afterward, Julia's mouth dropped open, and her eyes grew to the size of ping-pong balls.

"No, no, no, ho, ho, hold up," Julia said, waving a hand. "This woman just pops up out of the blue, talking about she wants to give you half a million dollars to marry her gay brother? This stuff don't happen to real people."

"It happened to me," Austen said, sipping from her coffee.

"Why in the hell would you even consider such a thing? You told her to kiss your ass, right?"

Julia didn't know anything about Austen's fall from grace. She didn't want her friend feeling sorry for her, treating her like she was a charity case.

"No, I didn't quite tell her to kiss my ass."

"Okay, you said something more like, 'Fuck you, skank? Screw you, bitch?' What?"

"I said I'd think about it."

"And exactly why did you say that?"

"Julia," Austen said, getting up from her stool and stepping away from the breakfast bar. "There are things I haven't told you about my situation. I haven't sold a house in I don't know how long, which means I'm not making money."

Julia stood. "But when I asked you if you were okay with —"

"I lied. I wasn't okay with money, and as of right now, I'm just about broke. I've depleted all my savings, I've sold all my furniture."

"Why are you selling all your furniture? Please don't say for money to live."

"Okay, I won't, but that's why. And more to the point, in two days, I might not have anywhere to keep what little I have left because my place has been foreclosed on."

Sorrow appeared on Julia's face as she sighed deeply. "Why didn't you come to me? I could've helped you." Julia looked around her place, like she was picking out a spot to stick a cot. "You know what? You can stay here till you —"

"No. You have a two-bedroom condo and a daughter," Austen said. "I truly appreciate it, but you already have someone to take care of."

"So that's why you told that lady you'd think about it?"

"Yeah," Austen said. "I know what I should do, but I needed my best friend's input just to make sure."

"Austen," Julia said, shaking her head. "I don't want to be the one to tell you to do this if —"

"You aren't telling me," Austen said. "I really just need to know what you think. Please. I really value your opinion."

Julia shook her head. "I hate to say this, but if you have no other options, baby, I really think I would do it."

34

I sat having lunch with Sissy at the café in the downtown Ritz-Carlton. We ate there with a view of the huge lobby, with its water fountain, sofas and chairs, and the massive windows overlooking the bustling Gold Coast just outside. Sissy said nowhere else made a better Caesar salad.

That was what sat before her now. I had the tuna salad on whole wheat with a side of coleslaw and water with lemon.

We were supposed to be having a quaint little lunch filled with family conversation, but I should've known that would never be the case with Sissy.

She had already received two phone calls, returned four texts, and was talking on her iPhone, while her BlackBerry sat beside her plate, ready to buzz or ring at any moment.

"Okay, yes. Sure, uh huh. And I will hear from you when?" Sissy said. She was wearing a pastel pink suit with a white blouse.

"No later than this evening. Good. Looking forward. Good-bye."

Sissy disconnected the call. "I was just told that Procter & Gamble have approached a few of our board members. They're saying they're willing to pay them double what their shares are worth to sell."

"Do we have anything to worry about?" I asked.

Sissy took a long sip from her glass of water. "Not if we get your shares, Cobi. And that gives us two weeks before your birthday, but you already know that, and that plan is in action, so finish telling me about the convict."

"Stop it. Eric is our brother, and you need to start calling him by his name."

"It's hard. 'Convict' just sounds so much better." Sissy smiled, then managed a straight face. "Okay, sorry. So you said he finally told you what he was in for."

"Grand theft auto," I said, taking a small bite of my sandwich.

"Wow. And you let him stay in the house. I'm surprised you didn't wake up this morning to see that he had stolen Daddy's Mercedes."

"No. He definitely didn't steal Daddy's Mercedes," I said, happy I didn't have to lie.

"So how long is this little experiment really going to last?"

"It's not an experiment, and you know it. Eric is living there and will continue doing so until he feels comfortable enough to move out on his own."

Sissy shook her head and pushed more salad into her mouth.

"What?" I said.

"I think you need help with this. I think your vision is clouded by what you want to happen, and you don't see what most likely will."

"You have a pretty harsh opinion of him for someone who has never even met the man. You need to meet him."

"I don't want to."

"But you're going to. I won't have my sister avoiding my brother."

"It's not a good idea. You know me. And if I meet him, I'm going to be me. Are you ready for that?"

"Wouldn't have it any other way."

"Cool."

Sissy's BlackBerry started to ring.

"Don't pick it up," I said.

"I won't," she said, looking at the screen. "I just want to see who it is before I ignore the call." Then, "Oh, Cobi, sorry. I'll make it quick, but this is the call I've been waiting for."

"Of course it is," I sighed.

After several minutes of back and forth, Sissy said into the phone, "I'm glad you've come to that decision. I'll make sure and tell him, and we'll be getting back to you." Sissy disconnected the call, sat back in her chair, and looked very satisfied.

"Okay, what just happened there, Wonder Woman?" I asked.

"I have some very exciting news," Sissy said with a smile. "You have yourself a wife."

35

Eric arrived early at the Artist's Café. The day was a beautiful one, so he sat outside at the tables and chairs beside the sidewalk.

This morning when he woke at seven, he rose in bed, grabbed the phone, and called Jess's number again.

When she answered the phone and discovered it was him, she was silent.

"Jess, you can't do this to me. You have to tell me something."

"There's nothing to say. Maybe you should just stop calling me."

"What? No. You stopped coming to see me. You kept our daughter from me, and now you're trying to take her," Eric said. "You need to tell me what's going on now."

"I can't, Eric. You wouldn't understand. Please, just leave us alone."

"I got your address when I got your phone number. I'll come over there. Jess, I need to see you and the baby, and you need to tell me what's going on."

There was silence for a long moment. "Fine," Jess said, and gave Eric a time and place to meet her.

Now, Eric had been waiting ten minutes, sipping from a complimentary glass of water.

He straightened his T-shirt and wished he had better clothes. There were no holes in the shirt he was wearing. It wasn't dirty. Neither were his jeans, but he felt like a bum and was sure he looked like one. He lowered his head, wondering what he would say to Jess when he finally saw her.

A moment later, he heard someone call his name. He looked up and saw a beautiful woman, wearing a beige business suit. The woman's hair was pinned up, a single curl falling down one side of her face. She wore dark sunglasses and glossy red lipstick.

If it hadn't been for the tiny dimple in her left cheek, Eric wouldn't have known it was Jess. She looked drastically different from the days when he dated her, when all she wore was jeans and T-shirts like he did.

Looking at her for the first time in years painfully reminded him just how much he missed her. Eric stood from his chair and motioned to give Jess a hug. She allowed it but didn't give him one back.

Eric pulled Jess's seat out for her and waited till she took it before he sat back down.

He smiled. "You want something to eat? I ain't never been here before, but the food looks pretty good."

"I don't have time."

Eric wrapped his hands around the half glass of water. "So how you been?"

Jess looked over her shoulder as though worried someone was following her. "Eric, you said you needed to talk, so maybe you should talk."

"Fine. What happened to us? You and Maya was coming to see me, then you just all of a sudden up and stopped. Now you trying to do this thing by taking Maya."

Jess closed her eyes and frowned as if her answer caused her pain. When she opened them, she said, "I can't do this anymore. I want you out of my life. And I'm filing the petition because I want you out of our daughter's life as well."

"What! Jess, I loved you. I still do," Eric said, standing, reaching across the table for Jess. She backed her chair away.

"I'm sorry. I truly am, but it's not working."

"You can't just leave me and tell me you're taking my daughter with you because it ain't working. There has to be more than that."

"Let this happen, Eric," Jess said sadly. "It's better for everyone."

"I won't let you do it."

"You don't have a choice. It's already happening."

36

Blac sat alone in his cell, on a chair, staring at a wall. It was almost lights out and the cell doors would be closed soon.

He had just come back from speaking on the phone to his girl Theresa. She was so excited that she screamed through the phone and told him she was going to make his favorite meal, give him a bath, a full body massage, and anything he wanted after that.

The phone pressed to the side of his face, Blac smiled, grateful that at least there would be someone there at the gate to pick him up. He didn't even know if Eric had that. He hadn't heard from him since he got out, which led Blac to believe Eric's so-called twin brother didn't come through for him.

That's why there was a frown on Blac's face as he stared at that dirty cement wall in front of him. He was excited about getting out tomorrow, but he had been betting on somehow being able to use Eric's filthy rich brother to put his hands on the $150K he needed to save his ass. If this Cobi character decided to disappear, then Blac would be back to the drawing board, and that would be a bad thing. He just wanted to be done with this chapter of his life and move on to something better.

Blac had a twenty-six-year-old little sister, Wanda, that he loved dearly. She had an eight-year-old son named Johnny. He hadn't seen his nephew since the last time he was a free man, years ago.

Wanda and Johnny lived in the small town of Racine, Wisconsin. Blac hated to think about it, but he was what drove them out of Chicago.

The late-night visits by thuggish men, rolling up in pimped-out cars, unexplained stacks of money appearing in the house he lived in with Wanda led her to believe that Blac was not a good influence on her or Johnny's life.

She told Blac she was certain of that the morning Johnny, at four years old, came running down the hallway, playing with a gun. Wanda was in the kitchen cooking breakfast for the boy when she heard a loud click.

When she spun around, she saw her son giggling and pointing a gun that was just about as big as he was, at her.

Later that night, Wanda had sat her older brother down and explained to him, "If your gun had been loaded, I would be dead right now. And who knows, maybe even Johnny, too. Stay here if you like, but I can't take it anymore. I love you, Joseph." Wanda refused to call him Blac. "But I can't have you influencing Johnny like that, wanting to grow up to be like you. I won't let you and the streets take him from me."

Wanda had a friend who found her a job way down in bum-fuck Wisconsin of all places, and she packed herself and Johnny up as quickly as she could and got out of Chicago.

Before she left, she asked Blac to come with them, start a new life there.

Blac snickered, turned away, like he hadn't given it any thought at all, when he actually had. He shook his head and said, "What the hell would I look like hanging out in Wisconsin? Nope. No thanks. I ain't no dairy farmer."

When he turned to look back at Wanda, there were tears on her face. "You're gonna end up in trouble if you stay, Joe. You gonna end up in trouble or dead."

37

His hands in his pocket, his head lowered, Eric walked a line back and forth across his room.

When he heard a knock, he stared at the door but did not move.

The knock came again. Eric walked over and opened the door to find Cobi there.

"What are you doing locked up in this room again? We live in a mansion. There are other places to do things, you know."

"Prison mentality," Eric said.

"How did your meeting go this afternoon with —"

"Jess," Eric said. "It ain't go very good."

"Let me get you out of here. We have acres of land out there. Let's take a walk."

The night was warm, and the sky above was speckled with stars.

Eric told Cobi about the meeting, about how nicely Jess was dressed and how embarrassed he felt because he was wearing the same clothes he wore three years ago, when he was thrown in prison.

Cobi appeared saddened by what Eric told him but remained quiet.

Eric looked just as sad. "She said I just need to leave her alone and let this happen. What the hell does that mean?"

"You can't just wait on her. You have the letter from the attorney," Cobi said. "I'll call him, so we can find out exactly what's going on."

"How can she say I'm unfit to see my daughter?" Eric said, distress in his voice. "I love my little girl and treated her the best I could. Why would Jess do this?"

"You were in prison for three years, right?"

Eric nodded.

"And the child is four years old now?"

"Yeah. She just made it last month. You wanna see a picture of her?" Eric said, digging into his back pocket. He pulled out his wallet and slid out the old photo of Maya and handed Cobi the picture.

"She's gorgeous. Look at that smile, and those dimples. She's beautiful, Eric," Cobi said.

"She is, isn't she," Eric said proudly.

"Maybe Jess thinks you been away too long. Maybe that's why she's doing this,"

Cobi said, passing the picture back to Eric. "I really don't know. We'd have to speak to a family law attorney. If Jess is filing a petition, there's going to be a hearing. I know a good man who practices family law. I'll get him to represent you."

38

The next day Eric and I walked in the house around three in the afternoon. I took off work today, because I had the appointment with Sissy and the mystery woman I was supposed to be marrying, but I also wanted to start the process of helping my brother keep his daughter.

This morning, I knocked on Eric's door to wake him up, but he had already dressed and showered and was sitting on the edge of his bed.

"You're up early," I said.

"Still on prison time."

"You have plans today? I got somewhere I want to take you."

We ended up at my favorite clothing store. AERO was located on Michigan Avenue. They carried the finest designers from all over the world, and they even had a spa, where I often went to get a facial, mani-pedi, and a massage.

I knew the owner, Monica Kenny, so I always received five-star treatment.

Standing outside the big glass doors of AERO, Eric stopped me just before I pulled on one of the handles.

"What are we doing here?"

"We're getting you some new clothes."

"No. I don't need none."

"You told me the only clothes you had were the clothes on —"

"I wasn't saying that to get you to take me shopping. I ain't like that, man. And I don't need none of your charity."

"Then what, Eric?" I said. "You wanna walk around wearing the same jeans and T-shirt?"

Eric lowered his head. "I don't wanna take no handout from you, man. I need to earn it."

"Fine. Whatever I buy you today, or from now on, we'll look at it as a loan."

"I'm gonna need a way to pay it back."

"I'm one step ahead of you. My sister has a little influence in the family company," I said, smiling. "I'm sure we'll be able to find you a job there."

The owner, Monica — an attractive, shapely woman, with short-cropped curly black hair — almost passed out when she saw the two of us. I had called her earlier this morning and told her I wanted her to lay out a fashion show's worth of fine men's suits, casual clothing, and sportswear.

"Changing up your look?" Monica asked.

"I wouldn't quite say that," I told her. "You'll see. Oh yeah, and I have a surprise for you, too."

Seeing Eric and me, Monica gave me a hug and said, "So is this the surprise you were talking about? You've been cloned?"

"Very funny," I said. "Monica, this is my long-lost twin brother, Eric."

Monica stepped forward, looked at Eric's attempt at a handshake, blew it off, and gave him a hug. "Family of Cobi's is family of mine. I assume this is really who the clothes I laid out are for?" Monica said to me.

"Yup."

"Then why don't you go over to the spa? Charlene is waiting to take care of you, and I'll make sure Mr. Eric here gets everything he wants."

Eric and I walked back in the house at three carrying six thousand dollars' worth of clothes. He picked out jeans, jerseys, slacks, shirts, and even three beautiful Italian suits and ties to match.

On the way home, we stopped off and had

Eric hooked up with service and the latest iPhone.

Inside the mansion, we set down all of the bags. Eric shook his head. "What am I supposed to say, man?"

"Nothing, because you already thanked me a gazillion times on the way home."

Eric pulled the phone out of his pocket and started poking the touch screen. "Dude! I even got a phone. I can't believe it. Tonight, my boy is gonna be like, wow!"

"You're meeting someone tonight?"

"Yeah, I'm probably gonna be out pretty late."

"Well, have a good time."

Eric gave me a quick hug, clapped me on the back, and said, "Thanks again for the clothes."

39

Because Austen no longer had a car, a limo had been sent for her, which brought her out to the Winslow Hair Care Products corporate offices.

When Austen was given the okay by Sissy's secretary to step into Sissy's office, she saw that the woman was on a very heated phone call.

"Listen, I told you we will have the money! When have we ever been late?" Sissy raised her voice into the headset as she paced the office. Tiny, quarter-sized circles of perspiration dotted the blouse under her arms. She held up a finger to Austen, while giving her a forced smiled. "Well, you just hold them off as long as you need too, understood? Good!"

Sissy disconnected the call, pulled off the headset, and walked over to greet Austen.

"Sorry about that," Sissy said, taking Austen's hand.

Austen had made a point to put on a nice earth-toned spring dress and short heels to appeal to the man she was supposed to meet today. It's not as though she felt she had to sell herself, but over the last couple of days, she did realize that this deal was something that she desperately needed, and she wanted Mr. Winslow to feel as though he was getting what he was paying for, so to speak.

"Sorry that my brother isn't here yet," Sissy said. "He should be walking in the door any —"

Before Sissy could finish, her office door opened and in walked Cobi.

Austen had seen pictures of him in magazines before Sissy had given her the clippings. She had even seen him on the evening news a couple of times, but none of those sightings did him justice, Austen thought. Gay or not, Cobi Winslow was a beautiful man with his medium chocolate brown skin, his chiseled facial features, perfectly shaped head, and athletic body. It was sad, because yes, Austen felt her body warm a little at the thought of what he would look like standing there nude.

"Austen," Sissy said. "Let me introduce you to my brilliant big brother, Cobi Winslow."

Cobi took the four steps over to Austen,

displayed a beautiful smile of gleaming white teeth, and shook her hand. "Pleasure to meet you. Miss Greer, correct?"

"That's right," Austen said, enjoying the softness of his hand and the strength of his grip. "The pleasure is all mine, Mr. Winslow."

"Well," Sissy said, behaving like a proud mother sending her teenage son to his prom. "Looks like we've made a connection. Once I get the contract prepared, we'll have this deal done in no time. Till then, why don't we just all sit down and get acquainted?"

"You know what, Sissy?" Cobi said. "Would you mind stepping out for a moment and giving me and Ms. Greer a few minutes to speak alone?"

"Oh," Sissy said, surprised. "No. No problem," she said, making her way to the door. "Just . . . call if you need me."

After the door closed, Cobi paused a moment before cutting to the chase and saying, "So what do you think?"

"What do you mean?" Austen was caught off guard.

"If I know my sister, she has already explained every minute detail about this potential arrangement. You understand what will be happening, don't you?"

Though fully aware, Austen sounded uncertain. "I do."

"This in no way will be a traditional, fairy-tale marriage. Not even close."

"I'm not expecting it to be."

"And you're okay with that?"

"I am."

"Because you're having financial difficulties and this deal will rescue you from them?"

Austen didn't like it being summed up like that. It made her feel like the high-priced prostitute she told Sissy she wasn't. "I guess so. And how about you? I won't be the only one in this. Will you be okay with it?"

"I will."

"Because you're gay, and your father wanted you to marry a woman in order to receive your trust?"

"I guess I deserved that."

"You did," Austen said, trying to smile. "Is this something that you really want to happen?"

Cobi looked down at his shoes, then back up at Austen. "I don't necessarily think it's a good idea. You?"

"I feel the same," Austen admitted. "But just like me, if you had any other option at all, you'd take it. Right?"

"That's right," Cobi said.

40

After the meeting, I sat in my father's Mercedes, thinking about the woman I just met — the woman who would be my wife. She was beautiful, pleasant, and didn't seem to have any pie-in-the-sky beliefs as to what this would be. That was a good thing. I just hoped my sister knew what she was doing.

I picked up my cell phone and dialed Sissy.

"Cobi, she's perfect, yes?" Sissy said. I could hear in her voice how proud she was of her work.

"She's nice, Sissy. But there's no such thing as perfect. That's not why I'm calling. I need a favor."

"Well, considering what you're doing for me, I guess I owe you one. Shoot."

"I need you to give my brother a job."

Silence.

"Sissy."

"No. There are a million other places he can work."

"He's an ex-con. You know how hard it'll be for him to find work," I said. "And he shouldn't have to go through that, considering he has family that can employ him."

"You're his family," Sissy argued. "Find him a job at the state building where you work."

"Yeah, right. Our business is locking up people like Eric, not employing them," I said. "It would never happen, no matter how hard I tried. I need this from you. You said you owed me one."

"Cobi, I can't. I'm sorry."

"Sissy . . ." I said firmly. "I wouldn't ask this of you if —"

"Fine," I heard her blow angrily into the phone. "But he'll be cleaning toilets."

"No. You can do better than that. I'm signing my life away for two years. He can file records, answer phones, or something."

"Dammit, Cobi, all right. I'll find something. But if he does anything I perceive as questionable, he's fired."

41

Blac kissed Theresa's full lips, rode her with a little less force till she finished climaxing, then he lowered her legs, leaned over her, brushed her sweat-drenched hair from out of her face, and kissed her deeply again.

Theresa's eyes closed as she breathed. A content smile appeared on her face. She looked up at Blac. "I love you."

"I love you, too."

His only family was in Wisconsin, and if it wasn't for Theresa sitting outside that gate in her rusting Chevy Malibu to take him home with her he would've had nowhere to go.

Blac raised himself from the bed and stood in front of the mirror on her dresser. She sat up behind him, admiring his tight, well-built body.

Blac glanced at the reflection of the slightly overweight woman behind him. She had gained a few pounds since he had gone to prison, but they were all in the right places — her hips, her ass, and her breasts. Her hair was longer now — a weave of some sort, Blac thought. It looked nice, though, and he figured she might have done it a day or two ago just for his release.

Theresa wasn't winning no beauty pageants. She was a hard 5.5 on a scale to 10, but that's what Blac liked. A woman who didn't think she was too cute. A woman who wasn't getting hit on every time she walked through the grocery store. A woman who thought she could get no luckier than to find a man like Blac.

Yeah, Theresa was exactly what he needed, and as Blac slid on his jeans, without first putting on his underwear, he figured he'd stay here till he was able to drum up the money to give Cutty, then he would head out to Wisconsin.

He just hoped he could get it in time.

Blac was surprised he had not heard from the drug dealer or any of his boys yet. They knew where Theresa lived, and Blac was surprised not to find some black Hummer or huge GMC truck with smoked-out windows sitting in front of her house when they pulled up earlier.

Theresa knew about Blac's past, about his brushes with the law, but for the last year, he had promised her that he had changed and would not bring any of that criminal behavior back into her house.

If she got wind of him owing a drug dealer money, despite how much it might hurt her, Blac was almost certain she would put him out.

"You hungry, baby?" Theresa said, climbing out of bed and sidling up behind Blac. Her body was soft against his skin. Her erect nipples pressed into his back, started him going again.

Theresa sunk her small hand into the loose waist of Blac's jeans, grabbed his growing penis, and tugged at it softly.

"We could go again, then I could make you whatever you want to eat."

He could do that. His sexual appetite was enormous, his skill was masterful, and Theresa was easy. He could bring her to orgasm three more times without as much as a drop of sweat falling from his brow.

"We got all the time in the world for that, baby," Blac said, wrapping his arms around her and kissing her on the forehead. "Why don't you get that food together now, 'cause I'm starving. And get me the phone. I got an important call to make."

"Sure, baby," Theresa said. She grabbed a robe off a chair in the corner of the room and covered her naked body. She stepped out of the room for a moment, then re-appeared with the cordless phone. "Roast beef, potatoes, gravy, and green peas sound good to you?" Theresa said, handing the phone over.

"Perfect, baby."

Theresa smiled.

Blac patted her on the ass as she stepped out the room, giving him his privacy.

He pulled out the scrap of paper Theresa had written Eric's cell phone number this morning, when he called the house about their hanging out. Blac was happy that Eric did as he said — actually called the number Blac had given him the day before Eric was released.

Now Blac called Eric, and waited, a frown on his face, with the pressure of having to find $150,000 for Cutty.

When the call was picked up and Blac heard Eric's voice, a sincere smile appeared on his face. Not until then had he realized how much he missed his friend. "Hey, man! You coming by to pick me up for that beer tonight, or what?"

42

I sat on the living room sofa, thumbing through an *Essence* magazine to check out the new Winslow Hair Care advertisement while I thought again about the woman Sissy was having me marry.

Sissy said the contract would be ready for signatures tomorrow.

"I'm going to want the two of you to make at least two very public appearances before we announce the wedding — give people the impression that this has been going on privately, at least for a little while. Then I'm thinking a quick private wedding with just family and a few friends. Don't get me wrong. It'll still be beautiful," Sissy had said.

The home phone rang on the end table beside me.

"Hello," I said, picking up, noticing that the screen said it was a call from the front gate.

"Cobi."

A tingle went through my body at the sound of Tyler's voice. That always happened after not speaking to him for more than a day. I wished I was able to control that and not feel like a giddy schoolgirl whenever he decided to call or drop by to grace me with his presence.

"Tyler," I said.

"Guess where I am?" he said in a sing-songy voice.

"At my front gate."

"How did you know?"

"I'm psychic. I'm buzzing you in."

When Tyler walked through the front door, he looked and smelled as good as he always did. His wavy hair was freshly cropped, and his mustache trimmed. I loved when he visited me on the day of a fresh haircut.

After I closed the door, he stepped right up to me, placed a hand to the back of my head, and gave me a long, passionate kiss.

When he was done, I felt breathless and slightly dizzy. *Damn that schoolgirl thing,* I thought, smiling to myself.

"So, tonight is my lucky night," I said. "You found thirty seconds to spend with me."

"Business meeting with a couple of congressmen that was supposed to last all night wrapped up early, so here I am," Tyler said, extending his arms out to his sides, like he was ready for anything.

"You know I could've been busy doing something," I said.

"But you aren't."

"And your wife Kennedi and the girls won't miss you too much, you being gone tonight?"

Tyler took my face in his hands. "Cobi, how about we not do this. Tonight I'm free, and I want to be with you. Let's say we put everything else aside and just enjoy each other, okay? We can find a game, or a movie on TV, have a few drinks, and who knows? What do you say?"

He knew he was way too charming for me to deny, and he was right. I didn't want to ruin it. "Fine. What do you want to drink?"

Tyler smiled, walked over to the sofa, grabbed the remote to the flat-screen, and thumbed it on. "Scotch neat. Make it a double."

I poured us two short glasses halfway full with Black Label, walked them over to Tyler, handed him his, then sat down beside him.

He took a sip, threw an arm around me, and said, "Now why don't you tell me about your day."

I snuggled in next to him. "Okay, but I think I'm going to have to go back and get the bottle."

43

Eric and Blac sat hunched over beers inside a dimly lit, crowded bar on Fifty-fifth Street.

Blac wore jeans, a T-shirt, and a hooded zipper sweat jacket. Eric wore the peach-colored Boss shirt, designer jeans, and a new pair of black loafers Cobi had bought him earlier.

Blac's head was turned, looking out the storefront window of the bar. He shook his head, as though he couldn't believe what he saw.

"What?" Eric said.

Blac turned to him. "He gave you that motherfucking Audi?" Blac said over an old Rolling Stones tune that played loudly in the bar. "Just gave it to you, like, 'Here. Here's the keys. Take it.' "

Eric took a drink from his mug. "Yeah, kinda like that, but I ain't gonna keep it."

"You crazy? He don't even have to say he's giving it to me. Make the mistake and put the keys in my hand, it's mine. Hell, leave the keys on the counter or anywhere I can reach 'em, guess what?"

"I know. The car's yours."

"Damn, Skippy." Blac grabbed his beer, took a couple of swallows. "And look at you, all Sean Johned out, looking like Boris Kodjoe and shit."

"All right, you made your point. I'm lookin' kinda crazy right now."

"Naw, man. You looking good, for real. Which means dude wasn't lyin' about being who he said he was."

"Naw. He wasn't lyin'."

"So you gonna be living there?"

"Guess so."

"He a decent dude?"

"He's okay, but I don't know if he like me."

"So why he givin' you all that stuff?"

"Don't know. He says he wants us to be family, but I think maybe he's feeling guilty about him being raised like royalty and me being poor, and hopes tossin' me a few dollars will help him sleep at night."

"So you think he got a soft spot for guys who had a rough life, make him wanna hand out bags of money? Hell, take me over there. Introduce me to him," Blac said.

"Don't think so."

Blac turned away from Eric and faced the bar. He stared at himself in the mirror behind the stacked bottles of liquor, thinking that maybe he had come on a little too strong. He would have to try again. He couldn't afford to blow this.

Blac lifted his mug, took another drink, and wiped his mouth with his knuckle. He turned back to Eric, who seemed deep in thought. "I was just saying, he seems like a pretty cool dude, and to look just like you, that would be a trip to see. You really ought to let me meet him. Besides, I'd love to see this crib you in, if it's all that you sayin' it is."

"Trust me, Blac. That and more. Dude even got a maid. It ain't no joke."

"So . . ."

"So what?"

"You gonna let me meet your brotha, or are you ashamed to say you know me?"

"Naw, man," Eric said, punching Blac in the shoulder, smiling. "I ain't ashamed of you. You can meet him."

Blac smiled, too. "Introducing me to your brother means more to me than you'll ever know, dude."

44

Earlier, Blac gave Eric some dap when he pulled the Audi up in front of Theresa's house to drop him off. After getting out of the car, Blac's eyes were focused on the area around the dark street for any sign of Cutty's people.

"You all right, man?" Eric said.

Blac showed Eric a fake, confident smile. "I'm good. Holla at you later, right?"

Blac cautiously walked up to the small, two-bedroom house, inserted his key in the lock, and walked in.

He closed the door and double bolted it. He leaned back and exhaled. He told himself that things would work out. He had a good lead. This Cobi guy had loads of money to spare, and it didn't seem as though he had a problem parting with some of it.

Yeah, Blac would be just fine. He had nothing to worry about. Outside of coming up with a plan to get some of Cobi's money. But he had to think about that later, because what bothered him now was the fact that he had been out of prison for almost a full day and there hadn't been any word from Cutty. The man had to have known he was out.

Could there have been a chance that he just forgot about Blac? No. No way in hell. Then again, maybe in return for keeping quiet all that time, Cutty decided that Blac would not have to pay back the money for the drugs after all.

"Baby, is that you?" Theresa called from the bedroom.

"Yeah, just walked in," Blac said, heading to meet her, his spirits uplifted by the chance he was off the hook.

Blac stepped into the bedroom. Theresa was in a nightgown, in bed. The TV was on, showing a commercial for dog food.

"You have a good meeting with your friend, baby?" Theresa asked.

"Yeah, it was pretty good," Blac said, sitting on the edge of the bed, leaning over, and kissing Theresa. "How you doing?"

"Fine. Was just waiting for you to get home. You hungry?"

"I'm good. I had something while I was out," Blac said, standing. "Think I'm gonna take a shower then come in here and do some nasty things to you."

Theresa laughed. "Don't take too long, or I'm gonna have to come in after you."

Blac was in the hallway, his shirt halfway over his head, when Theresa added, "Oh yeah, somebody came by looking for you."

Blac turned around, stepped back in, and pulled his shirt back down. "Who was it?"

"A couple of guys, said they was old friends of yours."

"Did they say anything else?"

"They said they would be back."

"When?"

Just then three loud knocks came at the front door, startling Blac. Worry covered his face.

"You okay?" Theresa said.

"Fine. Just stay right here."

Blac nervously walked to the front door, pressed his ear against it, and listened. When the knocking came again, it panicked him so much he stumbled backward and almost fell. "Who is it?"

"Open the door, Blac. You know who the hell it is."

Blac reluctantly did as he was told.

Standing on the stoop outside was Bones, the thin, muscular man who had pressed the gun to his head four years ago. Beside him stood another, shorter man, wearing a long white T-shirt and a black patch over his left eye. Blac saw the bulges in the waists of both men's jeans and didn't have to be told they were carrying.

"Come on," Bones said. "Somebody needs to talk to you."

"Let me just tell my girl —"

"You don't gotta tell your girl shit," the shorter, one-eyed man said. His name was Rondo. "You just gonna be out here in the truck. Bring yo' ass on."

Blac stepped out of the house and pulled the door softly closed.

The two men walked on either side of Blac to the Cadillac Escalade parked at the curb.

Bones opened the back passenger side door for Blac.

On the backseat was Cutty, looking as he had looked four years ago: short and evil and pissed off. His hair was longer. Some of it stuck out from under a baseball cap, the bill cocked to the side.

Cutty's jeans were pushed down just below his hips. A scantily clad woman had her face in his lap, giving him a skillful blowjob. Blac noticed how the fake, bright pink fingernails of her hand slid rapidly up and down his erect penis.

"What the fuck you lookin' at?" Cutty said, as calmly as if he were reading a newspaper. "Ain't never seen a nigga get his dick sucked? Get in the fucking truck."

Blac got in on the other side of the woman and stared toward the front seat.

"You remember the little deal we made, right?" Cutty said.

"Yeah," Blac said, his eyes still forward.

"Look at me when I'm talking to you."

Blac turned to Cutty, trying not to follow that errant eye of his.

"I said, you remember our deal?" Cutty said, his right hand buried deep into the woman's weave, guiding her head as she continued sucking and stroking him.

"Yeah, I remember."

"Good. Just needed to make sure you did, cause if I don't get my 150K in . . ." Cutty held up his left wrist, glanced at his heavily jeweled watch. "Midnight will make nine days, bad things gonna happen. You clear on that?"

"Yeah."

" 'Preciate you keepin' your mouth shut, but business is business. You owe me, and law of the street say I gotta collect or make an example of your ass. I let you slide, then I'm the punk, and young fools be gunnin' for me. Can't let that happen. You understand?"

"Yeah," Blac said.

"Good. Now get out my truck so I can give this bitch what she been workin' so hard for."

Her mouth full, Blac heard the woman giggle.

"Yeah, okay," Blac said. He opened the door of the truck and started toward the house. He heard the truck door open and shut behind him again, then footsteps moving toward him.

"Hey."

Blac turned to find the man wearing the eye patch behind him, holding out a cell phone. "Cutty wants you to take this for when we need to contact you."

Blac took the phone.

"Number is taped to the back. Whenever that bitch ring, you better be picking it up."

45

I had told Tyler everything about what Sissy had planned for me. I told him the reasons behind the plan and how the family would supposedly benefit from the marriage. I then told him about my skepticism and my fear about going ahead with the whole thing.

"So what do you think I should do?" I said.

He was looking in my eyes, a sly smile on his face. "I know what I want to do to you."

"I just asked you a serious question," I said, pushing down his hand as he tried to undo the top button on my shirt. "I really want to know what you think."

Tyler grabbed the remote from beside his thigh and clicked off the game we had been watching. He stood and held out a hand. "Come on. Let's go to your room. There's something I want to show you."

I crossed my arms. "Can't you do any better than that? Seriously, I need to know what you think about this."

"Okay, okay," Tyler said, grabbing my arm and pulling me off the sofa. "We'll go to your room. You give me what I want, and afterward I'll tell you exactly what I think about your sister's little plan."

"Fine," I said, taking Tyler's hand and leading him toward the stairs. I glanced down at my watch, and saw that it wasn't even eight o'clock. Eric said he wouldn't be home until late. I would make sure Tyler was long gone by nine-thirty at the latest.

We had made love for almost forty-five minutes, taking our time like we always did.

Now, just finishing, we lay naked beside each other in bed, both of us breathing heavily, a light coat of sweat covering our bodies.

I was happy in that moment. Tyler had only been here, in my room, in my bed like this on a few other occasions when my parents were away on trips. But now I could have him over whenever I wanted, and I knew, soon, I would want him over all the time.

I wanted to ask him when, if ever, it would just be the two of us, but I knew he would avoid the conversation. Besides, I truly did need guidance about the situation with the woman I was set to marry.

"What are you thinking?" Tyler asked me, leaning up on an elbow and rubbing a hand over the shaved stubble on my chest.

"I want you to tell me how you think I should play this."

"Okay," Tyler said, lying on his back, crossing his arms behind his head. "You told me earlier, Sissy said the business might be in trouble, that P&G might be attempting a hostile takeover, and the shares that you'd receive once you marry might help you hold on to the company."

"Yeah."

"Do you think even with the additional shares, that she'll be able to save it?"

"Tyler, you don't know Sissy like I do. If you did, you wouldn't even have asked me that question."

"Then you answered your question. The shares are important, and you need to get them," Tyler said. "I would seriously consider this, Cobi. But even if you aren't sold yet, there is a benefit that you might not have thought of."

"What is that?" I said, disappointed, hoping Tyler would say marrying this woman was the last thing I should do.

"Do this, and you'll be married, a family man," Tyler said, sitting up in bed, looking at me very seriously now. "I know one day you want to be attorney general, and I even believe you made mention of political aspirations. This will help you be the man people want to see."

"You mean, lie some more? I don't want —"

"Cobi," Tyler said, laying a hand on my wrist. "I hate to say it, but what do you think you'll be doing when you marry this woman? You're lying then, you might as well take advantage of all the benefits. Also, it will help deflect any suspicion as to whether you and I have something going on."

"Are you worrying about being found out? You know how careful we are. Why would you even think —"

"Never think that we can't be found out. Do you know what kind of news that would make? A state's attorney and an Illinois state senator having a lurid, gay relationship — that would sell a lot of papers and make a lot of money for some people, and there are folks out there who know that."

"We're fine," I said, turned off by the direction of the conversation. "I would never put you in that kind of jeopardy. I don't appreciate you insinuating that."

Tyler laid back down and stared up at me.

"You know you're so handsome when you're angry."

"Shut up," I said, trying to push him out of bed. But he was all muscle and wouldn't budge.

"Come here and give me a kiss," he said, trying to pull me on top of him.

I climbed him and gazed down in his eyes. "So I'm going to go through with this, not just because you think I should, but for all the reasons I mentioned before you gave your opinion."

"I think it's a good idea."

"Me being married won't mess things up between us?" I asked, concerned.

"Does *me* being married mess things up for us?"

"You're lying in my bed, right." I laughed. "So it hasn't messed things up too bad."

"Once you get getting married, we'll share the same situation. Things will be even better."

"Yeah, I guess so," I said, not knowing if that would really be the case.

"There you have it. Now where's that kiss?"

I lowered my face and kissed Tyler. I wished he could just stay here the night. As I kissed him, I considered making that request, when I thought I heard a sound in the hallway.

"Hey Cobi, you in there?" It was Eric. He was just outside my door.

Filled with panic, I called loudly, "Eric don't —"

"We finished up early and —"

Eric must not have heard me, because there were two quick knocks on the door, and then it swung open.

46

After busting in on Cobi, Eric froze, unable to process what his eyes were seeing. His brother, naked, lying on top of another naked man.

Not until Cobi said, "Eric, please!" Did he snap out of his trance and pull the door shut.

He hurried to his room, feeling as though he had blown it, as though he had given Cobi reason to take back everything he had given him and to put him out on the street.

Eric stood, his door partially closed, until he heard Cobi's door open and the footsteps of the men move through the hall and down the stairs.

Eric stepped out after them and stood by the top of the stairs listening to the hushed voices of his brother and the other man. He felt so sick to his stomach that he pressed his hand against his belly, trying to settle it. What he had just witnessed was so very disturbing to him, but worse, it brought back those images, the ones he had worked so desperately all those years to forget. He pressed his hand harder into his belly, fought the horrific memories out of his mind, and listened to what was being said downstairs.

He wasn't able to make out everything, but he did hear Cobi say, "Everything will be all right, I promise. He won't tell."

He heard them say their good-byes. Eric quickly headed back to his bedroom, where he sat on the edge of the bed and waited.

A minute later, there was a soft knock.

Eric stood. "Yeah. Come in."

The door opened, and Cobi stepped in, wearing slippers, his work slacks, and an unbuttoned, collared shirt.

Eric looked at his brother with both sadness and disgust.

Reading his brother's expression, Cobi said, "What, Eric?"

Angrily, Eric said, "You talk that garbage to me about honesty and not keeping secrets, and you're doing that."

"I'm sorry you had to find out that way, but this is my house and I didn't have to tell —"

"Then you're a hypocrite," Eric said, stabbing a finger at him. "My past is my past, and I shouldn't have had to tell you, but you say you weren't going to let me come back here so I had to . . . but you're hiding that." Eric turned away from his brother. Under his breath, he said, "You're a nasty motherfucker."

"What?" Cobi said. "What did you just say?"

"I said, what you were doing, what you let him do to you is some sick shit."

"There is nothing sick about it. We were making love, and if you haven't realized yet, I'm gay. That's how we do it."

"Can you just get out?"

"I can't, not without us talking first."

"Just get out the room! I don't wanna talk!" Eric yelled and could not stop himself from being transported back to that little dark room twenty-three years ago.

It was his second foster home. His foster mother's name was Ms. Mosley. She was a loud, rude, hateful, uncaring, squat little woman. She told Eric several times that the only reason he was there was so that she could collect a check from the state.

Ms. Mosley had a boyfriend, a beady-eyed, mousey-looking man, named Calvin. Eric feared the man from the first time Calvin looked at him with those shiny, ratty eyes of his. Those eyes said he was a predator, that he had plans for Eric, and that it was just a matter of time before he executed them.

Ms. Mosley worked at the fish-packing plant. She'd leave at four-thirty in the morning when it was still dark outside, leaving Calvin asleep in her bed.

The first early morning Calvin entered Eric's room, Eric had suddenly woken up to the full weight of the heavy, grown man on top of him. Eric was on his stomach. His pajama bottoms had been yanked down to his calves. Calvin was fully erect, and was trying to enter Eric at the moment he was snatched from his sleep.

Eric yelled and squirmed, trying to flip his little body to get out from under the man, but he was too heavy, too strong.

Calvin was harshly whispering something over and over in Eric's ear, as he wrestled to spread Eric's little legs apart.

"Don't fight it, little boy, you gonna love it," he kept saying, his voice rough.

Eric continued to struggle with every ounce of his strength until the man pushed into him.

Eric screamed, never feeling a pain so extreme. He yelled and cried louder, until he couldn't cry anymore.

Afterward, there were the warnings from

"He said he would, so I can."

"No, you can't, or you wouldn't be calling me for advice."

"Not calling for advice."

"I'm giving you some anyway. If you're smart, you'll take it. Get him out of there. That way when he tries to sell your story for money, you can say that you never even knew you had a twin brother."

"I won't do that. I think I can trust him, and I know I have nothing to worry about."

"So why did you call me?"

"Good night, Sissy. I'll talk to you tomorrow."

"Cobi, wait."

"What?"

"You know there's no way I can allow him to work at the company now. He knows too much."

"Sissy, you promised," I said. "I just told him he had a job."

"Cobi, Eric is your brother, not mine. And just because you can't see straight, doesn't mean I can't. Already, with all that's going on, you're taking too much of a risk having him at the house. I won't take the same risk, having him at work. Good night, Cobi."

Calvin. "Don't you ever think about telling anyone about this." Then the threats. "If you do, I'll kill you."

Eric kept his mouth shut for the three years Calvin continued to rape him.

He had gotten to the point where when he heard the doorknob turning, his mind would just go elsewhere, far away. He liked to pretend he could remember back to when he was an infant, before he was put up for adoption, back when his mother might have loved him.

He would think those thoughts until after Calvin was finished, leaving him wet and sticky and in flaming pain.

"I'll see you next time," Calvin always said at the door, before stepping out.

Now Eric looked up at his reflection and saw that there were tears in his eyes. "He always said that," Eric said, noticing his twin brother in the mirror, the same tearful expression on his face.

Cobi walked up beside Eric, placing a hand on his shoulder, and asked, "Did you ever tell anyone?"

"Not until now."

"Is there anything I can do? I have a friend who's a therapist."

"No," Eric said, sounding grateful. "That was in the past, and that's where I want it

Calvin. "Don't you ever think about telling anyone about this." Then the threats. "If you do, I'll kill you."

Eric kept his mouth shut for the three years Calvin continued to rape him.

He had gotten to the point where when he heard the doorknob turning, his mind would just go elsewhere, far away. He liked to pretend he could remember back to when he was an infant, before he was put up for adoption, back when his mother might have loved him.

He would think those thoughts until after Calvin was finished, leaving him wet and sticky and in flaming pain.

"I'll see you next time," Calvin always said at the door, before stepping out.

Now Eric looked up at his reflection and saw that there were tears in his eyes. "He always said that," Eric said, noticing his twin brother in the mirror, the same tearful expression on his face.

Cobi walked up beside Eric, placing a hand on his shoulder, and asked, "Did you ever tell anyone?"

"Not until now."

"Is there anything I can do? I have a friend who's a therapist."

"No," Eric said, sounding grateful. "That was in the past, and that's where I want it to stay. I need to focus on now and getting my daughter back."

"Got some good news which should help with that," Cobi said. "My sister agreed to give you a job."

"What?" Eric said. "Are you serious? Doing what? No, don't answer that. It don't even matter. Thank you for that."

"Now what about us?" Cobi said. "Are we okay?"

Eric stared Cobi in the eyes, then said, "Sure, we okay."

47

Pulling the blankets up over my shoulder, I told myself I had nothing to worry about, that I believed my brother when he promised he wouldn't tell a soul.

I rolled over again to take a look at the clock on my nightstand. 11:32 p.m. She'd be awake, I told myself, reaching for the phone and dialing Sissy's number.

"Cobi," she said. "You should've been tucked in by now. What's going on?"

"He knows, Sissy."

"He? Who? Knows what?"

"Eric. He was supposed to have been out. Tyler came by. Eric came home early, walked in my room unannounced, and —"

"Cobi, no," Sissy sighed. "So what happened? Did you talk to him?"

"Yeah, not long ago. He promised he wouldn't tell anyone."

"You can't be certain that he'll keep quiet."

"He said he would, so I can."

"No, you can't, or you wouldn't be calling me for advice."

"Not calling for advice."

"I'm giving you some anyway. If you're smart, you'll take it. Get him out of there. That way when he tries to sell your story for money, you can say that you never even knew you had a twin brother."

"I won't do that. I think I can trust him, and I know I have nothing to worry about."

"So why did you call me?"

"Good night, Sissy. I'll talk to you tomorrow."

"Cobi, wait."

"What?"

"You know there's no way I can allow him to work at the company now. He knows too much."

"Sissy, you promised," I said. "I just told him he had a job."

"Cobi, Eric is your brother, not mine. And just because you can't see straight, doesn't mean I can't. Already, with all that's going on, you're taking too much of a risk having him at the house. I won't take the same risk, having him at work. Good night, Cobi."

48

Austen sat on the edge of her bed, her head resting on her folded hands. Her hair hung over her eyes, obscuring the legal-sized envelope from her vision.

It had been sitting next to her for almost twenty minutes.

Finally, she lifted her head, grabbed the envelope, tore it open, and pulled out its contents.

The contract was twelve pages long. Austen flipped through all of them, till she stared down at the last — the signature page. Cobi had already signed. A blank line indicated where she was to sign. All she had to do was find the courage.

Austen quickly thought about her options and just as quickly realized she had none.

"Hell with it!" Austen said, springing from her bed, the contract in hand. She walked toward the kitchen, needing to find a pen in a hurry, scribble her name there before she talked herself out of it.

She yanked a drawer, dug around a bit, and found a pen.

She flipped back to the signature page, set it on the counter, and prepared to sign. When she pressed the tip of the pen to the paper, she found she could not do it. She couldn't just sell herself for a half million dollars and go back on everything she believed.

Austen dropped the pen back in the drawer, slammed it closed. What she decided to do was rip the contract to shreds, maybe stuff it in a return envelope, and spend money she didn't have to send it back to that arrogant Winslow woman.

Yeah, that's what she'd do, Austen thought, when she was startled by a loud knocking at her door.

When she opened it, she was surprised to see two large Cook County sheriffs standing in front of her, badges on their chests, guns on their hips, and mirrored glasses over their eyes. Low chatter from a radio clipped to one officer's breast pocket buzzed annoyingly.

"Miss Greer?" the larger officer said.

"Yes? What's going on?"

"I'm sorry, but this property has been foreclosed on, and we are going to need you to vacate the premises immediately."

"I . . . I . . . I have," Austen tried to speak but was flustered. "I have things still here. Can't you come back tomorrow?"

"I'm sorry, ma'am. The county needs you out today," the other officer said.

"I need time," Austen said, feeling tears come to her eyes. She willed them back.

The larger officer glanced down at his watch. "We can give you three hours. What you don't have out by then, we will have taken out."

"Okay," Austen said, wiping at her cheek. "Okay. Can I close my door?"

"Of course, ma'am. We'll be out front in our car, waiting."

Austen hurried back into her bedroom and flipped on the light. She went to her dresser, pushed around the bottles of perfume, her jewelry, and other clutter, till she found the gold business card that Sissy had given her the other day.

The card trembling in her hand, Austen dialed the direct number into her cell phone.

A moment later, she heard, "This is Sissy Winslow."

"Miss Winslow, sheriffs . . . they're telling me I have to go."

"Miss Greer, just relax. Now what are you

saying?"

"I'm saying I'm being thrown out of my fucking house. You said you were going to buy it. Do something. Stop this!"

The phone pressed to her ear, tears spilling from her eyes, Austen could hear papers shuffling on the other end.

"Okay, as soon as I get off the phone, I'll call my people, send them over there, and we'll handle this. Have you signed the contract yet?"

Austen was quiet. She realized her back was against the wall, she was painted in a corner, between a rock and a hard place. Every lousy cliché she had ever heard she was now in.

"Austen, did you hear me? Have you signed the contract?"

Austen caught sight of a pen on her dresser. She grabbed it and quickly signed her name to the contract she was holding.

"Yes," Austen said. "Now send somebody over here to take care of this."

49

I lunched with Tyler at an open-air café downtown on LaSalle Street, trying to convince him that he had nothing to worry about when it came to Eric making our relationship known. There were at least a dozen other diners there chatting and enjoying their meals on the beautiful sunny day. Tyler seemed uncomfortable.

It took everything just to convince him to come out and be seen with me in public. He was very paranoid, and he sat picking at his tilapia, wearing dark sunglasses, and looking over his shoulder every now and again.

"And what if he does tell somebody, Cobi?"

"I told you we had a long talk last night. He promised he wouldn't."

"Promised," Tyler repeated with skepticism.

He was about to say something else when

my phone vibrated in my pocket. I pulled it out and saw that it was Sissy calling.

"Minor alteration in plans," Sissy said, her tone very businesslike. "Ms. Greer was put out of her condo this morning, so she'll be moving into your place today."

"Hold it. That doesn't work."

"She's been put out. Where is she supposed to —"

"Get her put back in. We're supposed to be buying her place anyway," I said, wanting that woman to be anywhere but in my home. I just wasn't ready. "Do something."

"It hasn't been put up for sale yet, Cobi. Besides, the two of you will have to be married in less than twelve days. What is the problem with her moving in now?"

"I'm not ready."

There was a pause. "Everything that's going on right now, none of us are ready for. She'll be at your place when you get home tonight. I'll put her in the last vacant bedroom. Call you later, Cobi."

My sister hung up. I slipped the phone back into my jacket pocket.

"Do you have any assurances, any guarantees your brother won't tell?" Tyler said, not missing a beat.

"No, other than the fact that he's my brother and I trust him. Why are you so paranoid, baby?" I said, reaching across the table for his hand.

He yanked away as if I was trying to do him harm. "Don't call me that out here!" Tyler looked around for a moment, then turned back to glare at me through those dark glasses. "You just need to make sure your brother doesn't open his mouth. We have too much to lose."

"Fine," I said looking in both directions to make him think I was as concerned about our secret being found out as he was. "We've been together this long, and we've been fine. We'll continue to be," I said, not realizing we were being watched.

50

Blac didn't know if the phone he'd been given was for his personal use, but he made the call anyway. The way Blac saw it, he was dealing with Eric to try to get Cutty's money back, so he was sure Cutty wouldn't mind.

Half an hour later, the Audi pulled up in front of Blac's house.

In the South Side bar Eric and Blac drove to, they sat at a corner table in the very back of the establishment. Only two other men sat at the bar, drinking beers and having loud, drunken conversation.

Eric ordered two beers and two cheeseburger plates from the overworked-looking waitress but was otherwise silent.

When the beers came, both men took drinks and lounged back in the wooden chairs.

"What's up, man?" Blac asked, almost afraid of the answer. "Everything ain't peaches and cream over in millionaire land?"

Eric looked up from his beer bottle. "Cobi found me a job. Well, his sister did."

"Damn, that's fast," Blac said. "Then why don't you seem happy?"

" 'Cause dude a punk."

"The man find you a job, and now you call him that. What did he do?"

"No. I mean, seriously. My brother's a punk, a faggot. A sissy on the down-low."

"Hell, naw. You got proof?"

"I walked into his room last night, and I find him all cuddled up in bed, naked with this thick, mustache-wearing, Captain Kangaroo–lookin' fool."

"They were fucking?"

"They just finished," Eric said, disgust on his face. "Glad I hadn't walked in five minutes earlier. Cobi was like, 'Nobody knows about this. You can't tell nobody, or it's my ass.' "

And here it is, Blac thought, trying his best to hide the smile that threatened to appear on his face. Since the day Eric had told Blac about Cobi, Blac had been wondering exactly what angle he would take to get this man for his money. Now he knew.

Blac was a sexual being. He loved sex and was blessed with the perfect body to express his passion and give pleasure to others. All that hetero-homo stuff was nonsense to him. Good sex was good sex. Whether he was getting his dick sucked, or eating pussy, riding a woman's ass, or riding a man's, it was still oral sex and it was still ass riding, and if it was halfway decent, somebody would end up coming and that was all that mattered.

During his countless stints in prison, Blac had broken in several men that became his bitches. They were reluctant at first, but once they got a taste or a feel of the nine and a half inches of black granite he was slangin', they couldn't live without it. And now, Blac just had to find a creative way of introducing Cobi to the best he would ever experience.

Blac lowered his eyes and shook his head, as though he was just as disappointed as Eric was at finding out the news. "That's messed up, dude. But you ain't gonna move out or nothing, are you? I mean, he still seems like a decent guy. He is your brother, and he did just get you a job."

"Naw, I ain't going nowhere unless he puts me out. Him being gay is gonna take some getting used to, but that ain't what's bothering me the most. He was all up in my face about this honesty nonsense, and he was the one lying about stuff. I'm just wondering what the hell else he's hiding."

"I'm sure that's it, man," Blac said. "So he still cool with us meeting?"

"Yeah, it'll be cool," Eric said, draining the last of his beer, then staring hard at Blac. "But, like I said, I wasn't supposed to tell nobody about this, you feel me. The senator he's fucking is all paranoid about them getting found out."

A senator, Blac thought. Damn, this just gets sweeter and sweeter. "Ain't nothing to worry about, playa," Blac said. "Your secret is safe with me."

51

Several hours after Austen was evicted from her condo, Julia stood over Austen as she expressed little enthusiasm for the pair of gold, open-toe Prada pumps she was trying on.

"Ooh, girl, they look fabulous. Stand up and see how they feel."

"I don't like them," Austen said, undoing the straps.

"What? Those are the ones you wanted. I'm about to spend my grocery money for the month on those things to make you feel better."

"And now you don't have to."

Not even an hour after Austen had called Sissy to tell her about the eviction, three brawny, uniformed men from a moving company showed up to move what little Austen had left down to a moving truck. When they finished, the place no longer contained even a matchbook of hers. Sissy showed up afterward, holding a Chanel shoulder bag. She walked in, pulled her dark glasses from her eyes, pushed them into her hair, and took a look at Austen, appearing generally concerned.

"I'm sorry this is happening, but the movers told me they have all your belongings. You can come with me now."

"Go with you? Where?"

"Your new home. The Winslow estate."

"No. I mean, I don't know," Austen said. "I'm not ready to —"

"You and my brother are more alike than you know," Sissy said. "Grab your purse and whatever else and you can tell me just how much you don't want to live at the estate on the way there."

"So this Sissy woman is still going to buy your property and make sure it's placed back in your name, right?" Julia asked, as they walked toward the exit of the shoe store.

"Yeah, she said she will."

"That's a good thing. And till then, the house I picked you up from . . . girl, it ain't like it was Cabrini Green. That mansion had it going on. You know I was dying to see what it looked like inside."

"It's the most beautiful house I've ever

seen," Austen said glumly. "It has everything, winding staircase, maid's quarters,
chef's kitchen, and the room they put me in
was damn near as big as my entire condo. It
has a separate sitting area that is more like
a living room. But to be frank, who cares?
It's not mine."

Stopping in the middle of the mall corridor, Julia grabbed Austen's hand. "Why
are you looking at it that way? I know the
situation isn't ideal, but —"

"But what?" Austen said. "I'm getting
married to a wealthy, handsome man. I'm
moving into a mansion, where all my needs
will be met. Yeah, I know it sounds like a
dream, but it comes at a cost."

"Nothing is free."

"I know. I just thought when and if I got
married, it would be to someone I loved."

"What?" Julia said, surprised. "I thought
you never wanted to give a man control over
you."

"I don't, but that doesn't mean I don't
want to fall in love," Austen said, sadly.
"This way that won't ever happen."

Julia sighed, set down her shopping bag,
and grabbed Austen's other hand. "Locked
up in this contract or not, know that when
it's time for you to fall in love, it'll happen.
Nothing's going to stop that. Will you at

least believe that for me?"

Austen rolled her eyes at her friend's desperate attempt to cheer her up. "Yeah, Julia. I'll believe love will still find me while I'm married to my gay husband just for you."

52

When Eric steered the Audi into the circular drive outside the front door of the mansion, he saw a woman standing outside, wearing a suit, her arms crossed.

He pulled the key out of the ignition and stepped out of the car, wearing some of the new clothes Cobi had bought him. He walked toward the house. The woman stood directly in front of the doorway with a nasty little smirk on her face, looking Eric up and down. "Well, I didn't really believe it until now."

"Believe what?" Eric said, still not knowing who he was talking to.

"The resemblance is uncanny," she said, slowly walking a circle around Eric, examining him. When she made her way back around, she held out a hand. "Sissy Winslow, CEO of Winslow Products, and Cobi's sister."

Eric took Sissy's hand and shook. "Hey,

Sissy," Eric said. "I want to thank —"

"Come with me, please," Sissy said, cutting him off.

Eric followed the woman through the house and around a corner. She opened a large wooden door and led them into a dark wood-paneled room with floor-to-ceiling bookcases.

Sissy closed the door behind them. "Eric, is that correct?"

"Yeah," Eric said, looking around the large library.

"Are you a reader, Eric?"

"No. Not really."

"Didn't take you for one," Sissy said. She stepped in front of him. "I'm going to get straight to the point."

Eric just stared at Sissy, starting to develop a dislike for her.

"I think you're trying to play my brother. I look at you, and to tell you the truth, considering the way you are dressed, if I were to have walked in this house and not known it was you, I would've sworn you were Cobi. But that's where the similarities end. You are a criminal, and have been since the first time you were caught stealing at nine years old, out of Toys "R" Us on Eighty-seventh and the Dan Ryan."

Eric looked at her, bewildered.

"I looked up your file. I know all there is to know about you," Sissy said, her arms crossed, casually pacing away from him. "You were put up for adoption, but no one wanted you. You were shuffled from foster home to foster home, got in trouble several times with the law before you were even seventeen. At eighteen, you committed your first violent crime and were sentenced to two years in prison. The list goes on," Sissy said, turning back to face Eric. "Shall I continue?"

"No," Eric said, not understanding why this woman was doing this to him. Isn't she the one that got him the job? Was there another sister? There had to be.

"Good." Sissy walked back toward Eric and stopped just in front of him, smiling. "I see you're driving my brother's car. He spent a little money on you, bought you some fine new clothes." She grabbed the collar of his shirt, flicked it. "Now what, you think you're him? You think you're on his level?"

"I never said that," Eric said defensively.

"You're a worthless nobody who had a hard upbringing. It reminds me of when Cobi and I were kids. He found this stray dog. He begged my parents to keep it, and they let him, but that dog was nothing but a mutt. Cobi gave it a bath, bought it a new collar, but the dog wouldn't train. One day when Cobi was feeding that dog, it bit him. The dogcatchers came and took it to the pound, and they put it to sleep," Sissy said, standing only inches from Eric's face, speaking in nothing more than a whisper. "You understand? I'm not going to let you bite my brother. I would sooner have you put to sleep."

"I don't know what you talking about."

"My brother and Senator Stevens . . . you saw them together. I swear, if as little as a peep gets out, I will have you carted off to jail for a crime so heinous that life imprisonment would be considered a light sentence. Do you understand me?"

Eric stood there silently, hatred now in his eyes.

"Do you understand me?" Sissy raised her voice.

"Yes," Eric finally said.

"And about what you were going to thank me for. I assume it was the job Cobi asked me to arrange for you," Sissy said. "Keep your thank-you. Like I told him last night, I don't want you working there. There no longer is a job for you."

53

When I walked in the house after work, I was surprised to see all the clothes that I had bought Eric folded neatly on the dining room table. Some of them were still in plastic, many of them still had tags, and the shoes were placed neatly back in their boxes.

"Eric," I called, setting down my briefcase.

He answered me from the top of the stairs. "Yeah."

"Can you come down for a moment, please?"

When Eric walked over to me, he was wearing the old jeans and T-shirt he had on when I picked him up from prison.

"Uh . . ." I said with a smile, trying to make light of what I knew had to be a potentially bad situation. "What's going on? Need a smaller size?"

"You should take those back, Cobi. Sorry about the ones I wore already. If they don't give you your money back, I can find a way to pay you for them."

"Stop it. What's this all about?"

"I'm sorry about stealing your car the first night I was here."

"I know. We went over that, and I already accepted your —"

"And you told me you wouldn't deal with me doing it again, and I promised you I wouldn't."

"That's right," I said, not following Eric's line of thinking.

"So why would you think I'm trying to take you for your money?"

"What do you mean? I don't think that."

"You think I'm gonna go to some newspaper or somethin' and tell them what I saw last night to try to make —"

"I don't think that. What would have you thinking" — and then it came to me. I was just surprised it took so long. "Hold it. Was my sister here today?"

"Yeah."

"Did she say something to you?"

"Yeah, she did."

I shook my head, feeling sorry for my brother. I could only imagine the disrespectful things Sissy probably said to him and how he must've felt to ask me to return all his clothes.

"I need for you to understand I don't

think that's what you're going to do. I trust you when you say that you wouldn't tell anyone, and my sister's thoughts are hers, not mine. You understand?"

"So you ain't never say any of that to her?"

"Eric," I said, walking over, taking him by the shoulders. "If I truly felt that way, how big of a fool would I be allowing you to stay here in my home?"

"A pretty big fool, I guess. And what about the job you told me she gave me. She said she ain't giving me no job."

"I'm sorry about that, Eric. That happened last night, and I didn't have a chance to tell you. But you will be getting a job, and it will be there."

"What do you mean?" Eric asked. "How?"

"I may not work there, but my name is on that company just like Sissy's. We're going to get you a position there, even if we have to do it without her knowing," I said, walking over to the table and grabbing an armload of the clothes. "You're going to need these for when you start."

"Are you sure?" Eric said, not looking very confident.

"I'm Cobi Aiden Winslow," I said, playfully. "I'd like to think that still means something. Now come on, grab the rest. We'll put these back in your room, then how about I take you and your friend out to dinner to make up for my sister?"

"I don't wanna mess up anything between you two. I'm just —"

"My brother," I said, answering for Eric. "Now come on."

54

Dinner smelled delicious, Blac thought, as he walked into the kitchen from the bedroom. He was wearing his usual, jeans, T-shirt, and do-rag tied over his shaved head.

Theresa was at the stove, her back to him, putting the finishing touches on the meal, as he rubbed the palms of his hands together in preparation for digging in. "Mmmm, mmm, smells fantastic," Blac said. "What you cook?"

"Shrimp, pasta, and grilled chicken breasts with a side of asparagus," Theresa said, not turning around. "But it'll just be a few minutes. Have a seat, baby."

Theresa came over to the table and had a seat across from Blac. Her new weave was pulled back in a ponytail. She looked cute, Blac thought.

"Like I said, we got a few minutes till dinner is ready," Theresa said, folding her hands on the table. "So I thought I could take this moment to tell you something I been wanting to say."

"Okay, baby," Blac said, throwing an arm over the back of his chair and leaning back.

"First, I'm gonna need for you to take that do-rag off your head while you're at my table."

Blac had to take a second to make sure he'd heard Theresa correctly. "But I always wear my rag at the table."

"I know. That's what I want to talk to you about. And I will, as soon as you lose the do-rag. Blac, I'm serious."

Hearing the conviction in her voice, Blac slowly untied the scarf from around his head. He balled it up and stuffed it in the pocket of his jeans.

"Thank you."

"Now what's this all about? I'm hungry," Blac said.

Theresa cleared her voice. "I been with you six years. The four years you just been away, and the two years before that. I been good to you, and you been taking advantage of that."

"Now hold on —"

"No, Blac. You listen to me. I'm talking," Theresa said, not harshly, but almost asking permission to continue. "All that shady stuff you got going on, like the other night. That stuff gotta stop. And I need to be treated better now. You have to do your share. Clean up around here, take out the garbage, and whatever else I need help with. I'm getting older, I'm tired of doing it all myself, and you ain't a child of mine, so I shouldn't have to. I need you to act like you want to be here, not that you have nowhere else to go."

This is complete and total bullshit, Blac thought, but he nodded his head, faked a smile, and said, "Okay, you right. I can do that."

"You can?" Theresa said, a smile coming to her face. She looked down at her folded hands, as if taking a moment to find courage. "So, like I said, I'm getting older. I don't do all I do for you and let you stay here because I need a roommate. I wanna be married, Blac."

Blac clamped his jaws together to keep from telling her just where she could go with that nonsense. "We had this discussion before and —"

"And we're having it again."

"And what happens if I say I can't marry you?"

This time Theresa didn't take time to prepare her answer, she just came straight out with it. "I gave you a few days to lay back and get treated like a king. I know what I'm worth, and I know what I deserve. If you can't get it together in the next few days, I want you gone," she said, getting up from the table.

Afterward, when Blac went out in the backyard to catch a breather and vent in private, his cell phone rang.

It was Eric saying that Cobi wanted the three of them to get together and have dinner tonight.

Blac walked back into the house and told Theresa he was stepping out. She nodded her head as though it made her no difference.

55

The dinner meeting was at a new spot called Histrionics. Blac had never been somewhere that looked as much like money as this place. There were white tablecloths, the waitstaff wore white waistcoats, and most of the diners looked like they were millionaires.

If Blac hadn't had as much self-confidence as he did, he probably would've been punked by all that money, bitched up, and not been as cool as he was tonight. But that wasn't him. Ex-con or not, Blac carried airs like his time behind bars had been time at an Ivy League institution, walked as though his jeans and T-shirt were the finest ever made.

When Blac and Eric were led to their table by the hostess, Blac spotted Cobi across the room right away. How could he have missed him? Blac had been looking at the identical face for two years now. But what he also noticed was how Cobi's eyes immediately locked on him.

"Pleasure to meet you, Blac," Cobi said, standing, reaching out a hand, when Blac approached the table.

Blac took it firmly and shook. He made a point of maintaining eye contact with Cobi. Maybe he was wrong, but he thought he felt an immediate longing from the man.

The three men sat down.

"So how do you two know each other?" Cobi asked, opening his menu.

Eric looked over at Blac. Blac recited the story Eric had prepared, of him being an old high school buddy and an out-of-work Ford autoworker.

By the end of dinner, Blac had Eric and Cobi laughing so loudly at made-up stories of family members that the hostess had to come over twice and ask them to quiet down.

Later, out of the corner of his eye, Blac noticed the long gazes Cobi was taking at him. When Blac looked at him while telling one of his stories, he saw Cobi's eyes watching his lips, and Blac made a point to run his tongue across them, keeping them shiny and moist.

He felt an instant connection with Cobi. The man was definitely checking him out and seemed interested in finding out more.

Blac just needed an opportunity to push a little harder to see if he was right.

Eric slapped Blac on the shoulder. "Man, you are too funny sometimes. You got me about to piss my damn pants," he said, pushing away from the table. "Going to the men's room. Be right back."

As Eric walked away, Blac and Cobi now sat at a very quiet table.

Blac knew the next few steps would be crucial in whether he was to succeed with his plan.

He let another moment pass. "When Eric told me he had a twin, I told him I had to meet you."

"Well, what do you think?" Cobi said.

"I think you're very interesting; quite handsome and extremely sexy."

If Cobi hadn't been drinking, Blac wouldn't have been so aggressive. But because of the tipsy glaze over Cobi's eyes and the limited amount of time he had to work with, Blac knew he had to move fast. He saw a suppressed, surprised reaction from Cobi, but it wasn't a negative one. Blac had not blown it, but he would have to continue very carefully to ensure he didn't.

Blac pulled his cell phone out and looked at it as though he was confused by the device. "I just got this phone, and I still have no idea what I'm doing with it. Do you have as much trouble with yours?"

"Nope," Cobi said. "Mine is pretty simple," he said, digging inside his breast pocket.

"Can I see it?"

Cobi handed his phone over.

Blac punched a few buttons. "This is a nice one. I wonder if I dial my number into your phone, and press Send, would my phone ring?"

This was the moment Blac would see if Cobi actually had an interest in him, or if it was just his imagination.

"Why don't you try it and see?" Cobi said with a drunken smile.

Expecting Eric to come back any moment, Blac hurriedly dialed his cell number into Cobi's phone. It seemed to take forever, but when his phone finally did respond, he smiled, and handed Cobi's phone back to him.

Cobi grabbed the phone, but also Blac's hand. He squeezed both extremely hard.

Now looking very sober, Cobi said, "Did my brother tell you anything about me?"

That caught Blac off guard, but he told himself to remain composed. "He told me you were a lawyer."

"Anything else?"

"That your family made the pomade I used to always use," Blac said, smiling sheepishly.

Still squeezing his hand like he was trying to crush his bones, Cobi said firmly, "Is that all?"

"That's all."

After a second, Cobi released Blac's hand. "Then how did you know?"

"Really?" Blac said. "You don't think people see, but we can see you."

"Who is 'we'?"

"We. You, me — us," Blac said, talking softly out the side of his mouth, watching as Eric made his way toward the table. "If I was wrong, I'm sorry. You can just delete my number."

Cobi was silent.

Eric was fifteen feet away, then ten, and at five feet away, Cobi said, "No. You weren't wrong."

56

I smiled as I walked down Rush Street.

I loved this street, with its bars and restaurants and the fun-loving people who partied here. It was close to the feeling I got when I walked through Times Square in New York, my favorite place in the world.

I stopped in front of a bar, looked through the window, and saw people laughing, drinking, and having a good time.

But I felt lonely at the moment and knew that was why I even flirted with Blac. I'd been pretending for so long not to be who I know I am, and instead, listened to Tyler, kept things a secret, and only saw him when he allowed.

It wasn't fair, I told myself. I had fallen in love with him but couldn't outwardly express it.

Couples walked past me on the sidewalk, enjoying the beautiful night. I envied them from my perch on the corner.

I snatched my cell phone out and punched in Tyler's number.

The phone rang four times, and I knew on the fifth it would be retrieved by his voicemail.

I stood there, angrily pressing the phone to my face, and listened to Tyler's recording telling me to leave a message. I thought of the evil things I could tell him, but when I heard the beep, I stabbed the End button.

I turned and aimlessly started walking slowly. The phone felt as though it was tingling in my hand.

I stopped at the next corner to wait for the Walk signal. A picture of Blac popped in my head. He thought he was too sexy for his damn shirt prancing around in that skintight deal, but he did look good.

I thought of giving him a call, but what would I do if he picked up? Most likely nothing. Say hi. But that could lead to something else, which could lead to still something more, which could then lead to what I wanted to be doing with Tyler tonight but was unable to.

I shoved the phone back in my pocket, then turned completely around, because I had gotten the haunting feeling that I was being watched. I turned in a slow circle, scanning the area, as if expecting to find some weirdo, staring right at me, but no one was paying me any mind.

57

After his shower, Eric brushed his teeth, ran his brush over his buzzed hair, and then toweled off. He wrapped the white bath towel low around his waist, grabbed his toiletry bag, and gathered his clothes before opening the bathroom door.

Remembering he forgot his toothbrush on the edge of the sink, he went back to grab it. His hands were full, and he felt the knot in his towel slowly loosen. Eric managed to grab the toothbrush with one finger without losing his towel or any of what was in his arms.

When he turned around to exit the bathroom, a beautiful woman wearing nothing but a long T-shirt and white ankle socks was standing in the doorway.

Startled, Eric dropped the toiletry bag. As he tried to catch it before it hit the floor, he dropped his clothes, then the toothbrush,

then the towel, leaving him completely naked.

Eric's eyes ballooned. He heard the
woman gasp as he quickly bent down,
snatched up the wet towel, and struggled to
wrap it back around his waist.

When he looked back up, the woman was
gone.

Either his mind was playing tricks on him,
or Cobi wasn't as gay as he said he was.

Eric stepped out, only to see the woman
leaning up against the wall, blushing, just
outside the bathroom.

"I'm really sorry about that, Cobi," the
woman said. "I didn't know you were in
there."

"I'm not Cobi."

The woman smiled oddly, as if waiting for
the punch line of the joke. When it didn't
come, she said, "What are you talking
about?"

"I'm not Cobi. I'm his twin brother, Eric,"
he said, trying to keep his focus on her eyes.
He could see the roundness of her ample
breasts, the shadow of her nipples, and her
legs, which were smooth and shiny. The last
thing he needed was to pop a rod wearing
nothing but a bath towel in front of this
woman.

"Oh, I'm sorry," the woman said. "I didn't

know he had a twin. Cobi didn't tell me."

"Well, he does," Eric said, definitely feeling himself coming to life down there. "I'm gonna go to my room now. Good night, okay?" Eric said. He wanted more information, wanted to speak to the woman more, but he didn't want to be accused of trying to come on to his brother's girlfriend, or piece of ass for the night, or whatever she was.

"Okay," the woman said. "Well, my name is Austen. Yours?"

"I already told you. Eric. My name is Eric," he said, smiling.

"Well, it's good to meet you, Eric," Austen said, holding out her hand to shake.

Eric looked down at it. If he tried to shake it, there would be a replay of what just happened in the bathroom. He smiled bashfully. "Uh, don't think I can do that without flashing you again."

"And who says that would be a bad thing?" Austen said, smiling slyly. "Good night, Eric."

58

As Austen sat down in the kitchen preparing to have breakfast that Stella made for her, she wondered if her encounter last night had been a dream.

It hadn't felt like it. She believed she had actually been standing in that bathroom when that man's towel fell, exposing that beautiful body, those tight pecs, those chiseled abs, and his long, thick manhood. No, that wasn't a dream, nor was the conversation afterward. Neither was the gigantic orgasm Austen gave herself, later in bed, while thinking about the mysterious twin brother named Eric.

Austen slept like a baby sucking on a bottle, although, during her fantasizing last night, she imagined herself sucking on something else.

This morning, she awoke to a soft knock on her door.

When Austen answered it, Stella, the

kindly older woman, asked her if there was anything she needed. And if she would like to come downstairs, either before or after she showered, Stella would be more than delighted to make her whatever she wanted for breakfast.

More than once, the thought had crossed Austen's mind to ask Stella if she knew Cobi had a twin brother, but she didn't want to seem crazy. So instead, she bit into a succulent strawberry and let her mind drift back to the image of Eric she had burned in her brain.

"Good morning, Mr. Winslow," Austen heard Stella say.

Austen snapped out of her thoughts to see Cobi walking into the kitchen, wearing a gray business suit.

"Good morning, Stella," he said.

"What would you like for breakfast?"

"Nothing for me, thank you," Cobi said, resting his hands on the chair back adjacent to Austen's. "But if you wouldn't mind, would you excuse us for just a moment please, Stella?"

"Of course," Stella said, wiping her hands on a towel and pulling the double doors closed behind her.

Cobi smiled at Austen. "First, let me apologize for not being here to welcome you on your first night here in my home."

"No problem. Sissy took me on a tour yesterday and introduced me to Stella and some of the other staff. Everyone has been wonderful. And something told me I'd be bumping into you sooner or later — today, tomorrow, or maybe on our wedding day." Austen laughed, trying to bring levity to the awkward moment.

Cobi joined her with an uncomfortable smile. "So everything is to your satisfaction, then?"

"No complaints."

"Okay. Good, then I guess I'll be heading —"

"But I do have a question or two."

"Okay," Cobi said.

"What am I supposed to be doing here? I mean, like during the day?"

"You own a real estate business, right?"

"Yes, but my office is in Hyde Park. I don't have a car."

"Then I'll have Sissy arrange for you to buy one. Then you can come and go to your office as you please, or do whatever else you'd like."

"So that's what this mainly is? Me doing whatever it is I want to do? Are there any obligations, any demands that must be met that I should know about?"

Cobi smiled. "I thought Sissy went over what was expected of you the other day when she —"

"She did. But what do *you* expect of me?"

Cobi paused, appearing clueless. "What I expect is just for you to do what Sissy expects."

"Okay, I can do that," Austen said, taking a bite of melon and crunching it between her teeth.

Cobi turned to leave.

"Oh, and one more thing. Do you have two names?"

"I don't understand," Cobi said, turning back to Austen.

"Is your middle name Eric, or are there two of you? The reason I ask is because I ran into someone in the hallway last night who looked just like you, and I almost had a heart attack when he said he wasn't."

"Yes," Cobi said. "Sorry, I hadn't gotten around to telling you about him. I have a twin brother and his name is Eric. He just moved in a few days before you."

Austen smiled. "Oh. You should introduce us. He looks like a nice guy."

59

Blac reached for his ringing cell phone. He was half asleep, in nothing but white boxer shorts, the bed blankets falling off of him.

He squinted at the screen before he answered it. Private Number.

"Hello?"

There was a moment of silence before a deep, menacing voice said, "Eight days and counting, motherfucker."

The call was disconnected, but Blac remembered the voice as Rondo's, one of the two men that came by the house the other night. He dropped the phone to the floor, recognizing the scare tactic. It wasn't necessary. There was enough fear in him already. A phone call or two would give him no more motivation than he already had to get that money.

Last night Blac had made progress — a major breakthrough. He was happy about that. So happy that he walked in the door, stripped off his clothes, and made Theresa come like seven times. She was twitching in bed, stuttering like she had Tourette syndrome.

When he got the chance, Blac planned to throw the sex on Cobi the exact same way. After a few rounds of Blac's skillful sex acrobatics, Blac thought, climbing out of bed, slipping on his jeans, and walking out of the small bedroom, Cobi would be whipping out his checkbook and forcing him to take money.

Blac walked through the living room, pulled open the front door of Theresa's house, stepped out on the porch that was nothing more than a slab of cement, and stretched his arms over his head. The sun was out and there was not a cloud in the sky.

He smiled, thinking about how well things went last night, but he knew he could not rest. Eight days would blow by before he knew it.

Blac pulled the cell phone from his jeans pocket and pulled up his text screen.

HAD A GREAT TIME. THOUGHT ABOUT YOU IN MY DREAMS. LET'S HAVE A DRINK SOMETIME.

Blac sent the text to Cobi but didn't expect a reply right away. He knew Cobi was probably having mixed feelings about the entire situation, considering Blac was his brother's friend, but when he got the text, Blac was sure he would be excited all the same.

Blac slid the phone back into his pocket, then caught sight of the mail sticking out of the small, rusty box hanging from the side of the house.

He grabbed the envelopes, stepped back in the house, and closed the door behind him.

He saw that the address on one of the letters was handwritten, as if by a child.

He looked closer and saw that the return address was from Wisconsin.

Blac carefully tore the letter open. He pulled out the single page and immediately saw that it was written by his nephew.

A wide smile on his face, Blac read the carefully penciled words, some of which had been erased and rewritten.

His nephew told Blac that he missed him and loved him, and whenever he got out of jail, he wanted Blac to visit.

Neither his nephew nor his sister knew when his release date was. Blac had refused to give them his address in prison, telling them to send his mail to Theresa. He knew hearing from them would only make his time harder to do.

At the end of the page, a note was written by Blac's sister. She told him how wonderfully well Johnny was doing in school and that he was on the baseball team. Wanda urged Blac to come to Wisconsin. She had plenty of space in her house, and they would love to have him there to stay.

Blac noticed the envelope contained a picture of his sister and his nephew. They stood arm in arm, both smiling brightly, waving at the camera.

Blac flipped the picture to see handwritten on the back, "We love you! Come home soon!"

He couldn't stop smiling as he walked the letter and the photo over to the fridge, placed them on the door, and held them there with a magnet shaped like a smiling slice of bread.

60

I sat at my desk, looking at the letter Eric gave me — the letter that informed him of Jess's intentions to have him stripped of his fatherly rights. I shook my head in disgust as I read the phone number of the law office that was representing her, wondering how she could go through with this.

I held the phone to my ear as it rang, remembering from the picture how adorable my niece was. I knew losing her would just about kill Eric.

"Hello," I said, after someone on the other end answered the phone. "May I speak to . . ." I looked down at the letter again. ". . . Kenneth Holden."

The woman on the other end told me that he was out for the afternoon.

I told her who I was, what I was calling about, and that it was imperative that Mr. Holden call me back as soon as possible.

I hung up the phone, feeling helpless,

wishing there was something more that I could do. Then I realized there was. I told Eric I was going to get him a job at Winslow, and that's exactly what I planned to do.

It would have to be without Sissy knowing, but I thought I could pull it off.

Paul Jennings immediately came to mind. He managed the records office and was a good guy. I had known him for three years, happily said hello to him whenever I saw him in the halls. Most important, he worked five floors below Sissy, and I trusted him to keep a secret.

I reached for the phone, preparing to call him, when it rang.

I picked it up. "Yes, Nancy?" I said to my assistant.

"Your sister is on line one, Mr. Winslow."

"Fine. Put her through."

"Morning, Cobi," Sissy said, her voice cheery.

"Sis," I said, not feeling anything close to how good she sounded.

"Just calling to see how things went the first night with your future wife?"

"That needs to be the second topic of conversation. There's something more important that needs to be addressed, Sissy."

"Okay, what is it?" Sissy asked, somewhat

reluctant.

"You had a conversation with Eric yesterday. What did you say to him?"

"What needed to be said."

"Sissy, don't play with me. I'm not in the mood. Just answer the question, please."

"He has to know that we're not just going to sit around here and watch as he takes advantage of you. You're spending money on him, giving him a place to live, and he's walking around thinking he's entitled."

"Sissy."

"I don't care what kind of thug he fancies himself to be."

"Sissy," I said again.

"He needs to know I'm watching him, and the first wrong moves he makes, I'm putting his ass —"

"Sissy!" I yelled into the phone. "First, how dare you. You're nothing but a hypocrite. How much money are you planning on spending on Austen? She's going to need a car, the dress you're going to buy, the ring, not to mention the wedding. What happens if she annuls the marriage the day after? Who would've been taken advantage of then?"

"She won't do that."

"You know that for sure?"

"I know women, and I know what position she's in. That's why I chose her. She won't do that. Now you were saying —"

"Second," I said, "Eric is my brother, and that's my house. I don't need you laying down the law there. Do you understand me?"

"But Cobi —"

"Do you understand, Sissy?"

"Yup. Fine."

"Good. Now we can move on to topic number two. And the answer is, that woman being in my house doesn't feel right."

"Really," Sissy said. "Exactly how are you expecting it to feel? It's going to be awkward at first. Unfortunately, we're going to have to make even more serious moves fast. The public needs to know about you. You have to be seen as a couple. So I need the two of you in my office within the next couple of days so we can go over plans on how to proceed from now until the wedding."

I didn't say anything.

"Cobi, did you hear me?"

"Yeah, Sissy. We'll be there."

I hung up the phone, truly feeling this was out of my hands.

I felt my cell phone vibrate in my jacket pocket. I fished it out to see that I had a text message.

It was from Eric's friend, Blac. Against

my will, I felt a smile appear as I read the text.

He thought about me in his dreams, huh? That was a line, mad cheesy game if I ever saw it, but it was still nice to know. Considering Tyler's neglect, this was much appreciated.

I moved to respond, thinking that maybe a harmless drink would be nice, then stopped myself. I needed to give that move some thought before I did anything. So instead, I picked up my office phone and made the call to Paul Jennings about getting Eric that job.

61

Eric parked the car in the Fifty-third Street Haynes Point parking lot and got out. The day was overcast, but a couple of college kids from the University of Chicago dorm building across the street were tossing a Frisbee in the grass and a few people were walking dogs. Otherwise the park was calm.

Jess had told Eric she would be waiting by the bench just before the bridge that led to the lakeside.

The call had come this morning, waking him out of his sleep.

"Meet me today at eleven-thirty. There's something I have to give you."

"Where?"

She gave him the location.

"You bringing Maya?"

"Eric, I have to go. I can't talk right now."

"But you called me. I wanna talk."

"Just meet me, and I'll tell you everything you need to know."

Eric stepped out of the parking lot and walked down to the path leading to a grassy area with wooden park benches. There he spotted Jess but saw no sign of his little girl. Instead, Jess was with a tall man wearing slacks and a sport jacket. Jess's back was to Eric. The man was facing and speaking to her. When Eric walked up, the man's eyes focused on him.

Jess immediately turned around. She wore business clothes: a skirt, jacket, and short heels. "Hello, Eric."

"Where is Maya?"

"Eric, this is Quentin," Jess said, gesturing toward the good-looking, clean-shaven, dark-skinned man beside her.

"I don't care who that is," Eric said, guessing this was a guy Jess had been dealing with and the reason she wouldn't talk about them getting back together. "I want to know where my daughter is."

"Quentin and I thought it best we not bring her."

"Jess, what are you doing?" Eric said, taking a step toward her. "What happened to us? We used to love each other, and now —"

"Eric, stop," Jess said. "That's disrespectful to Quentin."

"What?" Eric said, angry that she even

285

brought the man to this meeting, but to put him before Eric, the man she had been dealing with for years — the father of her child.

"Jess," Quentin whispered, but it was loud enough for Eric to hear. "Maybe you two should speak alone. I don't think I should be here."

"No," Jess said, grabbing Quentin's arm, then turned back to address Eric. "There's something I need to tell you."

"What?"

"I want Quentin to adopt Maya. That's why I brought him for you to meet."

It felt as though Jess punched Eric through the chest, reached in, grabbed his heart, and was trying to rip it out. He felt dizzy all of sudden and took two steps toward them, still not believing what he had just heard. "You don't . . . you don't mean that."

"Eric, you were in prison most of Maya's life. Biologically, you're her father, but you don't even know her. Quentin does, and he's ready —"

"Ready to take my little girl away from me?" Eric turned and appealed to Quentin, emotion heavy in his voice. "Is that true? You, as a man, who should know what a little girl means to her father — you trying to snatch my child from me? Or is Jess putting you up to it?"

Quentin didn't respond, but Eric believed he saw what could've been sympathy and understanding in his eyes.

"No," Jess said. "It's what we both want."

"Well, it ain't gonna happen," Eric said, shaking his head. "I'm that child's father. You even said it yourself, and you can't do nothing about it."

"That's why I'm filing to terminate your rights, Eric," Jess said, digging in her purse and producing an envelope. "The date and place for the hearing is in there."

62

Austen drove out of a Mercedes dealership with a seven-year-old beige Honda Civic that cost eight grand. Sissy had given Austen an allotment of $90,000 and told her to buy something befitting her status as Cobi Winslow's wife.

Julia sat beside Austen, her face screwed up, looking around the tiny cabin. "This looks like the car I drove in college."

"And that's exactly the way I like it." Austen smiled, whipping the car into the flow of traffic. "I just had a seventy-thousand-dollar car repossessed. That's not going to happen again."

"The Winslows aren't going to take your car from you, Austen. If that were the case, why would they have bought it?"

"Whether they take it from me for some reason, or I decide to give it back, either way, I won't miss this little thing."

"And why would you want to give it

back?" Julia asked. "You thinking about backing out on this?"

"I hate to say it, but the thought has crossed my mind," Austen said, braking at a red light. She turned to Julia. "The upside is, I would have my freedom. The downside, I would still have to pay my mother's mortgage, and I would need to earn money till this housing thing blows over."

"Yeah," Julia said. "Money you don't have."

"Then maybe I should get a job."

"Girl," Julia said, "nobody's hiring out there."

The light turned green. Austen sped the car along, smiled, and said, "We won't know for sure until I try."

63

Three hours later, Austen sat in the family room of the Winslow mansion, watching Oprah. She was startled by Sissy's voice.

"Can I speak to you a moment?" Sissy asked.

Austen turned on the sofa to see the woman standing in the doorway, dressed as always in a business suit and high heels.

"Sure, what's up?"

Sissy walked into the room, lifted the remote from the coffee table, and clicked off the TV. "What is that thing in the driveway?"

"It's the car I bought from the dealership. It's kinda cute, don't you think?"

Sissy did not look amused. "I thought I told you to buy what Ken, the salesman I directed you to, recommended. We cannot have you driving around in —"

"But I'm the one driving it, so shouldn't I be able to —"

"No, Ms. Greer. The answer is no," Sissy said. "I've spoken to Ken, and someone from the dealership will be by tomorrow morning to drop off the car you were shown."

Austen shot up from the sofa. "But —"

"There is no but. It's already done."

"Fine, it's your money."

"You're absolutely right about that."

"I'm going to finish Oprah in my room," Austen said, on her way out.

"Hold it. There's something else."

Austen stopped and turned. "What?"

"Why were you filling out job applications today?"

Austen froze. "Were you fucking following me?"

Sissy chuckled. "Do I look like someone who would be driving around, following a Honda?"

"Did you have me followed? What the hell do you think this is? I am not your property!"

Sissy smiled coolly. "You've signed a contract. But to me it seems you're looking for a job, because you'd rather not go through with what you promised. Understand, if you don't want to be here, there are plenty of women who would be more than happy to accept the deal we presented you with."

"Are there?"

"You aren't the only one who has lost everything and is desperate to be saved."

Austen was sure that remark was supposed to hurt. It did.

"Sissy, you need to understand —"

"From now on, it's Miss Winslow to you, and the only thing I need to understand is if we still have a deal. What will it be, Miss Greer?"

Angrier than she had ever felt, Austen took the seconds she was given to make a decision. "Yes, Miss Winslow, we still have a deal."

64

As he sat in the living room, staring down at the papers Jess had given him, Eric still couldn't believe what she was planning. Didn't she know that he wasn't going to just let her snatch his child from him to let some other man raise without putting up a fight?

"I said, are you okay!"

Eric looked up to see Cobi standing in the living room doorway, after he finally heard him practically yelling at him.

"I've been standing here for like thirty seconds calling your name," Cobi said, walking over and reaching for the legal papers Eric was holding. "What's got you all in a trance?"

Eric handed him the papers. "Jess says not only does she want to strip my rights to see Maya, but she wants her fucking boyfriend to adopt him. This can't happen, Cobi," Eric said, standing.

"Just try to be calm," Cobi said, glancing over the document.

"I'm done with calm," Eric said, pacing, his fists clenched. "This can't be legal."

Cobi looked up at Eric, shaking his head. "I'm afraid it is. But I called my friend, the family law attorney. We're meeting him tomorrow. And don't you worry, Eric. We're going to make sure we're ready for this."

65

After calling Tyler several times to discuss all that was going on and getting nothing but his voicemail, I broke down and called Blac back and agreed to meet him at Shady's, a relaxed little restaurant with a two-level outdoor patio, on North Halsted Street.

When he walked in, I was already stationed at the bar, sipping from a short glass of cognac and a glass of ice water.

He wore a sparkling, crisp white-collared shirt that made his dark skin look amazing, a pair of jeans, and black leather shoes. When he saw me, his smile was as brilliant as the shirt he wore. He came over and without hesitation, gave me a hug as though we had known and loved each other for years.

"I'm glad you called me back," Blac said, sitting on the stool beside me. "I was worried you wouldn't."

I turned to him. "I really wasn't going to. I didn't think it was a good idea meeting you like this. But then I said, why not? You seem like a nice enough guy."

"Why isn't it a good idea?"

"It's a secret I'm keeping from my brother. There's a lot of stuff going on with him right now, and I'm not sure if this is right."

"I understand, but why is it a secret just because you don't tell him about meeting me? It's not like you tell Eric every time you go out for drinks with a friend. Are those secrets, too?"

"He obviously doesn't know you're gay," I said.

"Does he have to? He obviously doesn't know you're gay either," Blac said. "You didn't tell him, why should I?"

I felt more comfortable about the meeting, seeing that Eric hadn't let slip what he had found out about me. I figured if he hadn't told his best friend, then he hadn't told anyone. "I guess you're right."

We talked more, had a few more drinks, then moved outside to the crowded patio.

During our conversation, I noticed that Blac seemed to know everything there was to know about me. "Gee, do you know the day I lost my virginity, too?" I said, a little concerned.

"Okay, I'm not some stalker or anything," Blac explained. "Eric said you were a great man, and I wanted to know what made you all that, so I Googled you. I hope you don't mind."

"No, I guess I don't," I said, a little flattered that he had taken such an interest.

"Prove you don't mind."

"How?" I said, smiling. Blac was standing in front of me, not six inches away. He was staring right at my lips.

"Can I have a kiss?"

By now, I had forgotten how many drinks I had. I wasn't sloppy drunk, but I was a little tipsy and feeling somewhat playful.

"You'll have to take it."

Blac smiled, leaned in, and among the dozens of people on the patio having drinks and enjoying music, Blac gave me a kiss. I parted my lips, invited him to probe deeper, and by the end of it, my head felt light. We had shared a beautiful kiss.

Breathless, I said, "Wow. That was nice."

"There's more," Blac said. I felt him take my hand, pull on my middle finger. "Maybe we can walk back to your car."

My imagination started to go crazy, forcing a smile on my face. "Oh, I don't know if that's a good idea."

"Let's go and find out," Blac said.

66

Eric sat at the kitchen table, the overhead stove lamp barely giving enough light for him to see what was on his plate. He was worrying again about the hearing the papers said he had to appear at. Cobi told him he would hire a family law attorney to represent him, and he was thankful, but to Eric, none of this was making sense. It felt unreal. Eric did nothing wrong, yet he was still going to be dragged before a judge. All he wanted was to see his little girl.

Eric took a bite of his sandwich, chewed it, and stared blankly at the space before him, when he heard a sound by the kitchen door.

He looked up and saw a figure standing in the dark space fifteen feet in front of him.

It was the woman from the other night. She walked over.

"Remember me?" the woman asked. "Austen," she said, leaning forward on the table.

"Yeah, I remember," Eric said, staring at her and offering nothing else.

Austen's eyes landed on his food. "Sandwich looks good."

Eric took half of the sandwich, set it on the napkin beside his plate, and slid it to the other side of the table. "Have some."

"No. I don't want to take your food. I shouldn't be eating this late anyway."

"Sit down. Eat."

Austen pulled a chair out and sat down in the dimly lit kitchen. She grabbed the half sandwich, took a bite, and smiled as she chewed. "So let me apologize for barging in on you the other night."

Eric paid the apology no attention.

"If it matters, I think you have a really great body," Austen said. "I really do."

"Thanks," Eric said, showing no emotion.

Austen looked anxious and uncomfortable. She shifted nervously and looked around the room as though waiting for something to happen.

"Don't worry, we're not being watched."

"You sure? Your sister had the nerve to have me followed today. Can you believe that?"

"I can believe that. She's not very nice." He wanted to tell Austen that Sissy wasn't his sister, but what difference would that have made? "Why did she follow you?"

"You tell me. She tells me to buy a car, I buy one. She should be happy I didn't spend the ninety thousand dollars she allotted. Then she follows me, sees that I'm putting in job applications, and tells me that I can't do that. 'Either you stick with the contract, or we'll put you out on the street.' Sorry, but I can't stand her."

"So are you going to stick with the contract?" Eric asked. He had no idea what this woman was talking about, but he decided to keep fishing for information.

"You know, it's not like I don't appreciate you guys making me the offer of marrying your brother."

"Marry Cobi?" Eric said.

"Yeah."

"You know he's gay."

"Of course, I do. He's my fiancé, right?"

Eric stared at Austen, wanting to know more but not wanting to sound as though he was interrogating her.

"I just . . ." Austen started to say, then wiped at her eye. Her voice cracked with emotion. "This is hard for me, you know. I've lost everything. I'm used to being independent, and the idea of some man controlling me . . . you just don't know how much I can't stand that."

"Cobi's trying to control you?" Eric said, feeling some compassion for her and remembering how his brother forced him to tell things Eric didn't want to say.

"No, no, not really. I've barely spoken to him. But your sister . . . I just don't know how I'm going to go through with this."

Eric kept his eyes on Austen. She wiped at her eyes again, and he handed her the last napkin he had near his plate.

"Thank you," Austen said, dabbing the corners of her eyes. "You're much nicer than your sister."

Eric didn't respond.

"And your brother. I don't think he's mean, but I like you a little better." Austen smiled, standing from the chair.

Eric stood and offered his hand.

Austen shook her head, then came around the table toward him. "What's this hand-shaking business?" Austen said, giving Eric a warm hug. "I'm marrying your brother, right? We're all going to be family in a minute."

It had been years since Eric had held a woman in his arms. It felt almost foreign to him. His hands on her tiny waist, her hair brushing against the side of his face, he breathed in her womanly scent, and said regretfully, "Yeah, we'll be family."

67

The next morning, Eric wore the shirt, tie, and slacks I suggested. He sat looking uncomfortable in the chair next to mine as we waited for Paul Jennings, the records department manager, to meet us in his office.

On my phone call with Paul the other day, we had a great conversation. I asked him if there was anywhere he thought he could fit my brother.

"Sure. Tell you the truth, John just left for graduate school. I was about to post his job, but if you say your brother is interested, now I guess I don't have to."

"That's great," I said, smiling, excited about telling Eric the news.

"I didn't even know you had a brother," Paul said.

"Yeah, I rarely mention him." I paused for a long moment, knowing there was no way around saying what needed to be said. "He's been in prison for the last three years."

"Tough breaks, huh," Paul said, not making the big deal out of it I thought he would.

"Yeah, you can say that. Will that be a problem, Paul?"

"If you're vouching for him, it won't be."

Now sitting in Paul's office, I looked over at Eric and said, "Relax. I told you, you're already hired. Why are you so nervous?"

"You said he knew I was in prison and that won't be a problem?" Eric said.

"He knows everything. Just relax."

The office door opened, and Paul walked in. He was a tall, blond man with blue eyes and a bright smile.

"And you must be Eric. Wow, Mr. Winslow, you didn't tell me you guys were twins," Paul said, extending a hand to Eric. "Good to meet you."

Eric stood and shook Paul's hand. "You too, Mr. Jennings."

I stood as well, shook Paul's hand. "Yeah, sometimes I forget to mention that."

The three of us stood in the small office, staring awkwardly at one another, searching for something to say. Finally, I laughed and said, "Well, what do we do now?"

"If Eric is ready, I would love to get him started today," Paul said. "We'll just get all his information, fill out his tax forms, stuff like that, and then we can show him what goes on around here and let him jump right in."

"How does that sound, Eric?" I asked. "You ready for that?"

A huge, childlike smile on his face, Eric said, "Yeah, I'm ready."

"Good," Paul said. "I'll take you over to the next office. Tiffany will get you started filling out the paperwork."

"Paul," I said. "You mind if I talk to you before . . ."

"Sure," Paul said to me. "Eric," Paul then said to my brother, "just go to the office next door. Tiffany is in there, and she'll happily show you everything you need to do."

Eric shot me a concerned look.

I sent him a reassuring one back, letting him know everything was fine. When he left, I closed the door, then turned back to Paul. "I truly appreciate this."

"It's your company, Mr. Winslow. I just work here."

"How many times have I told you, it's Cobi. Now like I told you before, this is something my sister doesn't know about and doesn't need to know about. She still has some issues with our brother she has to work out. So let's try to keep this a secret until they iron out their differences."

"Sure thing, Mr. Winslow."

68

One hour later, Sissy walked into her office for the meeting with me and Austen. She was carrying a cup of coffee. "Sorry, I'm late, you two. I have a meeting in half an hour." She set down her purse and briefcase. "So we'll have to get right to it." She grabbed a legal pad from her desk and sat down in the chair facing us. "Okay, I wanted to have a huge wedding since it's for my big brother, but there's just ten days till Cobi's birthday, so we'll have to do this a week from now. That means we're going to have to scale way down. Is that okay?"

"That's fine with me," I said.

Sissy turned to Austen.

"Whatever you think is best," Austen said.

"Good," Sissy said. "If you like, you can have as much input on dress and ring selection as you want. But I'm thinking the wedding should be intimate — only a few people there. We can rent some beautiful location downtown. Maybe we can take a couple of photos to leak to the press and some of the magazines. Yes?"

I hadn't even heard Sissy because my mind had wandered back to last night.

My driver's side seat had been reclined all the way. Blac was beside me, kissing me passionately. I was squirming and throbbing, and he was rubbing me, playing with my belt, playfully threatening to unbuckle it, which is exactly what I wanted, but I grabbed his hand and stopped him.

"I so want you to do that," I said, breathing heavily, smiling up at him. "But I can't let you."

"Why not? You scared of how good it'll feel?"

"Because I'm seeing someone. Well, kind of seeing someone."

"Why isn't he here instead of me?"

"It's complicated."

"Oh." Blac laughed, lifting his hand and caressing the side of my face. "He's married, isn't he?"

"I guess."

"He's at home with his wife and kids, and not here, because he's ashamed of who he really is."

"I'm not going to say that for sure."

"You don't have to, because you know it's

307

true." Blac traced the rim of my ear with the tip of his finger. "That's the kind of relationship you want? Locked in the closet? If you were mine, I would —"

I looked Blac directly in his eyes. "It wouldn't work between us."

"Why not?"

"Because we're different. We're from different worlds, and it just wouldn't work."

"Then why am I here right now?" Blac whispered seductively in my ear.

"You want me to tell you the truth?"

"That's exactly what I want."

"Because you're sexy as hell, and even though a relationship won't work, I think there could be something that does work between us." I gave him a quick kiss on the lips. "I shouldn't even be thinking that. I don't know you. You could be crazy, out to get me. That stuff really goes on."

The smile on Blac's face suddenly disappeared, along with his playfulness. He began to move away from me as though I had offended him. I grabbed his arm.

"What do you think I'm doing?" Blac said, angry. "You think I'm trying to take something from you, blackmail you for money or something?"

"I'm just saying, it happens to people and I don't know —"

"You don't know if I could be trying to do that to you, is what you're saying," Blac said, upset, going for the door handle.

I held tighter to his arm. "Don't go. If you say you aren't doing that, I'll believe you."

"I'm not," Blac said.

"Cobi!" Sissy said, snapping me out of my daydream. "I said will you be fine with photos published in some magazines, *Jet*, *Ebony*, stuff like that?"

"Yeah . . . yes," I said. "Sorry."

"Good. And there is a social event, fundraiser of some sort at the museum in a couple of nights the two of you should attend," Sissy said. "Can you do that? It'll be a good opportunity for the world to get their first look at you as a couple."

"Works for me," Austen said.

"Sure," I said, still having an issue taking my mind off of last night. I looked up and saw Austen staring at me, a mischievous smile on her face.

After the meeting, once Austen and I had stepped out of Sissy's office, Austen said, "You were really somewhere else, weren't you?"

"Yeah, I guess. Was thinking about a few things."

"Was it a guy?"

I shot her a disturbed look, feeling very uncomfortable. "I don't think that's appropriate conversation considering this situation."

"It's absolutely appropriate considering the situation. I was thinking about this last night. We're about to be married — man and wife. But we aren't going to share a lot of what comes with that. I mean, we aren't gonna be lovers, so why can't we be great friends?" Austen smiled, rubbing my arm. "So was he cute or not?"

69

Blac pulled Theresa's Chevy Malibu to a stop in front of the old building that used to be a Goodyear Tire store on the West Side of Chicago. Theresa had been happy to let Blac drop her off at work today and take the car, after he told her he needed to drive around and try to find a job.

She actually believed that I took that crap she said about me changing who I am seriously, Blac thought, stepping out of the car and walking up to the building.

The big store windows had long been knocked out and sealed up with bricks. The building was set far back in an abandoned warehouse park. Rusty, barbed-wire fence surrounded much of the area.

Blac knocked on the steel door four times, then paused.

A curtain swept back from the narrow, rectangular-shaped window in the door, and a pair of eyes narrowed on Blac, then disappeared.

When the door opened, Blac was taken to a large back room where there was a sofa, a table, and a desk pushed back in a corner. There were framed posters on the paint-chipped walls of Al Pacino as Scarface waving a machine gun. A solemn-looking pit bull terrier was chained on a short leash, gnawing on a bone in another corner.

"What you doin' here, Blac?" Cutty asked. He was lounging on the leather sofa, staring up a huge flat-screen TV mounted high up on the wall. He was quickly tapping the buttons on a PS3 controller, as was a dangerous-looking man with a missing front tooth who sat beside him.

Two big-bootied women in skintight jeans and fresh blond hair weaves sat on either side of the men. Their eyes were half open, and Blac assumed they were high on whatever Cutty had offered them.

"I said, why you standin' in my face, Blac?" Cutty demanded. "Unless you got my money and you ready to even up."

"Naw, I don't got it yet," Blac said, apologetic.

Blac didn't want to put all his time and energy in getting the money from Cobi, and at the last minute, the man gets wise and leaves him in the lurch. He needed a backup plan, a just-in-case plan, and that's why he had called Cutty this morning.

"I wanna know if you can hook me up with a little something to sell . . . on consignment."

The man next to Cutty turned and stared at Blac as though he had just committed the greatest sin of all.

Cutty paused the game. The room went silent as he stared down Blac and said, "Ain't that how you got in this shit to begin with? Why in the hell would . . ." Then Cutty stopped speaking. A look appeared on his face that suggested he knew Blac's reasoning behind the request. Cutty stood from the sofa, walked over, stopped just short of Blac, looked up in his eyes, and said, "You ain't trying to make loot selling drugs to pay me back, 'cause you know you won't have my money, is you?"

Blac thought about telling Cutty the truth. Maybe he would work with him, help him out, sympathize even. "No," Blac said, changing his mind. "I just got a lot of time on my hands, and I figured I could be makin' both of us some dollars in the meantime. That's all it is, on my word."

"I was about to say," Cutty said, turning back around, dropping himself back on the sofa with the drugged women, and picking up his controller. " 'Cause if you know you ain't gonna have my money, I might as well have Bones kill your ass now."

"That man ain't got yo' money, Cut," the man sitting beside Cutty said. He looked at Blac again with cloudy brown eyes. "You ain't gonna have Cut's money, is you?"

"I don't know what you talking about," Blac said.

The man glared at Blac for a long moment, as if testing his sincerity, then he said, "I say you have Bones kill his ass now. He playin' you, Cut, like he did the last four years he was inside."

Cutty slowly stood from the sofa, the controller still in his hand. "Is that what you think, Drake?" Cutty said to the man.

"Yeah. Sho' as shit. I can see it on his face. He playin' you."

"I wanna get this straight," Cutty said. "You saying I'm getting played."

"Yeah, and let me tell —"

Before Drake could finish, Cutty reared back, wound up, and threw a blow that caught Drake on the corner of his left eyebrow with the hard plastic controller. Blood streamed from the wound. Cutty leapt on top of Drake, and using the controller as an extension of his fist, he struck Drake in the face over and over again, till the controller was covered in the man's blood. The women scurried from the sofa, averting their eyes from the malicious beating.

Blac ran over to Cutty, grabbed him by the arms. "Cutty! Cutty! You're gonna kill him!" Blac yelled.

Drake's face was painted a shiny red, and his eyes and lips seemed to be swelling before Blac's eyes as he wrestled Cutty off the bleeding man.

Cutty angrily shook Blac off of him, glared at him with death in his eyes. "Don't have my money, motherfucker, and you gonna wish I took it that easy on yo' ass."

70

Austin Harris was the family law attorney I took Eric to meet. He was a tall, well-built, good-looking guy who always wore a serious expression. I had met Austin five years ago at a downtown function for local attorneys and seemed to bump into him around town at least a couple times a month. We'd have short conversations and always promise to get together for golf. Professionally, Austin Harris had a reputation as an outstanding attorney. I had referred scores of people to him, and they were all more than happy with his services. I knew he would take good care of my brother.

Austin Harris sat at his desk thoughtfully rubbing his chin after Eric told him his story. He picked up the papers Eric had given him and glanced over them again.

"So, oftentimes a petition for adoption is filed at the same time as the petition to terminate a parent's rights. You said she wants her boyfriend to adopt Maya."

"That's right," Eric said, his voice low.

"Okay, this is what's going to happen," Austin Harris said, leaning forward on his desk, looking directly at Eric. "The day after tomorrow, at the hearing, Jess is going to argue why your fatherly rights should be stripped. She will use the testimony of family and friends to support what she says and hope the judge sides with her."

"It's just a judge, then? One person that's gonna say yes or no to me being able to keep seeing my daughter?" Eric asked.

"That's right. Basically, she's going to try to discredit you. You need to tell me all the negative stuff now, what's going to look bad to the judge, so we can know how to defend against it."

"I told you everything," Eric said. "I was raised in the foster care system and been to jail a few times. That ain't reason to do this to me. Is it? Take my child."

"You were gone for more than half your daughter's life," Austin Harris said. "That might be her reasoning for wanting to try."

"I couldn't help that. I was locked up."

"Were you paying child support? Sending any type of financial aid?"

"I told you. I was locked up," Eric said,

317

distraught. "And even if I wanted to, she disappeared. I had no idea where she was the last two years."

Austin Harris stood from his desk, crossed his arms, glanced at me, then back to Eric. "You say you treated the child well. You never abused or neglected her or anything like that?"

Eric looked surprised by the question. "I would never do that. I love that little girl."

"Good. Then that's all they have, that you've been to prison. That's how they're going to try to take Maya. You say you're working now? You have a job?"

"Yeah," Eric said, pride in his voice. "At Winslow Products, in the records room."

"Great," Austin Harris said. "And you have a stable address?"

"Austin, he lives at the mansion with me," I said. "And will live there as long as he likes."

"That works," Austin Harris said, smiling. "They're going to try to say a man like you doesn't deserve his daughter. In two days, we're going to prove to them that you're no longer the man they think you are."

71

"That's right, she had our asses followed," Austen said.

Julia took her break in one of the back rooms of her salon, a lavender curtain pulled across the doorway as she and Austen sat at the table and spoke.

"Wow, I still can't believe that," Julia said, sipping from a can of Diet Sprite. "Feels like my civil liberties have been violated or something. That just ain't right."

"Who you telling," Austen said. After a moment, her eyes wandered up to the ceiling. A smile appeared on her face.

"Okay, someone's having a pleasant thought. Fill me in."

"It's nothing."

"Nonsense, it's nothing. What are you thinking about?" Julia said.

"Guess who I saw again last night?"

"Eric?"

"Right."

"The one you saw naked."

"Yes."

"The one with the great body and the big
—"

"Dick. Yes."

"Okay, just confirming." Julia laughed.
"Go on."

"It was late, and I wandered down to the
kitchen for a glass of water, and he was
there eating a sandwich. I was still pissed
about what his sister did and my situation,
so I just vented."

"And what did he say?"

"Nothing. He just sat there very calmly
and let me speak. Oh, and then he gave me
half of his sandwich. Wasn't that sweet?"
Austen said, smiling wider.

Julia stared at Austen oddly, shaking her
head.

"What?"

"Do you hear yourself? You're thirteen
again, and you have a crush on your boyfriend's best friend."

"Shut up. You don't know what you're
talking about," Austen said, trying to force
the smile from her face. She wasn't successful.

"I don't?" Julia said, scooting to the edge
of her seat and staring right into Austen's
face. "I can see some red in your cheeks,

girl. You're blushing!"

"I'm not!" Austen said, covering her cheeks with her hands. "Okay, the man is fine. Well, both of them are, but Eric happens to be straight, and sexy, and brooding, and . . ."

Julia said nothing.

"What, J?"

"You're about to marry Cobi. You're going to be living in his house, living on his money, money that will pay your mother's mortgage, that will get your home out of hock, and you're daydreaming about his brother. Austen, please, if you've never heard a single word I've said in the past, hear this. Leave Eric and his big dick alone."

72

I had been waiting an hour on the edge of the king-size bed, in a beautiful room, with a view facing Lake Michigan, anticipating our meeting.

Yesterday, I had made a reservation at the W Hotel on North Lake Shore Drive to spend some much needed intimate time with Tyler.

I texted him after it was made and immediately got a response text, letting me know that he would meet me here and that he was looking forward to seeing me.

I had called him four times today just to confirm, but he hadn't picked up his phone or called me back. I left messages, making sure to leave the time, the address, and the room number, but still there was no Tyler.

Tyler wasn't the sort of man to be tardy. Something was going on. Maybe he was still paranoid, or no longer wanted to continue our relationship, or both. Either way, I needed to find out.

I stood from the bed, grabbed my keys from the nightstand, and left the room.

Half an hour later, I pulled up in front of Tyler's northwest suburban home. I gazed up at the beautiful brick, four-bedroom house with the manicured lawn, surrounded by the white picket fence. It was a dream — the house and the family inside it — something Tyler had said he had always wanted.

But if it was a dream, I thought, pulling the key from the ignition of the Mercedes, *couldn't that also mean it wasn't real?*

I rang the doorbell, wanting to confront him. He needed to know how I'd been feeling regarding his absence in my life.

His wife, Kennedi, answered. She was a tall, beautiful, fair-skinned woman with dark, shoulder-length hair that looked as though she had just stepped out of the stylist's chair.

I had dropped by unannounced. I knew I wasn't to do that, even though Tyler had no problem just popping up at my place anytime he saw fit. But I didn't realize just how wrong I was till I was leaning in to give Kennedi a hug and a peck on the cheek. "Is he home?" I asked.

"Sure, Cobi. Come on in. He's out grilling dinner with the girls. Go on back. He'll be glad to see you."

I told myself I didn't think so.

I walked through the kitchen, slid the patio glass door back, and stepped out into the backyard. Tyler's back was to me. He was working over a smoking grill. He wore an apron, walking shorts, T-shirt, tennis shoes, and a baseball cap — the traditional dad costume.

"Look who's playing chef today," I said.

"Hey, Uncle Cobi," Tyler's daughters said in unison, turning from the grill and skipping over to me. Konni and Kara were six and eight years old. They were tall for their ages, and both had heads full of thick brown hair, parted down the middle and tied into pigtails.

I wrapped my arms around them and kissed their foreheads. When I looked up, Tyler was holding a meat fork in his fist, giving me a vicious glare.

"Girls, why don't you go inside for a while and give me and Uncle Cobi a few minutes to talk about work stuff, okay?"

"Okay, Daddy," the girls said, playfully bounding into the house.

Tyler waited till he saw the patio door close. "What the hell are you doing here? I told you never to come here unannounced."

"How could I announce my visit, if you

don't pick up the phone?" I said. "I mean, what's going on? Are you dumping me?"

Tyler looked down at the smoking meat on the grill and poked a couple of the steaks.

I stepped closer to him. "You know that I love —"

"Shut up!" He whispered harshly at me, alarm in his eyes. "I'm at home, Cobi. My family is just inside the house, and you're talking that shit. That's the problem with you lately. It's like you've forgotten just how much is at stake here."

"What are you talking about?"

"The thing with the kid who blackmailed you, your brother walking in on us — that stuff could blow up in your face. And now you have a chance to do something that could actually help your situation, but you don't want to do it. And you wonder why I'm distant."

"I told you, I'm going to marry her. I told you that, so you can stop ignoring me. Everything is going to be fine. Just come back to me. I miss you," I said, wishing I could touch him.

He looked down again, the bill from the baseball cap shading his eyes. "I don't think I can do that. Not right now. I think we ought to take a break from this for a little while."

"No. You told me you loved me, that you would consider leaving your wife —"

"Cobi!" Tyler said, grabbing me by the lapel of my jacket, yanking me into his face. He glanced at the house to make sure no one was watching. "Really, how much of a chance do you think there is of that actually happening? Do you think I would ever leave Kennedi and the girls?"

"You lied to me?" I slapped his hand off me and stepped back.

"I said what I wanted to have happen, but I knew it never could — know it never can. This is the way things are, the way they need to be, and you'll know that once you get married. We can talk about getting back together then."

"You cowardly motherfucker," I said, my voice low. I was boiling with anger. "You're man enough to meet me in hotel rooms, but not man enough to take ownership of who you really are."

"I am owning it," Tyler said. "This is who I am." He pulled at his T-shirt that read "Greatest Dad in the World."

"You are sorry and selfish." I laughed sadly. "Fine. Since you can't man-up, why don't I just go in there and tell your wife what you and I have been up to? Maybe she'll have something to say about that." I was expecting Tyler to jump me, try to poke me with that fork like he was stabbing those steaks.

"Whatever you want to do, Cobi," he said, and continued fussing with the meat. "But I know you love me, and despite how angry you are, you'd never want me to lose my family."

"I'm going to go in there and tell your wife," I said, pointing at the house with a trembling finger. "I swear. I'm going to do it."

"Don't let me stop you."

I turned and marched inside the house. I glanced at the girls in the kitchen, playing at the sink in some dishwater. "Where is your mother?" I asked, managing to sound calm.

"In the living room, I think," one of the girls said.

I made a beeline for the room. I let her finish her phone conversation before I ruined her life with what I had to tell her.

Kennedi smiled at me, and into the phone said, "Okay, girl. Well, I'll talk to you later, okay? Bye bye."

She punched a button on the phone, set it on the coffee table, and said, "Hey, Cobi, what's up?"

All that I had to say was on the tip of my

327

tongue. It could bring down this entire house, shatter Kennedi's make-believe reality, kill the girls' futures. All I had to do was tell this woman the truth. But Tyler was right. I did love him too much to want him to lose his family. I became the coward Tyler knew I was and simply said, "Just wanted to give you a hug before I left. See you next time."

I rushed out to my car, trying to hold my emotions until I climbed in and shut myself inside. I buried my face in my hands and tried not to cry.

Moments later, I pulled myself together, sniffled, took a deep breath in, released it, then pulled my cell phone out of my pocket, and dialed a number.

When the phone was answered, I said, "Blac, I have a room reserved. I want to see you tonight."

73

Eric stood just outside the living room doorway. Austen was in there watching television. As he waited, he wondered why Cobi was keeping the terms of his marriage a secret. He thought about asking his brother but wasn't sure if Cobi would tell him the whole truth and told himself, who better to ask about this than Austen.

Eric stepped into the living room, catching Austen's attention. She looked up at him and smiled.

"What you watching?" Eric asked.

"Evening news."

"You mind if I watch, too?"

" 'Course not." Austen scooted over on the sofa. Eric sat beside her and silently watched the TV. "The stuff you told me the other night, I didn't know any of it."

"What stuff?"

"About the contract, about you and my brother getting married, any of it."

Austen shifted her body around to Eric, a suspicious smile on her face. "How could you not know? You're his brother. You live in this —"

"I just moved in." Eric hesitated a moment, then told himself it made no sense to continue to hide who he was. "I just got out of prison. Three years ago I needed money to take care of my new baby daughter and my girlfriend, and I foolishly went out there and tried to steal a car."

"And you got caught," Austen said.

"Yeah."

"Me and Cobi haven't seen each other in thirty years. My mother put us up for adoption, and by some miracle or something, Cobi was walking through the jail and just bumped into me."

There was an uncertain look on Austen's face Eric could not read. "Why you looking at me like that? You think different of me now because I was in prison, right? I guess I can understand."

"No. I made my share of mistakes, too. Not putting away enough money, not planning for what's going on right now. So I'm broke, and I'm marrying your brother so I can save my house and have somewhere to live. But this is tougher than I thought it would be, and we aren't even married yet. I keep saying I don't feel like I have control of my own life."

"I feel the same way," Eric said.

"How is your daughter?"

Eric lowered his head. "Haven't seen her in two years. Her mother is trying to get my rights taken away. But Cobi is helping me do everything I can to get her back."

"I'm sorry," Austen said sincerely, placing a comforting hand on Eric's shoulder. "Why would she do that?"

"I don't know. I loved my daughter, treated her as best I could, and . . . I don't know. Maybe it was because I'm a bad person and she doesn't want her around me no more."

Austen gave Eric a sympathetic look and moved her hand to his arm. "I don't think you're a bad person, and I think you'll be able to see your daughter again."

"You're sweet for saying that."

"I'm a sweet person," Austen said, smiling.

"You are." Eric smiled and looked away.

"So is your girlfriend —"

"She's not my girlfriend anymore," Eric said, turning back to Austen. "Whatever we had ain't there anymore."

"I wish there was something I could do to make you feel better."

Eric didn't know how to take what Austen just said. It was suggestive as hell, but he knew she couldn't have meant what he wanted her to mean. He wanted nothing more than to grab Austen and kiss her. Hell, lean her back on that sofa and make love to her. That would've made no sense. She was to marry Cobi, so he put the thought out of his mind. "I guess I should go up to my room," Eric said, forcing himself to stand.

Austen unexpectedly stood with him. She stared in his eyes. Eric believed the look asked him to kiss her, but he knew he had to be wrong. "So I'm gonna go on up," Eric said. "Can I give you a hug . . . for . . . you know, listening to me?"

"I would like that," Austen said.

Eric slowly wrapped his arms around her. He felt her arms move around his waist. She pulled him close to her, and although he tried, he could not stop himself from being excited and growing in his pants. He was embarrassed, knowing that she felt him throbbing against her belly. He backed away slightly, but felt her pull him closer still as if she wanted to feel him.

"I'm sorry about that," Eric said. "It's been a long time."

"Don't be," she said, softly. "I would be hurt if you didn't have that response." Her lips were inches from his. This was the time, he told himself, but pulled out of the embrace. "I really think I should go, before I do something I regret."

74

Blac lay next to Cobi till the man's heartbeat started to slow and his body began to relax against the bed.

"That was amazing," Cobi breathed, his eyes half open, an extremely content half smile on his face. "I so needed that."

After leaving Cutty's empty-handed, Blac had been worried for his life, still not certain how things would go with Cobi. But lying there next to Cobi, Blac felt hopeful again. All he needed to do was continue to execute his plan to perfection.

"I'm glad I was able to help you, baby," Blac said. He scooted over to Cobi and gave him a soft kiss. Blac knew he couldn't just come out and ask him for $150,000 just for laying the pipe, no matter how good it was. He would have to ease Cobi into the idea of giving him money. It would be a small amount at first. Blac would continue to give him the best sex he ever had, making himself more valuable in Cobi's eyes. Then each time Blac asked for money, the amount would increase and so would the intensity of the fucking.

In a week, Blac would tell him he needed the amount required, just in time to pay Cutty off. Cobi would probably hesitate at first. Blac would threaten to leave, take away all the good sex Cobi had grown accustomed to, then Cobi would break down and give up the money. Why wouldn't he? Money like 150K was nothing to Cobi.

Blac suddenly jumped out of bed and walked naked over to a window. He heard movement in the bed behind him, knew Cobi had probably lifted up and was staring at his ass. That was fine with Blac.

He pulled back one of the sheer curtains and looked out at the lake. "This room ain't no joke." He turned around to face Cobi, who was sitting up in bed. "It must be nice living like you do."

Cobi grinned but didn't say anything.

Blac walked back over to the bed and gave Cobi a kiss good-bye. "I really gotta be taking off." Blac grabbed his jeans and slid into them. "The tow truck guy said —"

"Hold it. Tow truck? What are you talking about?" Cobi said, throwing his legs over the side of the bed.

"My damn car stopped a block from here. I called a tow truck to take it in and get it repaired, but I really wanted to see you, so I told them to come in a couple of hours." Blac looked down at his watch. "I really should be going." He made his way toward the door.

A moment later, Cobi was behind him, grabbing him by the arm. "Hold on. Are you going to be all right? Will the repairs be expensive?"

"I don't know," Blac said. "It's something with the transmission, so I don't know. Nine hundred, maybe more. Why?"

Cobi reached into his suit jacket pocket. He opened his checkbook, jotted something on one of the checks, tore it out, and handed it to Blac. "Get it fixed. That should be enough, but let me know if it's not."

Blac glanced down and saw that it was made out for $3,000. "I can't take this," Blac said. "We just made love, and it makes me feel like you're paying me off or something."

"Stop it. It's nothing like that. You need something, and I'm in the position to provide it. Is that so bad?"

"No. I guess not."

"Good. Now you get out of here before

you miss that tow. And like I said, don't hesitate if you need anything else."

75

Entering the house, I heard the TV on in the family room, so I walked in that direction, hoping Eric was in there.

I was surprised to see Austen on the sofa, watching an episode of *American Idol* she had recorded.

She looked over her shoulder, then stood, as if having to formally greet me. "Hey, Cobi, I was just —"

"Sit down, sit down," I said. "Sorry to interrupt your show."

"No interruption," Austen said, sitting again. "Just watching these kids sing for their lives, you know. You ever watch?"

"No. You ready for the fund-raiser tomorrow?" I said. I didn't really want to engage in a long conversation with her, which seemed wrong, considering I'd be married to her in just a week.

"Sure am. I love stuff like that."

"Good." I walked over to the sofa and sat

down beside her.

She looked surprised.

"I need an honest answer, okay?"

Austen nodded her head.

"Are you okay with what's going on? This feels cruel to me, like we're abusing you in some way, but my sister seems to think that we're benefiting equally. This is the last time I'll ask, so now is the time to say something. If you don't see yourself getting something out of this, I promise, I'll do my best to call this whole thing off."

Austen looked at me, her eyes filled with both gratitude and sympathy. "Your sister's right. We're all coming out ahead. Let's just make the best of it, okay?"

"Yeah, okay."

I stood outside Eric's door, wondering if this situation really was as simple as Austen saw it. Maybe it was. Hopefully it was. Time would tell, I told myself as I knocked on the door.

"Yeah," I heard Eric say.

I stepped in. He was in bed, fully clothed, his shoes on, sitting up, two pillows behind his back. His legs were crossed and his hands were folded in his lap. He didn't appear to have been doing anything more than just sitting there, staring at the walls.

"I wanted to let you know I called Jessica's attorney, and he still hasn't gotten back to me."

"Yeah, okay," Eric said, not seeming to care.

"Well, I just wanted to let you know that. I'm going to bed." I turned toward the door and was about to walk out.

"Cobi."

"Yeah."

"Who is the woman down the hall? And why haven't you let me meet her?"

"Oh, her name is Austen Greer. Sorry I haven't had a chance to mention her. It's a long story and —"

"It's okay. That stuff is probably none of my business anyway, right? I mean, why would I expect to know every little thing about you? This is your house, and you can do whatever you want in it."

I knew that Eric was taking a shot at me for forcing him to tell me about his conviction. He felt he was being treated unfairly. But he was right about what he just said, and the situation was what it was.

"That's right," I said, turned off by his ungrateful attitude. "This is my house, and you shouldn't expect to know everything about me or what goes on here."

76

Eric stood in the hallway outside Austen's door. He told himself it was wrong what he was about to do, but he knocked softly, keeping his eyes on Cobi's door.

The door opened, and Austen stood there wearing a sheer nightgown. Through the thin material Eric could plainly see the dark circles on her breasts, her nipples, standing plump and erect, and he could see the neatly cropped triangle of hair pointing to the place he wanted to be.

She stood in plain sight, not trying to hide behind the door or use her hands to cover herself. She confidently watched as Eric's eyes surveyed her body.

Pulling his gaze up from her beautifully manicured bare feet, he felt short of breath, knowing why he was there.

"What do you want, Eric?" Austen asked, as if she already knew.

"I don't know," Eric said, all of a sudden

at a loss.

"Yes, you do. Tell me."

"Can I touch you?" Eric's eyes locked on Austen's. He saw her swallow hard, saw her chest inflate with a huge breath.

"Yes."

He reached out, softly touched her face with the tips of his fingers. Her skin was so soft. He stepped closer to her, raised her face by her chin, and stared wantonly at her full lips. They parted slightly, Austen biting down gently on the lower one.

"Can I kiss you?" Eric asked.

Austen nodded and slowly closed her eyes.

He leaned in, pressed his mouth to hers, carefully at first, but when he felt her tongue slip between his lips, he kissed her deeper.

She pressed her body into his, her hips grinding against his, as Eric pulled up Austen's gown, grabbed her firm, round, bare ass, then pulled out of the kiss. He baby-kissed her on her cheeks, her lips, and her neck, till he felt her pulse there speeding and pounding.

"Come into my room, before we get caught," Austen said, breathless.

They stumbled inside. It had been years since Eric touched a woman in a sexual way. Now, this beautiful thing was standing in front of him, fumbling with the buckle of his belt with one hand, rubbing him through his jeans with the other. She undid the button, unzipped his pants, and took him out, her hand tightly around him, stroking him. It felt so wonderful, he thought he would explode that moment.

Lightheaded, he leaned away from her, took the bottom of her nightgown, and began to raise it.

Austen lifted her hands up, let Eric pull the gown up and over her head. She stood before him naked, her breasts full and round, her belly flat, her hips wide and curved.

It took every ounce of restraint for him to just stand there the few seconds he did without attacking her. Finally, he threw himself into her, his arm around her waist, lifting her off the floor, and kissing her deeply again. He carried her over to the king-size bed, lay her on the edge of it, threw her knees up, kneeled himself, then buried his face between her legs and lapped her juices.

Austen whipped her head from side to side, bit down on the knuckle of her fist to keep herself quiet, while pressing Eric's face further into her pussy.

She tasted as sweet as Eric imagined, and he knew what he was doing. Her clit was fat, and very sensitive, and Eric held it between his lips, sucked it gently while applying constant pressure to it with the tip of his tongue.

She moaned loudly, clawed at the back of his head, and then he felt her come.

"I want you," he heard Austen say.

"I don't have a condom."

"I do."

Austen was up off the bed, and back, pressing the tiny package in his hand.

Eric quickly undressed, climbed on the bed, and kneeled between Austen's thighs, wearing the condom. He lowered himself onto her and carefully inserted himself into her warm, wet crease. He slid all the way in and knew, just fucking knew, he would not last.

Austen began to whisper in his ear, "Fuck me, fuck me, baby, fuck me."

It was too much, and it felt too good.

She grabbed him, softly urging him deeper. He had never felt so hard, and sex had never felt so good. He tried pulling out. He was on the verge of losing himself. But she pulled him in further, clamped down around him, and slipped her wet tongue into his ear. He shut his eyes, grabbed hold tightly, and exploded.

77

Blac snuck quietly into Theresa's dark house and closed the front door. He started toward the bedroom, when the light suddenly snapped on.

Startled, Blac saw Theresa standing before him with her hand on the switch. She wore a nightgown and a scarf around her hair.

"Where you been?"

"Working."

"Working, doing what?"

Blac didn't want to lie to her, but she didn't have to know every move he made. "There are some really important things I gotta take care of, okay?"

"Like what?"

"Like whatever I say, okay? I say I'm working, all you gotta know is I'm doing that. Understand?"

Theresa stared right back at him but didn't respond.

"Do you understand?" Blac said again.

"The talk we had the other night, that didn't mean nothing to you?"

Blac looked at Theresa as though she had only the sense of a child. "I ain't got time for this. I'm going to bed."

78

After work, Eric drove south down Lake Shore Drive toward Blac's house.

Going to a job, he felt like he'd never felt before — confident, responsible, and good about himself. Eric also knew that having that job would help him look better in the eyes of the judge who would decide whether or not he would keep his rights to see his little girl, and that made him feel even better.

But there was something pressing on his mind — last night. And that's why he needed to talk to Blac.

Neither of them had eaten, so after Eric picked him up, he treated them to some sliders at White Castle on Thirty-fifth Street. The two men walked leisurely down King Drive, pulling small burgers from a paper sack as they talked.

"I gotta kick Theresa to the curb," Blac said. "I know we been together for years, and I'm livin' in her crib, driving her car, and all that shit, but if she think she gonna be crackin' the whip —"

"You love her?"

"What?" Blac asked, as though that possibility never crossed his mind.

"I said, do you love her?"

"Well . . . she cool, but . . ." Blac slid one of the burgers out of its cardboard box and took a bite, gesturing with it. "I mean, sometimes she can be all right. I guess you might could say I love her sometimes."

"She met you when you got out of prison, right?"

"Yeah, so?"

"She be setting out that ass, too, don't she?"

"Yeah, Theresa don't have no problem putting out," Blac said, wiping mustard from the corner of his mouth.

"And what she asking for in return?"

"Dude, last night she was askin' me where I been, and she talkin' about one day she wanna get married, and I should be doing more around the house and —"

At a red light intersection, Eric stopped walking. "So you sayin', because you don't wanna tell her where you going, you gonna kick your girl to the curb?"

Blac tried to reach for another burger, but

Eric snatched the bag back and crumpled the top together in his fists. "Answer the question first, Blac."

"Why you all concerned about my relationship all of a sudden?"

"You brought it up."

"Naw, but you really all off into this. There's somethin' goin' on with you," Blac said, leaning closer to get a good look into Eric's eyes. "We been about this close, twenty-four-seven for the last two years. I know when something's up. What is it?"

Eric surrendered the bag to Blac. He spotted a bench to sit on. "Let's go over there."

They sat with their butts on the backrest, their feet on the bench. Eric told Blac what Austen told him about Cobi's arrangement. How he was going to pay her to marry him so Cobi could get his trust fund.

"Trust fund, huh?" Blac said. "How much is it?"

"I don't know."

"Okay, he got this woman livin' at the house, he gonna marry her to get his trust fund," Blac said. "What's the problem?"

"The woman's the problem. Like I told you, she's fine as hell, and somehow —"

"You fucked her."

"Yeah, I fucked her. And I feel guilty as shit, but —"

"But what?" Blac said, a smirk on his face.

"I loved Jess, and I always felt she was sitting out here waiting on me. I never thought about being with another woman. Turns out, she with some dude. I'm by myself, and now this woman is here, and —"

"You slept with her one night. Don't go telling me you falling all in love."

"I ain't in love. It feels good to be with her, and I kinda like this girl, is all. But this is the woman my brother is supposed to be marrying, and while he trying to help me with Maya, giving me a place to live, a job, I'm fucking his fiancée."

"Your brother's gay. Trust me, he don't care."

"How in the hell would you know he don't care?"

Blac hesitated a moment, then said, "It ain't rocket science. Punks don't like women, all right?"

"I haven't known the dude long, but I've known him long enough to know how he would see it if he found out. It's the fucking principle. I gotta break this off now, before something really gets started."

79

Austen and Julia had spent the last half hour browsing through Neiman Marcus. The two stood near the fitting rooms with a short rack of dresses they'd selected for the affair Austen was attending tonight with Cobi.

Austen stood in the three-way mirror, holding a sequined dress up under her chin.

"What do you think?" Austen said.

"Too nineteen-twenties. Tie a couple of bananas to it, and you'll look just like Josephine Baker."

"Whatever," Austen said, passing the dress back to Julia. "Give me that one. The black one with the silver."

Julia picked through the last few dresses Austen hadn't tried on and held out the black one. She took a quick glance at the price tag and said, "Uh, you probably don't want it."

"Why not?"

"Because it cost a little less than the

Honda you bought the other day."

Austen smiled and took the dress from Julia. "In that case, I'm trying it on."

Julia followed Austen and stood just outside the fitting room door. She could see Austen's feet and the top of her hair.

"So the other day you were all about trying to spend as little of Cobi's money as possible," Julia said, on her tiptoes, trying to get a look at the dress. "And now you're trying to buy the most expensive piece in here. What happened?"

After a little rustling from inside the fitting room, Julia saw Austen holding up a black AMEX card over the door.

"Okay, yeah, so what? You knew the man had money."

Austen stepped out wearing the perfectly fitted black silk dress with one bare shoulder.

Standing on her toes to simulate heels, Austen spun in a circle and did a short modeling run for Julia.

"Girl, that dress is hot!"

"Thank you, darling," Austen said, batting her eyes. "That means I'm getting it."

After buying the dress, Austen and Julia walked into the women's restroom. "I'm still waiting for you to tell me why the change all of a sudden," Julia said.

Austen placed her bag on the diaper changing station, then walked by all the stalls, softly pushing each door open, checking to make sure they were empty.

Julia watched Austen suspiciously. "Please tell me exactly what you're doing?"

"I told you, we've been followed before," Austen said, relaxing a little after making sure they were alone. She walked over to the door, locked it, then came back to Julia, who was leaning on the edge of a sink.

"I found a new reason to stay."

"Exactly what do you mean by that?"

Not telling Julia about Eric being an ex-con, because she knew how judgmental her friend was, she said, "I accidently slipped and fell on top of Eric's dick last night."

"What?" Julia said, shocked.

"It was my bad, but we made the best of it."

"Geez," Julia said, pacing away from Austen. "All the shit that's at stake for you and you're risking it for sex. Can you stop playing for a minute? This is serious shit."

"Oh, you wanna stop playing?" Austen said, instantly stone-faced. "Fine. Let me stop fucking playing and lay it all out here. These people have just bought me like a piece of property. It feels like that bitch Sissy knows exactly where I am every minute of the day and to whom I'm speaking. They tell me what to do, how to do it, and when, and I'm not even married to Cobi yet. I needed something that was mine. I needed a choice, and I needed to be the one to make the decision. And the decision I made was not to be put up like some perfect little doll in a glass case. If Cobi were straight, and he was fucking me, then I wouldn't screw Eric. But he's not, so I am. That's all there is to it."

"So when does it stop?" Julia asked.

"It just started. Last night was the first —"

"I said, when does it stop?"

"I don't know. If I have any say, I don't think I'll be quick to end it anytime soon."

"You know you're playing with fire," Julia said, giving Austen a long stare. "And when you do that, shit gets burned the fuck up."

80

To say that I felt like everyone's eyes were on me and Austen the moment we climbed out of the limo was an understatement.

I felt handsome in my simple black tuxedo and tie, but Austen was downright dazzling. Her hair was pinned up, her makeup was flawless, her lips were a sparkling red, and that black dress was something that could've been worn by Halle Berry or Kerry Washington on the red carpet Oscar night.

The event was held at the Field Museum on the lakefront.

Beneath the high ceilings, ice sculptures, balloons, and champagne fountains, we stood among the busts of Roman emperors and ancient columns.

A full band of musicians dressed in matching tuxedos, complete with horns and stringed instruments, played beautiful, up-tempo, big-band jazz.

Austen and I spent most of our time walking arm in arm among the hundreds of other well-dressed, well-paid professionals.

I had bumped into more old friends, associates, and former coworkers than I had expected. Upon seeing Austen on my arm, they all smiled brightly, hugged me, or shook my hand and asked who the gorgeous woman was.

After about half an hour of that, I leaned in to Austen and asked rather loudly, in order to be heard over the band music, "You doing okay?"

She smiled and said, "I'm having a fantastic time."

As I continued to walk about the museum, smiling, laughing, talking, and drinking with Austen and my friends, I experienced something I never had before. I wasn't sure what it was, but it felt like a strong sense of pride for simply being seen with this beautiful woman. As if simply having Austen by my side made me a better, more confident man.

When I introduced her to other men as my fiancée, they seemed to look at me in a different light. Before some of the men walked away, they would nudge me with an elbow, and whisper from the sides of their mouths, "Fine-looking woman," or "Dude, she's a ten," or "You're a lucky man, Winslow."

I wondered if this feeling of manliness had been something my father experienced when out at some function with my mother. And as I stood gazing at Austen, I wondered if this feeling, this moment, was what my father so desperately had wanted me to experience.

He had to have known that forcing me to marry a woman would never change me from gay to straight, but I was beginning to wonder if that had even been his intention. Could he just have wanted me to see what I had been missing all my life?

"What?" Austen said, noticing the trance I had fallen into. She was truly beautiful. Gay man or not, I was not so blind I couldn't see that.

"You are beautiful," I told her.

She looked surprised, blushed a little, then leaned in and gave me a peck on the cheek. "And you are one of the most handsome men I have ever met."

I instantly inflated with pride, grabbed her hand, and was about to lead Austen toward a couple of friends, when someone grabbed me by the arm. I turned and was shocked to be looking directly into Tyler's smiling face.

"You've been gallivanting around here all evening and can't even stop to say hello to your old friend," Tyler said. Kennedi was standing at his side, looking beautiful as always.

"And who is the mesmerizing woman standing beside you, Cobi, you old dog?" Tyler said.

"Tyler, Kennedi," I said proudly, "please allow me to present Austen Melrose Greer, my fiancée."

Kennedi cupped a hand over her mouth, then said, "Oh, no. Where have you been keeping this beautiful woman locked up?"

"He has a special cave under the basement, where I do all the dishes and laundry," Austen said, stepping around me and Tyler to give Kennedi a hug. Tyler gave me an approving nod. Kennedi whispered something to Austen, then rested a hand on Tyler's shoulder. "I'll be back. I'm going to the ladies' room."

"I'll go with you," Austen said. "Give these guys some time to talk."

Austen grabbed my hand, squeezed it before leaving, as if we were a real couple. When the two ladies left, I felt strangely alone, even though I was standing right beside Tyler, the place I had wanted to be for so long.

Tyler looked left and right at all the people in the museum, then took one step closer to me. "She's wonderful, Cobi. Sissy did a great job."

"Well, you know Sissy," I said, not looking at Tyler. I ran a finger around the rim of my wineglass instead.

"You're doing the right thing, you know. I've been watching you. I've seen the reception you've been getting from everyone, and I know you have to have noticed yourself. Do you see the difference that a woman can make?"

"I don't know what you're talking about," I lied, knowing full well now what Tyler meant.

He laughed, still knowing me better than I'd like him to. "Play with me if you want," he said. "But once you get married, you'll see what I mean. More professional opportunities will start to present themselves, friendships, more powerful alliances will be made, all because of that woman." Tyler moved closer to me, looked directly into my eyes. "And maybe some old relationships can be rekindled."

81

The next day, Eric sat in the passenger seat of Cobi's Mercedes.

He was dressed in a dark jacket, tie, and white shirt. He rode beside Cobi quietly as his brother drove him to the family law court building.

"So, just like that?" Eric asked, this morning, while he was standing in Cobi's room, letting Cobi knot the tie around his neck. "If the judge says my rights should be taken, that's it."

"Yeah," Cobi said. "Just like that."

"I'll never be able to see my little girl again."

Cobi looked Eric in the eyes, tightened the knot in his tie, then said, "Let's worry about that if it happens."

"No," Eric said, grabbing on to one of Cobi's wrists. "Does it really mean what she says it does, if she wins?"

"Yeah, Eric. Jess's fiancé can adopt Maya.

You will no longer have any rights pertaining to her. You'd only be able to visit her if Jess and her boyfriend allow it."

Those words echoed in Eric's head, no matter how hard he tried to force them out.

Cobi pulled the key from the ignition of the Mercedes and said, "We're at the courthouse, Eric. It's time to do this."

82

The hearing took place in a small room. Jessica Freeman and her supporters sat on one side of a long conference table. Eric, myself, and Austin Harris sat at the other end. In front of us, on the other side of the table, sat an older, clean-shaven man. His name was Judge Peters.

Beside Jessica sat a tall, good-looking, attentive man who held her hand. Jessica's mother was there, as well as a younger sister and a girlfriend.

Everyone was briefed by the judge as to how the hearing would proceed. Testimony would be heard from Jessica and those who represented her, then Eric and anyone who represented him. Sadly, I was the only person to speak on his behalf. After that, the judge would render his verdict.

"I don't feel good about this," Eric leaned over and whispered to me.

"Everything's going to be fine," I said,

steadying him, holding on to his arm. "I told you, I trust Mr. Harris. He's a good attorney."

Jessica's little sister, Lisa, was called to speak first. The judge asked her to give her account of how Eric treated his daughter.

Eric leaned over to me again. "Why they asking her that? She know how well I treated Maya. Ain't that just gonna help my case?"

"Let's hope so, Eric," I said.

Lisa stated her name and swore that the testimony she was about to give was truthful.

She began by saying, "One day I stopped by Jess's house, because I knew she had to work and Eric would be there by himself with the baby. When I knocked on the door, nobody answered. I didn't leave because I knew Eric didn't have a car, so wherever he went with Maya, I knew it wouldn't have been far. Five minutes later, Eric walked up to the door, but I didn't see the baby with him. I asked him where she was. He told me he had only planned to be gone twenty minutes, so it was easier leaving her at home.

"The second he opened the front door, we could hear Maya screaming. She was only a year old. Eric had left her home alone in their bed, and she had fallen to the floor."

"What?" Eric said loudly, astonished. He clamped his hand down on my arm. "No!"

"Eric, what's wrong?" I whispered.

"That's not right," Eric said to me then to our attorney.

"Mr. Harris," Judge Peters said. "Is there a problem with your client?"

"That never happened. I ain't never leave Maya alone, and she knows it," Eric said, angrily cutting his eyes at Lisa.

"Your Honor," Austin Harris said, "the witness's testimony is false."

"Miss Hampton," Judge Peters said to Lisa. "You are aware that you are under oath, and that there are harsh penalties for perjury."

"Yes, Your Honor," Lisa said.

"Are you certain?"

"Yes, I'm certain, Your Honor."

The judge inhaled deeply, looked at both parties, then said, "Fine, continue."

"What?" Eric said, his voice loud, filling the entire room. "I ain't do nothing —"

"Mr. Harris, are you going to contain your client, or will we have to continue without him?" Judge Peters said.

"But Judge," Eric said, "she's lying. She knows I never did anything like —"

"Mr. Reed," the judge said. "It seems your attorney didn't explain to you how these proceedings work, so I'll do it this one time. I ask each witness for their account. They tell me what they believe is the truth and the whole truth. After which, it will be up to me to decide whether or not someone has lied and whose case I favor. Every witness is entitled to state what they believe is fact without being interrupted, just as you will when the time comes. Is that perfectly clear, Mr. Reed?"

Eric didn't answer, just sat there scowling at Jess and her sister.

"Mr. Reed, you will answer the question."

"Eric," I said, nudging him. "You need to answer."

"Yes," Eric grunted. "It's clear, Your Honor."

Jessica's fiancé's testimony was short. He said he loved Maya from the very first day he met her, and if he was so blessed, and given the opportunity, he would adopt her and raise her as if she were his own.

After Quentin, Jessica's best friend, Jackie, was called. The heavy woman spoke with hate and conviction when she said, "I was right there when Eric said he didn't want that baby, that he never wanted it. Little Maya was right in front of us. Jess was feeding her, and that fool, Eric, just walked back and forth yelling how he didn't want to be responsible. He kept saying it wasn't his baby anyway, and why couldn't she just take care of it herself, because he never asked for the little bastard. That's right," Jackie said. "He said, little bastard!"

"This ain't right. This ain't right," Eric kept saying under his breath to me. The emotion in his voice sounded like he was near tears. "Why are they lying like this? Mr. Harris, you gotta do something."

"Eric," Austin Harris whispered, turning to him, sympathy in his eyes. "Like the judge said, we have to give them their say, and then you'll have yours. It's all we can do."

Jess was next to testify. She stared at Eric, and the look said she would do everything in her power to ensure that Eric never saw his child again.

"I cried every night," Jessica said. "Wanting Eric to just accept our baby, but he wouldn't. It didn't bother me that much when he called me names, when he ignored me, or yelled at me. But when he did that to Maya, I couldn't take it. I hung in there, because I told myself she would need her father — want her father.

"I remember after I had the baby, he never told me or Maya that he loved us. He acted like we were a burden, like his life would've been so much better without us."

"She's lying!" Eric yelled, shooting up from his chair, stabbing his finger at Jess. "You know I would never —"

"Mr. Reed!" The judge yelled right back. "This will be your final warning. You will take your seat and respect this hearing, or you will be removed!"

I grabbed my brother by the arm and forced him back into his seat.

"Miss Freeman," Judge Peters said. "Please continue."

She did. "Despite that, I stayed with him. When he was locked up, I stayed and carted Maya down to that prison every two weeks. But one Sunday at church, I met Quentin.

"We became friends. I realized I was not a burden, that my child was not a burden," Jessica said, wiping tears from her face. "I wanted Eric to be there for Maya. Like I said, I begged him, but he wouldn't. So I decided to stop forcing him. I stopped taking Maya to that prison, and on that day, I told myself I would never again drag my child to that place to see someone who didn't even want her."

After Jessica's case had been heard, I spoke on behalf of my brother.

I did so after hearing the horrible things Jessica and her family had accused my brother of. I knew that he was not capable of those things. I couldn't prove it, but I knew just by the way he spoke about his daughter, that he could never treat her like that. But Eric was an ex-convict. And as I spoke, I feared that when having to decide whose side to believe — that of an upstanding woman like Jess, who worked to put herself through college while raising a baby, or a man who spent the last three years of his life in prison — they would naturally believe Jess.

After my testimony, the judge asked if Eric had anything to say.

He was so angry and hurt, all he did was shake his head, smear tears from his eyes, and mumble, "They lying. They all lying."

It was no surprise to me, after the judge took a short recess to deliberate, that he came back with a verdict in favor of Jess. Jess had won, and as of that moment, Eric no longer had the right to father his child.

I drove Eric home afterward. He sat silently, bent over, his head in his hands the entire trip. I wanted so much to say some comforting words — anything that would make him feel better, but I knew there was nothing that could be said to ease the pain of losing his daughter.

I pulled up in front of the mansion and

cut the engine. I turned to Eric. He was sitting straight now, looking out the window at the house.

"How are you doing?" I asked.

"Fine," he said, his voice low, emotional. He did not look at me.

I reached over, placed a consoling hand on his arm. "It'll get better. We can try —"

"Try what, Cobi? This morning you just told me there wouldn't be shit we could do if the judge took my rights. Did that all of a sudden change?" Eric said, anger in his voice, a tear coming to his eye.

I looked at him, not knowing what to say.

"Did it?" he yelled.

"No." I felt like a failure for not being able to stop this from happening. "Is there anything I can do? Anything at all?"

"Don't mention this to me no more. Forget about me ever having a little girl, okay," Eric said, pushing open the car door. "And I'll try and do the same."

83

After the last argument Blac had with Theresa, he had been making a point to stay away from her.

He had heard all that mess Eric was talking. Did he love Theresa? Was it worth treating her better? Blac didn't know about all that. He was too busy and too focused on trying to get Cutty's money so he could save his ass.

Like Blac had told Eric, Theresa was cool enough, but he didn't think she was so cool that she could go bossing him around and demanding to know exactly when he would walk in the house. That's where he drew the line.

Earlier, Blac had taken the bus down to the Greyhound station.

He could've simply called down there and found out how much a ticket to Racine, Wisconsin, would've cost, but he needed to get out of the house. Going down there would make him feel like he was one step closer to actually getting out of Chicago.

The old man behind the counter told Blac the ticket would be $99 one way.

That was doable, Blac thought, walking to a corner of the bus station where he saw a bench. He pulled out his cell phone, had a seat, and dialed his sister's number. When he heard her voice on the other end, Blac smiled wide and said, "Hey little sister, what's going on?"

She sounded ecstatic to hear from him and to find out he was released, which made Blac even happier. He listened as she told him how much she missed him and how much Johnny had been asking about him.

"Yeah, I got the letter you guys sent me with the picture. He's gettin' big, ain't he?" Blac said, pressing his other hand to his ear, trying to hear his sister over the noise of the bus station.

She asked him when he was coming to visit Racine.

"I want to do more than visit. If you still sayin' it's okay for me to live there, that's what I want to do."

Blac held the phone away from his ear a moment, smiling, while Wanda howled with excitement.

"But it's gonna probably be another

couple of weeks before I can come. Got some stuff in Chicago I gotta finish, then I'll be headin' over."

Wanda asked him if they were dangerous things. Blac sensed worry in her voice.

"Ain't nothin' you have to be concerned about. Big brother gonna be just fine, and then I'll be there in the country with ya'll where I can stay out of trouble. Okay?"

Wanda seemed to be okay with Blac's assurances. She told him to hurry and that she loved him, and when his nephew came home from school, she would tell him that he called.

"Love you, too," Blac said, disconnecting the call and slipping the phone back in his pocket.

When Blac stepped off the bus a block away from Theresa's house, the sun had already started to go down.

It was still early, so he didn't expect to hear Theresa's mouth, but as he walked slowly along the sidewalk, he thought more about what Eric said. He really questioned now whether Theresa was wrong to expect the few things she had asked.

It had been late when he came in that night, and well . . . he had been out doing things he shouldn't have been doing. So she did have reason to be suspicious, Blac told himself as he walked onto the path that led up to the door.

If things were the other way around, wouldn't he have expected to know where she was going, or at least, expect her in at a decent time? Damn right, he would've. She would've had to have told him exactly where she was, with who, for how long, and knowing Blac, he probably would've had her take cell phone pictures and send them to him, to confirm that her ass was where she said.

Blac laughed as he pulled his key from his jeans and prepared to slip it into the front door lock.

But before he did that, he finally accepted he had been wrong. Theresa loved him. He realized that. She was only acting that way because she cared about him and wanted him to be a better man for himself and for her. So Blac decided, starting tonight, he would ease up, and actually try to give her what she asked.

Blac sunk the key in the lock, turned the knob with an actual smile on his face. He told himself he would surprise Theresa with his new attitude. But after opening the door, it was Blac who was surprised when he saw Theresa walking into the living room from the kitchen, carrying a cold glass of cola for a large potbellied man sitting on the sofa, watching TV.

Blac closed the door, pausing a moment to try to understand what was going on in front of him.

"Hey, Blac," Theresa said, setting the glass of soda down on a coaster before the man.

The guy had broad shoulders, a round head of freshly buzzed hair, and fat cheeks like an infant.

"Who the fuck is this?" Blac said.

"This is Franklin," Theresa said, sitting on the sofa beside him. "He was just going to finish his refill of pop, then he was going to go."

"Hold it. He ain't going nowhere till I know why he here now."

"It's cool, brah. I don't mean no harm," Franklin said, offering a fat-fingered hand for Blac to shake.

"Trust me, doughboy, I ain't fearin' no harm from you," Blac said, ignoring the hand. "But somebody need to speak up in this house, before I —"

"You aren't doing nothing, Blac," Theresa finally said. "If you have to know, Franklin is the last man I dated before you got out of prison. We dated for a year."

Blac felt his body warming with jealousy and forced himself not to do anything physical about it.

"I would still be with him, but he started taking me for granted, treating me like I didn't matter — kind of how you're treating me now — so I let him go. That was six months ago, but he's been coming around, saying that he's changed, and asking for another chance. I asked him to come here tonight to tell him I'd give him one, but only if you don't start acting right."

"What?" Blac said, unable to believe what he was hearing. He stepped closer to the sofa, his fists clenched at his side. "You tryin' to play games with me? You know what I'll —"

Franklin stood from the sofa, his wide body now between Blac and Theresa.

"Ain't no disrespect, brah," Franklin said, more serious. "Theresa with you now, I know that. It's your situation to mess up. But if you think I'm gonna stand here and watch you threaten her, you got another think coming, motherfucker."

Blac walked right up in Franklin's face, stared him dead in the eyes. Franklin wasn't trembling and seemed ready to back up what he was saying.

Blac turned to Theresa. "So this is who you want?"

"No, Blac. I want you. But I'm not gonna

pretend that you're treating me right when you're not."

"Fine. Fuck it! Fuck you, and this fat-ass honey-bear-bottle-looking motherfucker!" Blac said, then stormed out of the house.

84

I met Blac at the W Hotel again. We showered together, and he made love to me like it was an event in the Summer Olympics and he was trying to win a gold medal.

Afterward I was famished. I devoured the panini sandwich I ordered, but Blac did nothing more than pick at his spinach pizza.

We were both wearing the hotel's plush white bathrobes.

"What's wrong? You've barely said two words to me all night. Something on your mind?" I asked.

Blac looked up at me, as if wondering whether or not he could tell me. "I'm having problems with the woman I stay with. She put me out."

I took a moment to ask myself if he was telling me this because he wanted help from me. I took another second to look him over, and saw that he was genuinely distraught by what he was saying. "What, that means you have no place to stay?"

"Guess not," Blac said, shame in his voice.

I walked over to my slacks draped across the back of the hotel's desk chair and went into my pocket. I pulled out my checkbook.

"What are you doing? You can't do that again," Blac said, getting up and following behind me.

"You said you're homeless. You're going to need money to get a place." It was the right thing to do, I told myself. And it was what I wanted to do. He was not only my brother's friend, he was my . . . my sexual associate now. It wasn't as though I was going to allow him to stay at the mansion, but I wasn't going to have him out on the street either.

"But I . . . I didn't ask for any," Blac said, seeming astonished by my generosity.

"You don't have to ask. You need it, and I have it to give," I said, placing the point of my pen to my check. "Is this just a spat? You need just enough for a week or so, or will you be moving out permanently?"

"We're done. I'll need to get an apartment or something."

"Will ten thousand work?"

Blac nodded. "Ten thousand will work just fine."

85

Eric sat in his car, staring at the tattered picture of Maya. He wiped the last tear from his face. The thought of being with his daughter was what got him through his time in prison. He stayed strong inside for her. Since he'd been out, he'd been trying to be a better man for the same reason. But what was the point? He worked the job Cobi got him, but what was the point in that, either? His daughter was taken away from him, and Jess lied to do it. That shit wasn't fair, and Eric couldn't let that slide.

He stuck his daughter's picture back in his pocket, pushed open his car door, and walked the path up to the house Jess lived in.

It was a nice big brick house in a quiet neighborhood, with a large front lawn and a black wrought-iron fence. It must've belonged to her boyfriend, because Eric knew Jess couldn't afford anything like that.

Eric stabbed the doorbell several times, then stopped, looked through the sheer curtains of the living room window. A lamp was on, and Eric thought he saw movement inside.

"Jess! I know you're in there." He banged on the door with the side of his fist. "You lied. You took her from me. Now come the fuck —" He paused when he heard sounds behind the door. "I hear you in there. Come out! Let me see Maya!" He yelled louder. He started banging on the door again. "I ain't leaving till you let me see her."

Ten minutes passed, and Eric pulled himself from the front stair where he had been resting and prepared to bang on the door again till Jess answered or the thing fell over.

He stepped to the door and raised his fist, but stopped himself when he heard the squeal of brakes, and a car pulling to the curb behind him. He turned. A police cruiser stopped in front of the house.

Both doors opened, and two fit officers were walking across Jess's lawn toward the front porch. One, the shorter of the two, had his hand on the butt of his holstered weapon as though he had no problems drawing and using it.

"I ain't doing nothing but trying to see

my daughter," Eric said, slowly raising his hands shoulder high.

The door of Jess's house opened behind him. He turned to see Jess holding the storm door open.

"Ma'am, did you call the police?" the taller, dark-haired officer asked. Eric saw that his name badge said Williams. "Is he causing a disturbance?"

"Tell him I'm just here to see Maya, Jess. The daughter you lied and had taken away from me," Eric ordered.

"I don't know what you're talking about," Jess said.

"You know exactly what the fuck I'm talking about!" Eric said, lowering his hands, and moving toward Jess as if to attack her.

The shorter officer was quickly up the stairs on the porch. He grabbed Eric by the arm, wrenched it behind his back, almost bringing Eric to his knees.

"Stop!" Jess said, stepping out onto the porch. "No! He didn't do anything," she said to the officers.

"If he didn't do anything, ma'am, you wouldn't have called us," Officer Williams said.

Jess looked at Eric, still being subdued.

"Can I talk to him a moment? Privately, please," Jess asked.

The officers exchanged looks, then released Eric.

"We'll be right here, just down the stairs, ma'am," Officer Williams said.

Holding his arm, Eric walked over to Jess and sadly asked, "Why did you do it?"

"I don't know what you're talking about, Eric. I didn't do —"

"Stop fucking —"

"Eric!" Jess scolded, looking quickly to the officers whose narrowed eyes now focused on him. In a quieter voice she said, "I'm sorry you lost Maya, but that's over. What you need to worry about is what's happening right now."

"Fuck now. I want you to let me see my daughter," Eric said, his voice lower. "So fuck now and fuck those officers."

"Really. You just got out of prison. You continue to do this, and it could violate your parole," Jess said. "I know you just lost Maya, but do you want to lose your freedom, too? Take what you got left and be happy with it, and leave, okay?"

Eric thought about what Jess just said. He looked down the stairs at the officers staring up at him. What did he really plan to do now? Run through Jess, storm in the house, and take his daughter? The police would have him facedown on the living room floor, cuffed before he knew it, if they didn't shoot him in the back first. He couldn't deny what she said made sense, so he turned back to her, and said, "Yeah, Jess. Okay."

86

It was a beautiful spring day out. Not a single cloud dotted the baby blue sky overhead, so I chose to eat my bag lunch outdoors on the front steps of the court-house building. I was still troubled by what happened yesterday with my brother. I heard him come in late last night. I was tempted to walk down to his room, check on him, but he told me not to mention the situation again, so I respected his wishes.

As I took a bite out of half of the sandwich Stella made me, I caught a glimpse of someone sitting down very close to me.

I turned to see a middle-aged, balding man with a bad comb-over and square-framed glasses sitting next to me, turning the pages of a *Chicago Tribune*. He held the paper open wide in front of him, almost as though he was trying not to be seen. I slid away from him a little and went back to my lunch.

A moment later, I heard the paper crinkling loudly beside me. Then, "Hey . . ."

I turned around to see that the man had folded the paper into a neat rectangle and was leaning toward me.

"Aren't you a district attorney?"

"State's attorney," I said, correcting him, showing a bit of a smile. "Would shake your hand, but I'm eating, sorry. Cobi Winslow."

"I know. Young hot-shot attorney, who happens to be from a family of millionaires. You don't remember me?"

I smiled, trying to place his face, feeling badly that I couldn't. "Sorry . . ."

"Wow," the man said. "I don't know how I should take that. My name is Steven Ballard. Funny, you put a man in jail for two years, and I'd at least think you'd remember his name."

Immediately, I scooted away from him, desperately trying to place his face, scared I was in danger of being harmed.

"No, no, don't worry," Ballard said, reading my expression and my actions. "It wasn't a violent crime, more of the white-collar variety."

"I'm sorry," I said, gathering my lunch.

"But I was innocent."

"With all due respect, Mr. Ballard," I said, standing, "if you were innocent, you wouldn't have been convicted."

"I was innocent, Mr. Winslow, but you don't believe me now, just like you didn't believe me then. No matter," he said, smiling. "Before you go, can I show you something?"

"I'm sorry," I said, looking around, making sure there were still people around to witness this man if it came to that.

"No, you need to see this," Ballard said, standing and pulling a small, greeting-card-sized envelope out of his jacket pocket. He looked at me with a somewhat deranged smirk on his face. "You're gonna love these." He opened the envelope, pulled out a handful of snapshots, and handed them to me.

"What are these?" I said, afraid to take them.

"Take a look. I'm sure you'll enjoy them."

I hesitantly took the photos, looked down at them, and felt my heart skip. I couldn't believe what I saw. A picture of myself and Blac on the patio of a restaurant, kissing. I feverishly shuffled over to the next photo. Another one of Blac and me walking into a hotel.

"Keep going. There's more," Ballard whispered.

I continued to flip through the thin deck

of photos, then stopped, wide-eyed at the picture before me, knowing the irreparable damage that would be done if this were to ever get out. It was an image taken by a zoom lens, through a window, of Tyler and myself, naked in bed together, having sex.

87

"I told you, he wouldn't give the pictures to me," I said, frantically pacing back and forth through my father's office.

Sissy leaned against the edge of the desk, her arms crossed, her face balled into a mask of anguished thought. "I know it's not what you want to hear, Cobi, but we have to do what he says and pay him the money he's asking for."

I halted. "I'm not fucking paying him! That's not happening. You gave money to that boy and —"

"And he went away. And that's exactly what this man will do — go away."

"No."

"Half a million is practically a deal considering the damage he could do. In case you've forgotten, there will be a very well publicized wedding in five days. You want to take a chance of this man showing up, passing out these photos to all our guests? Just meet him tomorrow night like he said, and —"

"I said no, Sis! I would rather suffer the consequences of whatever he's planning than to roll over again and pay to cover up who the hell I really am. There just has to be another way."

"There is no other way, Cobi!" Sissy said, standing from off the desk. "If there is, tell me and we can consider it, but if not, we need to cough up this money."

We stood at a stalemate we'd never resolve when we heard a knock on the office door.

"Who's there!" Sissy said, marching toward the door.

Eric stepped into the office.

"What are you doing here?" Sissy said, speaking to Eric as though he were a child. "Did you hear any of what —"

"Don't pay him a cent," Eric said, a stoic expression on his face. "I know how to handle this."

Blac lay on his back as he stared up at Theresa's naked body through partially closed eyes. She gyrated on top of him, holding his palms to her large bare breasts, as she moaned.

She had already come twice, and she quickened the rapid pace of her tiny thrusts. "Oh, baby, I think I'm coming again," Theresa said, bearing down harder on Blac's hips.

He raised his behind further off the bed, forcing her to give herself over to him once again. "Come on, baby. Come on!" he urged, pounding himself up into her. Suddenly, she threw her head back, screamed, then her body started to convulse until she fell over forward onto him.

Blac wrapped his arms around her, kissed the side of her face.

"Do you love me?" Theresa murmured.

"You know I do, baby," Blac said. And for

the first time, finally admitted to himself that he truly did.

After he left Cobi last night, he was happy there was a $10,000 check in his pocket, but he was still upset with Theresa. He didn't want to crawl back to her house, as he was sure she was expecting him to, so he bused it over to Stony Island Avenue, and stayed in a ratty motel off of Eighty-first.

There he lay on top of what he figured to be a filthy blanket. He thought about Theresa and why she did what she had.

She was making a statement, Blac knew. She wanted to bring to his attention her value. It was a bold move on her part, he thought, and it had actually worked.

When Theresa came home from work earlier today, the house was spotless, a dinner of boiled hotdogs, Kraft macaroni and cheese, and canned peas was on the stove, and a warm bubble bath had been drawn.

Blac had even bought a bouquet of $9.99 roses and set them on the center of the table.

Theresa had burst into tears before she fully made it through the front door.

Blac fed her, bathed her, and now was just finishing thoroughly making love to her.

Theresa rose off of him, just to look down into his face. Sweat plastered strands of her hair to her forehead, but she looked beautiful that moment to Blac.

"I didn't wanna do that yesterday," she said.

"Shhh," Blac said. "You been with me before I was in prison, and you here now. You've always been good to me, and you deserve the same. From now on, I wanna give the same to you."

"Are you for real, Blac?" Theresa asked, her face brightening. "Don't be playing with me."

"I'm not playing. I wanna get my life together. I was thinking about moving with my sister and nephew in Wisconsin and —"

"You leaving me?"

"I was thinking about going, but now I'm thinking I wanna stay here and see where things can go with us, instead."

Theresa happily pressed her body back into Blac's, giving him wet kisses all over his face.

He held her tight, knowing his sister would understand and would even give her blessing to Blac if he was genuinely serious about giving a relationship an honest go. He felt he was.

Blac pressed his mouth to Theresa's, giving her a long kiss, when his cell phone rang.

He blindly grabbed it from off the nightstand, held it up, eyed the screen, and saw that it was Eric calling. He answered the phone. "Hello."

"Blac," Eric said, sounding troubled. "My brother has a situation I'm gonna have to deal with tomorrow evening, and I wanna know if I can get your help on it."

Blac questioned whether Cobi had told Eric about the two of them. No, that made no sense, considering how scared he was of his brother finding out, Blac assured himself. "Dude, whatever you need. You know I got your back," Blac said.

89

At work, Eric sat in the cafeteria, staring into his thoughts. A tray of food sat untouched in front of him. What happened yesterday at Jess's continued to eat at him. Jess had Maya taken away, so he no longer had a daughter. It's what he had to tell himself now, in order not to go crazy. Besides, there was something else he needed to focus on. Like what was to happen later this evening.

After hearing what was said in Sissy and Cobi's secret meeting yesterday, Eric knew he could not let his brother be taken.

When Eric said he would take care of it, Sissy scrunched up her face, looked at him as though he wasn't capable of taking care of himself, let alone anything to do with Cobi, then said, "And exactly how will you do that?"

"I'll go to the meeting as Cobi in his place."

"What do you mean?"

"What do you think I mean? I'll say I'm him."

"And then what?"

"And then do what needs to be done," Eric said.

"Pay him?" Sissy said. "Because that's what needs to be done."

"No. This man, whoever he is, needs to be spoken to."

"I don't understand what you're saying, Eric," Cobi said.

"This guy ain't shit. He's a criminal. He's strong-arming you, punking you. The only way to deal with fools like that is to punk them back."

"What do you mean?" Sissy said, stepping in front of Cobi, as if to protect him from any more of Eric's ridiculous ideas. "Do you mean get physical? Hurt this man? Do you understand if you go as Cobi, then it will be assumed that Cobi perpetrated whatever acts you commit?"

"I understand that," Eric said. "But what is the man going to do, go to the police to say he was assaulted while he was in the middle of trying to blackmail someone?"

"No," Sissy said, waving off the entire idea with her hands. "There is no way that we're going to allow —"

"What other options do we have, Sissy?" Cobi said. "And don't say pay him, because I told you, I'm not allowing that."

"Fine, Cobi," Sissy said. "I don't know what the hell is going on with you. Maybe it's guilt, or maybe this criminal here," she said, nodding toward Eric, "has brainwashed you. But whatever it is, you need to get yourself together, or you may find yourself in the very place he just crawled out of." Sissy gave Eric a long look of disgust, then stormed out the room.

Now, pulling himself out of his thoughts, Eric picked up his tray, walked it through the cafeteria, and without having had a bite, dumped his lunch into the trash. It was time he got back to work.

90

Austen sat beside Julia in front of a glass case at Tiffany.

A light blue velvet cloth had been spread in front of them by a smartly dressed saleswoman wearing a gray skirt suit and glasses. She stepped away from the case and let Austen and Julia make a decision.

There were two diamond rings sitting on the cloth. One was a four-carat princess cut with matching side stones, the other was a four-and-a-half-carat round.

"So which would you choose?" Julia said, not looking at the rings, but directly at Austen.

"I've been with rich men before. And they were all more concerned about their money than about me. And as you can see by what I've gone through, money comes and goes."

"So to answer my first question," Julia said. "If you could choose to marry either of the twins exactly as they are now — Cobi being gay, and Eric being poor — oh yeah, but with one change: Cobi is straight. Which would —"

"No. You can't just change Cobi to straight."

"I just did, now answer the question. Cobi's a rich, straight man, and Eric is a poor guy. Who would you marry?"

Austen smiled a little at the thought of the two men. "And I know them the way I know them now. They have the same personalities as they do now?"

"Yeah."

"Then it's not even close," Austen said. "It would be Eric."

"Girl, you let that man's piece drive you crazy. Even if Cobi were rich and straight?"

"I know Eric's had a hard past and has done some things he's not proud of, but he's trying to make those things right. I like who he is. I think he's a good man," Austen said, blushing a little.

"Ugh, you sicken me. It's a good thing you don't have to choose."

"Ladies," the saleswoman said, appearing back before Julia and Austen. "Have we made a decision? I know it's incredibly hard, because —"

Austen covered her eyes with one hand, pointed a finger toward the rings, and began with "Eenie, meenie, minie, moe . . ." When she finished reciting the children's rhyme, she uncovered her eyes to see that she had picked the solitaire. "Okay," Austen said. "Wrap it up."

91

It was 7:57 p.m., and Blac sat watching Eric sitting nervously behind the wheel of the Audi. Blac had never seen him look so frazzled.

He had his Cobi costume on — suit and tie — and would meet the blackmailer in his car, give him the briefcase of money that was sitting in the backseat, get the pictures and memory card in exchange, and that was to be it. Obviously, the money wouldn't actually be given to the man. Eric would threaten him into giving over the pictures because he would be afraid of what Eric would do to him. If that didn't work, then Eric would simply beat him until he handed the stuff over. At least that's the way Eric explained it to Blac. It was a brutal plan, but in cases like this, sometimes brutality was the only answer.

But for some reason, Eric didn't seem like he was up to the task, Blac thought, as he watched the clock on the dash hit 7:58.

The meeting was to take place in the rear parking lot of an abandoned grocery store. Eric and Blac were parked in front and down the street a half block from that store.

Eric told Blac the man would be in a dark blue Ford Fusion. The man wanted Cobi to come alone and bring the money. Eric was to park next to the man's car and climb into the passenger seat to make the exchange.

"You all right, Eric?" Blac said. "It's almost that time for you to be doin' this."

"Yeah, yeah, okay," Eric said, wiping a palm full of sweat from his brow. "I guess you gonna have to get out the car now, so I can drive around."

Blac looked at Eric. If he didn't want to admit it to himself that was okay, but Blac couldn't ignore what was obvious. "You can't do this, man."

"What you talkin' about?" Eric asked, offended.

"Dude, you look scared as shit. You can't do it."

Eric reached up, wrenched the rearview mirror around to take a look at himself. "Yeah, I don't know what's happenin', man, but I need to get it under control," Eric said, reaching to the backseat for the brief-case.

Blac reached back, grabbed the handle of the briefcase before Eric. "Let me do it."

"What? I can't —"

"Afford to let somethin' go wrong, because now you got somethin' to lose."

"I don't know what you talking about."

"You got a reason to stay out of prison now, dude. You got a brother, you got money, a job, you got a future. I ain't saying somethin' gonna go wrong, but if it does, you don't want to have your ass back behind bars."

"And you do?"

"No. But I ain't givin' up as much as you if I go back. I told her I love her last night, but Theresa ain't goin' nowhere. And I ain't planning on fucking this up," Blac said, giving the briefcase a tug. "Just let me go, get it over with, and we can talk more about it later."

Eric barely resisted as Blac pulled the case from his hand.

"Don't worry about drivin' around," Blac said, pushing open his door. "I'll just walk."

A fearful look on his face, Eric said, "You know the car to look for? You gonna be okay doing this, right?"

"I'm cool," Blac said, already outside of the car, slamming the door.

Eric watched Blac trot off, carrying the

briefcase down the street and around the building.

After he was out of sight, Eric slumped back in the seat of the car. He slapped a hand to his forehead. "What the fuck did I just do?" he said. He grabbed the car door handle, pulled it, opened the door slightly, thought of getting out and stopping Blac, then hesitated. He closed the door and fell back into the seat.

Blac was already out of sight. He fucked up. Plain and simple.

When Cobi needed help, Eric played the hardened criminal, took on the obligation, like doing deals like this was what he did every day before lunch. But what did he ultimately do? He punked out and had to hand the job over to Blac.

Eric thought about what Blac had said, and he realized he was right. Eric did have something to lose now. A brother, a place to stay, a gig he liked, and a woman that he was really starting to feel something for. Eric didn't think there was a lot of danger in what he had planned to do for Cobi. There surely wasn't as much danger as some of the things he'd done in the past for himself, but for some reason, he wasn't able to go through with it.

Eric leaned up in his seat, looked out the

window in the direction Blac went. He pulled his cell phone out of his pocket and thought of texting Blac to see how things were going, but how stupid was that, he thought. Eric had turned his phone off in preparation for the encounter with the man, so when he looked down at the screen, he was surprised to see that he had more than half a dozen missed calls from Cobi.

Eric thought about retrieving one of the voicemails but decided against it. Whatever Cobi had to tell him, it was too late now. Eric had to deal with what was happening that moment, so he stuffed the phone back in his pocket.

Settling back into the seat again, Eric closed his eyes and knew all he could do now was pray that everything turned out all right.

Moments later, the car door opened and slammed shut. When Eric opened his eyes, Blac was sitting in the passenger seat, laughing, breathing heavily, a huge grin on his face.

"Come on. Let's get the fuck out of here." The briefcase was on his lap, and he was pulling out a small envelope from the back pocket of his jeans and passing it to Eric.

"What happened?"

"It went down like it was supposed to.

Met the motherfucker, told him I wasn't givin' him the money, and told him to hand over the pictures. He said no, so I whupped his ass till he coughed them up, then I broke the fuck out."

Eric glanced at what was in the envelope, then closed it when he saw bare brown flesh and the tiny memory card. "How you know this all of them? He could have copies, and now he's probably more pissed and —"

"And he ain't gonna do shit," Blac said, fishing something else out of his front pocket and handing it to Eric.

It was the man's driver's license. A tubby, middle-aged, eyeglass-wearing man named Steven Ballard stared back at Eric from the ID card.

"Motherfucker was wearing a wedding ring. I told that fool if Mr. Winslow is ever threatened by him, or anybody else with some damn pictures, I was going to come to his house one night when he was out of town and have a slumber party with his wife, and if he had kids, I was gonna include them, too."

Eric didn't like the thought of that, didn't like the thought that Blac was capable of thinking that. That must've shown on his face, because Blac said, "I was just joking, man. But he don't know that, so we got the pictures, and your brother keeps his money. Now start the car so we can get the fuck out of here."

92

When they pulled up in front of Theresa's house, Blac immediately noticed the SUV with the tinted windows parked across the street.

Eric shifted the car into park, turned to Blac, and held out his hand.

Blac gave Eric some dap.

"Dude, can't thank you enough for what you did back there."

"Ain't nothin'. That's what boys are for, right?"

After Eric's car rolled down the street and disappeared around the corner, the big SUV's doors opened. Two men stepped out, walked across the street and up to Blac. It was Bones and Rondo.

Blac quickly looked over his shoulder at the house. There was a light on in the living room window, but it was always on. He just hoped Theresa wasn't in the front room, watching.

"What you want, man?" Blac said. "I told you I'm gonna have your money. I still got four days. Why the fuck you here?"

"Four days?" Bones said. He turned to Rondo, chuckled then said, "You hear that? Man think he got four days." Bones turned back to Blac. "Fool, that money due tomorrow. You looking at last year's calendar or something?"

"Hold it. Hold it! Cutty said I had ten days after the day I got out to get the —"

"That's where you wrong right there, playa," Bones said, holding up a hand. "Cutty said you had six days, not ten."

"What!" Blac said. "You're lying. You were right there. He said ten. How the fuck am I supposed to come up with that money four whole days earlier than —"

"Hold on, son," Rondo said, stepping in front of Bones. He lifted the front of his jersey to reveal the revolver he had stuffed in the waist of his jeans. "You need to access yo' uncrazy side before somebody wind up dead out here."

"I'd do what the man says," Bones said. He slapped a hand on Blac's shoulder. "You're gonna get that money just like you planned on gettin' it before, just have it by tomorrow. And then, Rondo and myself gonna be back tomorrow night, just like we here now, to pick that shit up. Got it?"

"You gotta call Cutty and tell him —"

"Ain't no callin' Cutty," Bones said. "Either it's gonna be you givin' me and Rondo the money, or you not givin' it to us, and some nasty shit happening to you that's gonna most likely leave you dead, or wishing you was. You got it?"

"I ain't gonna have that money," Blac said, knowing he hadn't invested enough time with Cobi to expect him to give up that amount of cash.

Bones squeezed Blac's shoulder, gave him a phony smile, then said, "Well, then, I'd advise you start saying good-bye to family and shit."

Blac watched as the two men walked back to the truck, speaking low to each other and chuckling.

Blac let himself in the house, walked back to the bedroom, stepped in, and took off his clothes. He crawled into bed, rolled on his side away from Theresa, folded his hands under his head, and tried to think of a way to get that money tomorrow. His life depended on it.

A moment later, he felt Theresa's arms around him.

His body tightened.

"You all right, baby?" Theresa asked. Her

voice was soft and concerned.

"Just stuff on my mind," Blac said.

93

I sat in my father's study for two and half hours believing I had sent my brother back to prison.

I paced, stared at the clock, prayed, yelled, and almost cried.

I had called Eric several times telling him to abort the plan, that we would just pay the man the money and avoid having something go wrong — someone getting hurt, the police getting involved, and my brother finding himself back behind bars.

I would never forgive myself, I kept thinking. With each minute that passed, I told myself that would be what happened. It was the reason Eric didn't pick up his phone. He had gotten arrested and soon would be calling from the police station.

I should have listened to my sister, I thought, standing from behind my father's desk, walking over to the wall where an antique clock hung. I looked up at it. Eric was already half an hour late.

I closed my eyes and prayed.

"Lord, I'm sorry for putting my brother in this position. It was wrong of me to think that my freedom and my life are more valuable than his, and to put him at risk to suffer again, as he's done for so much of his life. Jesus, if you find it in your will to bring my brother back to me just once more, I swear, I will never so easily send him away, and I will do everything in my power to keep him out of the jails that have so long imprisoned him. In your name, I pray, amen."

"That was touching, bro," I heard someone say from behind me.

I opened my eyes and spun around to see Eric standing just inside my father's study, a smile on his face.

I ran over to him and hugged him tight. "You made it back!"

"Course I did," Eric said, clapping me on the back a few times. He held out my briefcase to me. "It's all there. And . . ." he said, pulling out an envelope from his suit jacket pocket, "the pictures."

I gave them a self-conscious look.

"I didn't look through them," Eric said. "Just checked real quick to make sure it was what he said."

"I appreciate this, Eric, but even with the pictures, how do we know —"

"That he ain't keep others?" Eric finished for me. He reached into his pants pocket, pulled out the man's driver's license and handed it to me. "I scared him pretty bad. Told him if he ever thought of doin' what he said, I was gonna pay him a visit."

"And he believed you?"

Eric balled up his face into an angry scowl. "This is the face of a hardened criminal. Wouldn't you believe me if I threatened you?"

"It looks more like the face of a gay state's attorney, so I don't know how scared I'd really be." I laughed.

"Well, you don't have nothing to worry about no more, okay?"

"Okay," I said, staring at my brother. "You heard my prayer, right?"

"Yeah, kind of sappy."

"I meant every word of it."

"I appreciate that, for real."

"It's just how I feel."

Eric smiled bashfully. His cell phone rang. He dug in his pocket, pulled it out, and looked at the screen. "It's Jess," he said, surprise on his face, looking uncertain as to whether he would take the call.

"Well, answer it."

"Hello," Eric said. And after a moment, "Yeah. Yeah. I can do that."

I stood in front of him, hoping she was giving my brother some kind of good news.

"Okay, bye," Eric said. He slipped the phone back into his pocket and stared blank-faced at me.

"Well, don't keep me in suspense. What did she say?"

"She wants to meet tomorrow."

94

The next day, Eric pulled the Audi into the parking spot facing the public park. He shut off the car and looked out on the grassy area. There were kids running around, playing on the swing sets, chasing their dogs as their parents sat on nearby benches watching them.

He stepped out the car, just as Jess pulled up beside him in a black Infiniti sedan with tinted windows.

The driver's side door opened, and Jess stepped out, wearing a denim jacket, jeans, and heels. "Morning, Eric," Jess said, walking around the car, toward the back door.

"What's going on, Jess? Why'd you ask to meet me here?"

Jess ignored the question, continued around the car, and opened the back door.

From the other side of the car, Eric said, "You ain't going to answer my question? You call the police on me. Now this. Why you ask me to come out here?"

Jess looked up at Eric from over the roof of the car. "Have a little patience and you'll find out," Jess said, lowering her head into the car.

From his side, Eric couldn't see into the dark windows, so he slowly walked around the car to see what Jess was up to.

He got a glimpse inside the backseat. First he saw a pair of little legs, a portion of a child's car seat, then as Jess hoisted her from it, Eric looked into his daughter's face for the first time in two years.

The child was bright-eyed and more beautiful than Eric remembered. She had big, black pupils, a button nose, and a dimple in her cheek, just like her mother's. Her hair was shiny and brushed back into one long, thick, braided ponytail.

She wore a pink outfit that matched the ribbons around her braid.

Jess set Maya down in front of her father.

Eric stared down at the little girl, wanting to cry at how beautiful she was.

"Do you know who that is?" Jess asked Maya.

Maya looked up at Eric with her big eyes and scooted a little closer to her mother, grabbing her leg. She shook her head, shyly stuck a finger in her mouth, and in a soft voice said, "No."

Eric laughed.

"That's your father. Can you give your daddy a hug?" Jess said, kneeling down to Maya. "Give your daddy a hug, then we'll let you go play on the swings."

Maya looked over her shoulder at the swings and all the kids playing on them, then turned to Eric, extending her arms.

Eric laughed again, quickly kneeled down, and took his little girl in an embrace. He squeezed her as tight as he dared, and as much as he fought it, he could not stop a tear from falling from his eye.

Ten minutes later, Jess had told Eric everything. They sat on a bench just outside the playground, and watched Maya play with the other children.

"So you're admitting it," Eric said, a hurtful expression on his face. "You and everyone else who testified against me lied. Why the fuck you telling me now, Jess?" Eric said, his voice low.

Jess lowered her head in shame, then looked up. "The guilt. It was wrong, I know that. You're her father. I know you love her, and you never mistreated her, but —"

"But what?" Eric stood from the bench.

"But I couldn't have her grow up the way

I did. You know my —"

"I know, your old man was in prison, and all he did was disappoint you. But I ain't your old man."

"I wasn't taking any chances. You were gone. I was raising her alone. I wasn't going to take a chance on that being my life, her life," Jess said, standing in front of him. "It killed me to do it. To tell my family to lie, to sit in that room and lie myself."

"So what are you going to do about it?"

"There's nothing that can be done."

Eric grabbed Jess tight by the shoulders. "What do you mean, nothing? You can go back —"

"I can't. It's done. And even if I could, I wouldn't. The steps I took were wrong, but I think the decision was right."

Eric released Jess, turned his back on her in disgust. "Then why you bring me here?"

"I wanted you to see Maya. And if you want, I want you to continue to see her."

Eric spun around. "But you had my rights taken."

"That doesn't mean you aren't still her father," Jess said. "We can start slow, a couple of times a month. You can come by and visit her if you like."

Eric glared at Jess, hoping he was hiding at least some of the hate he was feeling for her that moment. "I don't know. I'll have to think about it."

"I can understand how you feel, but —"

"No, you can't! You lied and took my daughter away from me. That didn't happen to you, so don't say you know how the fuck I feel."

"You're right," Jess apologized. "But I don't want you not to see Maya, because you're mad at me. She didn't do anything wrong. And I know you won't have rights, and legally, Quentin will be her father, but you can still be in her life. What do you say, Eric?"

Eric looked across the park and watched his little girl playing on the slide. He had missed over half her life already. He didn't want to miss any more. "Fine. I'll see her when you let me."

"Good," Jess said, seeming genuinely happy. "But there is one condition."

"What is that?"

"If you ever get in trouble with the law again, it will be the last time you see Maya."

95

Late that afternoon, Blac stood outside the building Cutty used to run his drug operations, waiting for the man to finally tell him exactly when he needed to deliver his money to him.

Blac had been ringing Cutty's cell phone since the moment he had gotten up this morning. The man didn't answer, so as a last resort, Blac borrowed Theresa's car and drove down to his spot.

After he knocked on the front door, Blac was met with resistance from two of Cutty's men that Blac hadn't seen before. Blac had to convince them he wasn't leaving till he spoke to Cutty. The men told him to wait and they would see what they could do.

Ten minutes later, Cutty sauntered out, wearing sunglasses, sagging jeans, and holding an unlit blunt between two of his fingers.

"Deadline for my money ain't till eight o'clock tonight, but obviously you got it early. That's the reason you standin' there, right?"

"Look, Cutty," Blac said. "I don't know what's going on, but I'm not supposed to have your money for another four days. You said the clock started —"

"You tryin' to tell me what the fuck I said?" Cutty pulled a lighter out of his pocket and lit the tip of the marijuana cigar he was holding. He took a puff, held the smoke in a moment, exhaled, then in a lowered voice said, "The other day you came by here asking for some shit to sell because you knew you weren't gonna have my money, didn't you?"

"No, Cutty, I swear —"

"Don't lie to me, Blac," Cutty said, pointing at him with the blunt. "You didn't have my money and you was thinking you could sell enough of my shit in time to pay me what you owe. Problem is, my man Drake picked up on that. He made that comment about you playing me, which is why he got his ass whupped. People hear I'm getting played, same people start to think I'm getting soft, and I can't have that shit. Folks start thinking they can put a bullet in my head, take my position, just like I did to that pussy Booky Bear. So to send a message, I had to shorten your deadline. I know

421

it's fucked up, but it don't matter. New deadline is tonight at eight."

"Cutty! You can't do —"

Cutty yanked off his sunglasses, turned his evil eye on Blac, the other drifting off slightly skyward. "You don't tell me what the fuck I can't do. Like I said, deadline tonight. Have my money and we square," Cutty said, drawing smoke from the blunt and holding it in. "Don't," he said in a strangled voice. "I'm sorry, but yo' ass will be made an example of."

96

The day had been going perfectly until I had gotten the phone call that dragged me out to this bar and had me sitting, waiting for Blac.

Earlier today, I had a late lunch with Sissy at Wishbone, one of my favorite West Loop restaurants, where we discussed more of the wedding plans.

It would be in just three days, and because of that, my sister decided to scale it all the way down to a private function with just our closest friends. "We can have a public affair once we get your shares and make sure Winslow Products is out of the woods."

"How is company business? Are we still the owners, or have we been taken over?" I said, joking, but not really.

"As long as I'm living, you'd know I'd never allow that, Cobi," Sissy said with conviction. "P&G is still buying whatever shares it can get its hands on, but I've convinced most of our board members not to sell just yet. Don't worry, we're still in control."

"Good. I knew I had nothing to worry about with you in charge," I said, taking a bite out of one of my buttery corn muffins.

"You seem like you're in just a wonderful, click-your-heels-together mood today. What's got you so bright and shiny? I imagine not having to pay off yet another blackmailer."

"That's right, and you still have to thank Eric for his part in that."

"Sure," Sissy said. "On the day I find out what his part in it actually was. You never know. He could've been the one running the scam."

"Whatever. Just be happy with me right now. It's a good time. I have you, my brother, and this thing with Austen isn't necessarily the nuclear bomb I thought it was going to be."

"Oh," Sissy said, a smile of surprise on her face. "So you're liking her now, huh? Who knows. Maybe in five years, you two —"

"Yeah, don't go that far. But she's nice, and I do like her," I said. "And Eric called me an hour ago. I know this means nothing to you, but the mother of his child decided to allow him to see his daughter. Isn't that wonderful?"

"No. You were right, that means nothing to me," Sissy said, poking her fork at her catfish.

"You're going to grow to love him one day," I said confidently.

Sissy looked up at me with a face as serious as I've ever seen on her, and said, "Cobi, understand this. I know he's your brother, but there is simply something about that man I do not like. He does not deserve to be considered part of this family. I think if you continue to see him that way, he will cause you great harm, and for that reason, I will never, ever grow to love, like, or even tolerate him. Okay?"

"Yeah, okay," I said, holding the stupid smile on my face, trying to pretend Sissy wasn't as serious as she said she was.

After lunch, and for the next six hours, I was receiving phone calls and text messages from Blac at the rate of about a dozen an hour. I avoided them. I didn't answer the calls or check the voice messages. I simply ignored the texts, until half an hour ago, when he called me six times, back to back to back.

"Hello!" I answered the phone angrily.

"What is it? Why are you calling me like this?"

"I need to see you," Blac said. He didn't sound the same. I detected worry, almost fear in his voice.

"Well, if I'm not picking up your calls, or returning your texts, don't you know that means I'm busy?"

"Cobi, I said I need to see you. I really need to see you, please."

Sitting at the bar of a small place called Eva's on South Wabash, I told myself I wasn't going to wait a minute longer than the time we had agreed upon.

I had told myself that I was going to start distancing myself from Blac because of the situation with the photographs. It was a close call, but thanks to Eric, I had managed to escape it.

If one clown with a camera was able to capture pictures of me with another man, how hard would it be for another? I could no longer expose myself like that. Tyler had been right all along. Maybe I needed to be as paranoid as he was.

I glanced down at my watch and saw that it was eight o'clock on the dot. I pulled a ten-dollar bill from my wallet and was prepared to toss it on the bar to pay for my beer, when Blac walked right up to me and tried to give me a hug and a kiss. I pressed my hands into his chest to keep him back. "What are you doing? Not in here."

"Fine, then let's get a room," Blac said. He looked jittery and scared.

"No. We're not getting a room."

"C'mon. I promise I'll make it worth your while. The best you ever had it."

"I said no. Now, either sit down so we can talk, or I'm leaving."

Blac looked left and right, as if he thought someone was after him, then sat down beside me.

"Have a drink," I said.

"Don't want a drink, but I need something from you."

What else could this man want, I thought? I gave him sex and a total of $13,000. What else was there? "What is it, Blac?"

"I need money. Like tonight."

"How much?" I asked out of curiosity, not because I intended on giving it to him.

"A hundred and fifty thousand dollars."

I smiled, knowing this was a joke. When he didn't smile with me, I said, "You're joking, right?"

"I'm not joking. Does it look like I'm joking?" he said, sweat starting to appear on his brow.

He looked like a desperate, frightened man on the verge of doing something stupid. "What in the world do you need money like that for?"

"Don't have time to explain. I'm in trouble, and I need it, and you're the only person I can get it from."

"Then you're not getting it."

"Look," Blac said, grabbing my arm hard. "I told you I'm in trouble. I need this!"

"For what? What did you do?" I said, speaking in a harsh whisper.

"Drugs," Blac finally admitted. "Drug deal gone wrong, okay!"

"Drugs! And you want me to give you money for drugs? If word got out, do you know the damage that could do to —" I stood up, shaking my head. "No. I'm sorry, but you're on your own on this one."

"Sit down, Cobi," Blac said.

"I told you —"

"I said sit your motherfuckin' punk ass down," Blac said, forcefully. "Now listen," Blac said, digging in his back jeans pocket, pulling out a yellow envelope, and laying it on the counter. "I'm about to make you an offer your ass would be smart not to refuse."

97

Yesterday, when Blac took that briefcase from Eric and started around that abandoned grocery store to meet the blackmailer, the thought of stealing that half million dollars only crossed his mind once. But it crossed very slowly.

He could've taken it, paid Cutty his money, had $350K left, then headed down to Wisconsin and even taken Theresa with him. They could've bought a small house or something, lived off the rest for a good little while.

As Blac turned the corner and spotted the blue Ford Fusion, he asked himself, would he have actually been able to get away with it? If Blac did choose to play it that way, Eric would've surely told Cobi, and with all the money and resources that Cobi had — not to mention the fact that he was a fucking state's attorney — Blac would've been nabbed and thrown back in Joliet before he crossed the Illinois state line.

So he didn't steal the money but instead walked up cautiously to the driver's side of the Ford like he had intended.

The pudgy, balding, bespectacled man had his eyes trained on Blac from the moment he came around the corner. From the driver's seat of the car, he leaned over and said, "Who the fuck are you?"

"Mr. Winslow sent me. I got the money," Blac said, hoisting the briefcase up so the man could see.

"Get in the fucking car!"

Blac laughed to himself. The man was trying to act hard, but Blac knew he was scared shitless. He could tell by the bitchy high tone he heard in his voice and by the way the gun the man was pointing at Blac was trembling.

"Easy," Blac said, opening the door and lowering himself into the passenger seat. "We don't want nobody gettin' killed out here."

"Shut up. Open the case. Let me see what's inside."

"You got the pictures?"

"I got the gun," the man said, pointing it in the direction of Blac's face. "Open it."

Blac did what he was told. The man's eyes lit up at the clean, crisp, neatly stacked bills that filled the briefcase.

"Now close it and hand it to me slowly."

Again, Blac followed orders, measuring the man's every movement, knowing his opportunity was about to come.

"Easy," the man said, reaching with his other hand, while still holding the gun on Blac.

Blac lifted the case, then quickly turned it wide. Using it as a shield, he forced it into the gun, thinking if the man did manage to squeeze off a shot, the case and the bills inside might at least render the bullet nonlethal. But the man did not shoot.

Blac wedged the gun and the man's hand between the briefcase and the seat. Then with his free fist, Blac struck the man three times hard in the face.

Steven Ballard dropped the gun, his nose squirting blood from the last blow.

Both Blac and Ballard scrambled for the weapon that slipped down between the two front seats, but Blac came up with it and pointed it in between the man's eyes, a wicked smile on his face.

He took the pictures off the man, as well as his license, and left him with the warning that he would come to his house and kill his family if Cobi was ever threatened again.

The thought hadn't struck Blac till he was

halfway around the building, then it hit him all of a sudden. What if Cobi wasn't as agreeable as Blac hoped he would be?

Blac dropped to his knees and quickly sifted through the thick envelope of photos. There were pictures of himself with Cobi, and snapshots of another good-looking guy with a thick mustache. Blac took a longer look at the man's face and figured this had to be the senator Eric told him Cobi was fucking. Blac's leverage had just gotten stronger, because the photos were juicy as hell, shots he was sure Cobi wouldn't want to be leaked to the public.

He divided the pictures evenly into two piles, slipped what he would give to Eric back in the envelope and pocketed his.

Now as he sat at the bar with Cobi, he was glad he had thought to give himself this bit of insurance.

Cobi sat there on his stool, shocked, staring down at the photos. He looked up at Blac. "How did you get these?"

"I need that money tonight, or you'll see those pictures on the Internet and every fucking TV station in this country."

"I said, how did you get these?" Cobi said, waving the photos in his fist.

"Eric."

"You're a liar. Do what you want with the

pictures. I won't be blackmailed. I'm not giving you the money. I don't care what kind of trouble you're in," Cobi said, standing from the stool. "And from now on, stay your ass away from me and my brother. Now that he has me, he no longer needs people like you in his life." Cobi turned and started away, but Blac ran up, grabbed him by the arm in the middle of the bar, and spun him around.

"Eric don't care for you like you think he does."

"You don't know what the hell you're talking about, and I'm still not giving you the money," Cobi said.

"Really?" Blac said, spitefully. "If he did, why is he fuckin' your fiancée?"

98

It wasn't true, I told myself as I hysterically burst through the front door of the mansion. I had sped home, telling myself that Blac had made everything up. Eric hadn't given him those photos, and he definitely wasn't having sex with Austen, the woman that I was starting to believe could make me appear, at least to the outside world, normal — the woman I was going to marry.

I stumbled onto the second floor, breathing hard, fighting the images that danced through my head. Was it a jealousy of the flesh that enraged me? No. I was gay. I didn't want Austen like that. It was the principle of the entire matter. I welcomed Eric into my home, accepted him as my brother, found him a job, and how did he repay me? By allowing his criminal friend to jeopardize all that I worked for and fucking Austen in my house?

No! It cannot be true, I thought, mere steps

from Eric's door. I threw the door open to find his room empty.

I felt foolish. I had allowed Blac to manipulate me into believing things that I should've known could've never been true. Eric was my brother, and although we've been apart all our lives, he wasn't the kind of man to —

I froze when I heard a groan coming from Austen's room.

I spun around, raced down to her door, pushed it open, disgusted at what I saw. Austen was in bed, naked, on her back, her legs hiked in the air, my brother, holding himself above her, pushing himself into her, both of them, sweating, thrusting, moaning so loudly, and so lost in themselves, they must not have heard the noise I made entering the house and must not have noticed me standing in the room with them.

I stood there in utter shock for a moment. Finally finding the strength to speak, I yelled, "Eric, get the fuck out of my house!"

99

Blac parked Theresa's car one street away from her house. He cautiously walked through two backyards and made his way to the back of Theresa's house.

Moving through the driveway, he listened for the voices of any of Cutty's men toward the front of the house. Not hearing anything, Blac continued in that direction.

Standing out front, he didn't see the truck down either side of the street.

Feeling his heart start to slow, he walked up to the front door.

He was easily past his deadline by two hours and was surprised Cutty's men had not been camped out front, ready to shoot him on sight.

It would be only a matter of time if he didn't get Cutty's money, Blac thought, sliding his key into the front door lock. He needed a plan. Cobi wasn't going to budge, so Blac had no choice but to go to the other man in the photos, the senator.

He would do that first thing tomorrow morning, he thought, pushing the door open. And if this senator was a smart man, he would give up the money without a hassle, and everything would be fine.

As soon as Blac entered the house and closed the door, he knew something was terribly wrong.

One of the lamps in the living room was on the floor, the shade crumpled, the base shattered. There were sofa cushions scattered about, and two of the kitchen chairs were flipped over.

Blac froze, his eyes wide, his pulse revving again.

There had been a scuffle. Someone had been in this house. He thought to call out to Theresa, but he kept his mouth shut. They could still be there.

Blac moved quietly but swiftly to the closed bedroom door and pressed his ear against it.

He heard muffled crying sounds and knew they were coming from Theresa. What was happening in there?

He wished he had carried with him the gun he had taken off Ballard, but it was stuffed under the mattress in the bedroom.

He gripped the doorknob firmly and told

himself that however many men were in there, he would have to fight like hell and kill if it came to that.

Blac threw open the door, slamming it against the wall behind it, and was startled to see no one.

The room was a mess, drawers hung open from the dresser, the nightstand was toppled over, the portable TV lay on the floor, the tube smashed in.

"Theresa!"

He heard sniffling. It came from the other side of the bed.

He ran around it. There on the floor, Theresa lay curled in a ball, covering her face. Her shirt was ripped, exposing most of her bra, and her jeans had been yanked down to below her hips.

Blac threw himself down on the floor with her. "Theresa," he said, gently taking her by the wrist, pulling her arm away so he could see her face. What he saw sickened him.

Both of Theresa's eyes were purple and swollen almost completely shut. Her face was bruised in several places, and fresh blood still streamed from her nostrils and a gash in the center of her bottom lip.

"Who did this?" Blac said, scooping her up in his arms, trying to control his rage. "Who did this to you?"

No answer came as tears spilled out of the swollen slits that were Theresa's eyes, and then between her sobs, she said, "Someone named Cutty."

100

I sat on the edge of my bed, head lowered, still stunned by what I had seen.

I didn't know how Blac had gotten those pictures. I didn't believe him when he said he had gotten them from my brother, but maybe I should've. Blac hadn't lied about Eric fucking Austen, so why would he have lied about the other?

I couldn't bring myself to even think about Blac's attempt to blackmail me. What required all of my attention now was the situation with my brother and Austen.

Eric had left soon after putting on his clothes.

I stood there, my arms crossed, and watched him shamefully get into his jeans, pull on his shirt, and step into his shoes. He was silent the entire time, never once looking at me or Austen.

When he was finished, he looked over at Austen, and said, "Sorry."

"Don't speak to her!" I ordered.

He immediately averted his eyes to the floor and started walking toward the door, near where I stood.

Eric paused, as if about to say something before he walked out.

"Just get out," I said, before he could open his mouth. "There is nothing I want to hear from you."

He walked out, leaving me and Austen in the room alone.

By that time, she was standing in a bath-robe, staring at me. "What should I do?" she asked in a meek voice.

I turned and walked out, slamming the bedroom door behind me.

From my bedroom, I called Sissy, told her everything that happened except the part about the blackmailing. I didn't want to be scolded by Sissy about sleeping with Blac.

"You put Eric out, didn't you?"

"Yes."

"I don't want to say I told you so, but —"

"Then don't. Just don't, Sissy."

She insisted that she be allowed to come over and take care of this.

"Fine," I said, then disconnected the call.

Sissy had gotten here fifteen minutes ago, let herself in, and had come up to my bedroom.

She made me stand from my bed and give her a hug. My knees barely felt strong enough to hold me up.

"We're going to get through this, okay?"

"Yeah," I said, not believing that.

"Just stay in here, and I'll take care of everything."

That was only moments ago, and only now did I feel confident in my strength to stand, and the courage to find out what happened.

I slowly walked toward Austen's bedroom door and stopped just outside of it.

I saw Sissy standing in the center of the room. There was an open suitcase on the bed, and Austen was filling it with her clothes.

"Move it. We don't have all night," Sissy said.

"Why did you do it?" I said, stepping through the door.

Sissy and Austen both turned to me, surprised to see me standing there.

"Cobi," Sissy said. "Don't you think it'd be better if you just —"

"You were sleeping with my brother," I said, ignoring Sissy. "Why did you do it?"

Austen finished rolling a pair of socks into a ball, set them in the suitcase, and said, "It just happened. You had me locked up in this house, controlling every aspect of —"

"No one had you locked up, and no one was controlling you," I said. "You had complete freedom. Don't go blaming this on me."

"Complete freedom?" Austen chucked sadly. "Your sister had me followed everywhere I went."

I couldn't believe that, and the look I gave Sissy said as much.

The look Sissy gave me back did not deny the accusation.

"Your brother and I were both going through a lot. He didn't want it to happen, he didn't push for it. I did. I needed someone, in that way, you understand. I needed that kind of attention, and I sure as hell wasn't going to get it from you, was I, Cobi?"

"That wasn't part of the deal."

"But do you understand what I'm saying? I needed to feel love, or something close to it right now. Eric needed the same thing. And I bet you did too, didn't you?"

"I have nothing to do with this."

"But you do. You're always out late at night. I see you stepping out all dressed up, and for what? Business meetings? No. You're getting your needs met. You have someone to listen to you when you talk about your problems, someone to hold you."

"Did Eric talk to you about —"

"No," Austen said. "Eric didn't say anything about your personal life or about who you date. But I know you're seeing someone. Everyone needs someone, and for you and your fucking sister over there to think that you can sign me to a contract, lock me up in a room, and expect me to behave like a nun, you were very wrong."

"Okay, bitch," Sissy said, stepping up. "I've had enough of —"

"I'm sorry, Cobi," Austen said over Sissy. "I truly am sorry for this happening. And I'm sorry that I've fallen for your brother, because it was wrong. But don't either of you say you've never found yourselves in situations where you were involved with someone you had no business being involved with."

I felt Sissy's eyes all of a sudden on me. I thought about Blac, and of course I thought about Tyler. Blac was Eric's friend, yet I slept with him behind my brother's back. Austen was nothing more than my friend at the moment, so was I being hypocritical, considering Eric slept with her? And the Tyler thing was something I couldn't even compare. I knew he was married, had a family, yet I continued seeing him, even considered ratting him out to his wife.

I turned and walked out the room.

"Cobi," I heard Sissy calling from behind me. She stopped me in the hallway. "What are you doing?"

"I don't know."

"You want me to finish having her pack her things and get her out of here, right?"

I took a moment, thought about all that was going on, all that was just said, and I even thought about Eric, who was Lord knows where, and then said, "No. Let her stay for now."

101

The next morning, Blac sat parked outside the gated subdivision, where he believed Senator Tyler Stevens lived.

He found the man's home address early this morning after searching the Internet for better than two and a half hours.

Last night, Blac had carried Theresa out to the car and sped her to the nearest emergency room.

There, the doctor told him that she had not been raped, only badly beaten. She had a mild concussion, bad bruising, a very fine facial fracture that would heal on its own, but no major breaks.

The doctor said they would bandage her up and release her later in the day with pain medication, and that Blac should expect her to have a full recovery.

That was at 1:30 a.m.

Afterward, Blac walked out to the parking lot, his cell phone to his ear, listening as his phone rang the number he had dialed.

"I knew my little visit would get your attention," Cutty said. "Got my money, yet?"

"What the fuck is wrong with you? *I* owe you the money. She ain't got nothin' to do with this."

"Your ass wasn't around, so we did what we needed. But be grateful, Blac. Your girl got a nice, fat ass, and Bones was really wantin' to fuck that. I held him off this time, but next —"

"Won't be no next time, okay. I'm gonna have your money, but I need one more day."

"Aw, Blac. Isn't this how all of this shit started?"

"I'm gonna need one more day!" Blac yelled into the phone. "Haven't you done enough? Give me the goddamn day so I can get your money and we can be done."

There was silence on the phone. Blac held it worriedly up to his ear, waiting.

"You know what?" Cutty finally said. "Okay. Fine. But we found the cutest little thing when we was in your girl's house. On the fridge, there was a letter with a picture."

Blac froze, the phone to his ear.

"You got a sister and a little nephew in Racine, Wisconsin, don't you?"

"Motherfucker, don't you even think —"

"Told you, bitch. Don't tell me what to

think. You have my money by tomorrow, or me and two of my boys gonna come back and fuck your girl so bad, all the thread in the world won't sew that pussy back up. And if you still ain't got my loot, we gonna take a little trip out to the address on this letter and make this a family affair. Clock is tickin', motherfucker," Cutty said, then disconnected the call.

Now, sitting behind the wheel of Theresa's Chevy, Blac watched as a Lexus LS 430 pulled out of the gate of the subdivision. He had gotten a good look at the driver and saw that it was indeed Tyler Stevens.

Blac started the car, stepped on the gas, and sped up the quiet, residential two-lane street. In seconds, he overtook the Lexus, cut the wheel hard to the right, and swerved in front of the big car.

The tires of both cars squealed as the vehicles screeched to a halt, and Blac was quickly up out of his car, his door hanging open, as he ran toward the driver's side of the Lexus.

As Blac approached the car, he heard the power locks engage, and saw as the driver's side window rolled up the last inch and sealed completely.

"Open the door! I gotta talk to you," Blac

yelled at the window.

Tyler looked frightened, cowering away from the door. "Who are you?"

Blac reached into his back pocket, pulled out the single, extremely graphic photo of Cobi and Tyler having sex, slapped it up against the window so the man inside could see, and said, "This is who I am. Now open the fucking door!"

102

I sat in my office at work and realized I still had no idea just how much of a role Eric played in this. I had to find out from him. To this point, I had put off doing that, because the last thing I wanted to discover was that Eric had been involved in some plan with Blac all along to rob me of my money. I had prayed that was not the case and even asked Austen that this morning, after filling her in on everything that was going on.

We were at the kitchen table. I had called her down and told her that I needed to speak to her.

"I know I haven't known him long, but I know he's not that kind of person, and you should know that, too, Cobi," Austen said.

"I know I should, but I'm just not certain anymore."

"He's never told me, and I know the two of you just found each other again, but by the way he talks about you, I can tell your brother loves you," Austen said. "He really does."

It was good to hear that, even if I wasn't sure it was true.

"How do you feel about him?" I asked.

"What do you mean?"

"Last night you said you didn't mean to fall for him. Do you have feelings for my brother?"

Austen hesitated, seeming afraid to hurt my feelings.

"You can tell me. I won't be jealous."

"Yes, I do have feelings for him," Austen said.

"And if I freed you from this contract, would you continue to see him?"

"I don't want to be freed from this contract. You know I need the money."

"You should've thought of that before you fucked my brother," I said coldly.

I reached across my desk, grabbed my office phone, and tried to dial Eric but was unable. I needed, wanted to speak to him but just couldn't find it within myself to get past my feelings of resentment and betrayal.

The phone rang and startled me out of my thoughts.

I snatched it up.

"Mr. Winslow," my secretary said, "Senator Stevens is on line one for you."

This was the wrong time. I didn't feel like talking to him right now, but said, "Put him through."

When I heard the line click over, I said in my best cheery voice, "Hey, how —"

"Some thug practically ran me off the road, demanding I give him three hundred thousand dollars or he's going public with some very sensitive pictures. What the hell did you do, Cobi?"

103

Blac sat in the emergency room waiting area.

A nurse told him she would be bringing Theresa in a wheelchair to be discharged in just a few minutes.

While sitting there, Blac checked his watch. It was already 6:00 p.m. Senator Stevens had just two hours left to get the $300K together.

Blac had upped the price. He needed more, considering all the shit he had gone through and what he expected he would need to give him and Theresa a clean start. There was no way he would feel comfortable leaving her where she was after the comments Cutty said Bones made about her. He thought about maybe still going to Wisconsin and taking Theresa with him. Whether he did or not, the $150,000 he would keep for himself would make things a hell of a lot easier.

This morning, after Blac had finally gotten the senator to roll down the window, he told the man his demands.

The senator sat there quietly, obediently nodding his head as if Blac had a gun on him. He was much easier to handle than Blac thought he would've been.

"And where do you want me to bring the money?" the senator asked.

"There's a J & J Fish on Cottage Grove."

"I don't know where that is."

"Find it, and bring the money there at eight o'clock, or you're gonna see these pictures on tomorrow morning's news."

104

Eric was too troubled to go to work today. Instead he sat in a McDonald's, watching the news on a wall-mounted flat-screen TV while sipping a Coke.

He was exhausted.

He had slept in his car last night after Cobi put him out.

He and Austen weren't supposed to have gotten caught. They weren't even supposed to have had sex last night. But Eric was so happy to have seen his daughter, to know that he would be able to continue seeing her, that he wanted to share that with Austen.

Eric stood there in her bedroom after telling her the good news.

She hugged him, kissed him on the cheek, then said, "I'm so glad for you. You deserve another chance with her."

Austen stared in his eyes, and Eric could feel the sincerity in what she had just said.

The way she looked at him made him feel like she really cared what happened to him, and he couldn't remember the last time someone made him feel that way.

"I want you," he said.

"Then what's stopping you? Your brother's not here."

"This can't ever happen again," Eric said. "He's done too much for me. This is wrong, and he would be so hurt if he ever found out. I don't want to do that to him."

"He won't find out," Austen said, pulling Eric into her, and kissing him deeply.

Eric took another sip of the watered-down Coke and stared down at his cell phone. It sat beside a crumpled double cheeseburger wrapper.

It was the phone that Cobi had been charitable enough to buy him, just like the clothes on his back and the shoes on his feet. In return, Eric slept with his fiancée.

He banged his fist angrily against the table for being so stupid.

He had thought about calling Cobi several times today, but remembering how angry his brother was last night, he knew Cobi wouldn't want to hear from him.

The guilt was really starting to eat at him, so Eric picked up the phone. He'd call anyway. At the very least, he could apologize and ask Cobi if he wanted him to bring his car back, or just leave it somewhere with the keys in the glove box.

Eric had punched in the first three digits of Cobi's number when his phone lit with an incoming call.

"Hello," Eric said, quickly pressing the phone to his ear.

"Eric, it's Austen. Your brother doesn't want to call you, but he's gotten himself into a very bad situation. Can you come now? He needs you."

105

"It's already six-thirty. That leaves me just an hour and a half to decide what needs to be done," Tyler said, pacing anxiously back and forth across my father's study floor. He had been here for the last hour, trying to decide what to do. He turned to me. "Goddammit, Cobi!" he said, striking his palm with his fist. "How did you let this happen? You slept with that man?"

"He told you that?"

"What do you think? Why did you do it?"

"You weren't around!"

"I see. Now both our lives are about to be ruined because you couldn't keep your dick in your pants."

That stung, as I'm sure Tyler intended, but I was no longer in the mood for being blamed. "I'm sorry, Tyler, but what's done is done."

"What's done is done!" Tyler said, suddenly rushing across the room at me. Before

I knew it, he had me by the collar, pushing me backward, until I slammed into the wall behind me. He was in my face, his fists still wrapped around my shirt, his knuckles digging into my neck. "This is my life! Do you know what will happen if my wife finds out about this? She'll leave me, and I'll never see my daughters again. Do you understand that?" Tyler yelled, spit flying from his lips onto my face.

"Tyler —" I said, grabbing his hands and struggling to breathe. "Let me go."

"I said, do you understand that!"

"My brother said let him go!" I heard Eric's firm voice say from behind us.

Tyler looked over his shoulder. He was still holding me, but his grip had loosened some.

"He's about to ruin my life," Tyler said to Eric.

"If you don't let him go, I'm gonna ruin it," Eric said. I looked over Tyler's shoulder, saw Eric there, his eyes narrowed, his fists balled at his sides, as if ready to attack.

Tyler let me go.

I grabbed my throat and massaged it as air filled my lungs.

"Do you know what he did?" Tyler said, pointing, as he stepped disgustedly away from me. "What he did with his boyfriend, Blac?"

Eric looked at me, questioning, surprise on his face.

"I'll tell you, Eric," I said, my hand still around my neck.

I finished my story fifteen minutes later. Eric told me Blac had been the one who had gotten the photos from Ballard and how he must've kept some of them.

Eric and I sat on the sofa, Tyler still pacing back and forth, his arms crossed over his chest.

"I know what I did was stupid," I said, "but —"

"I should've never sent him when I told you I was going to be the one to get the pictures," Eric said.

"But if I was going to sleep with Blac, I should've told you."

"I ain't judging you. I did wrong, too."

"That's wonderful that there's no judging going on," Tyler said sarcastically. "But I'm not giving that thug three hundred thousand dollars of my money. What do we do?"

"I don't know," I said, standing. "If I had just paid off the first guy, Blac would've never gotten ahold of those photos and —"

"We need to do something," Tyler said. "I'll call the police before I hand over one dime, and they'll be waiting for him when he shows up."

"No," Eric said, standing with me and Tyler. "Don't do it like that. Keep the police out of it."

"Why?" Tyler said. "They'll put him away, and I'll never have to worry about him again."

"I know Blac," Eric said. "You cross him, yeah, he goes back to jail, but what's to say he doesn't keep a few of those photos just in case? Call one of his boys on the outside, and make sure the pictures get to the right people, and then your secret is out anyway?"

"Then maybe he needs to be taken out," Tyler said.

Eric looked at me oddly, then said to Tyler, "What do you mean 'taken out'?"

"You know, taken care of. You're a criminal. Isn't that what you do? Don't you have a gun hidden around here, somewhere?"

"I think you been watchin' too much TV," Eric said.

"If he can do what you say he might, and he's not taken care of, how do I know I'll ever be safe?" said Tyler. "How does your brother know? Even if I were to give him the money, what happens when he blows through it? What's to stop him from coming back to us, insisting on more? Cobi and I will forever be indebted to this man, unless something happens to him, and you know it."

I stared at Eric. I saw his eyes glaze over, as though he were seriously considering the nonsense Tyler was saying.

"Stop it!" I said. "That is ridiculous. Eric, you were about to suggest something before Tyler started talking that madness."

Eric blinked a number of times, seeming to snap out of the place he had gone. "I'll go over there and talk to him. Like I said, I've known him for a while. If there's anyone he'll listen to, it's me."

106

Blac stuffed more of Theresa's clothes into a large duffel bag that sat on her bedroom dresser.

When he had gotten her home from the hospital, he sat her down in the living room, stared at her bruised and bandaged face, and told her as much as he dared about why she had been beaten.

"Those were Cutty's drugs I got caught with, and he wants the money back now. But don't worry. I know someone who's gonna give me what I owe, plus some more. Enough so we can leave, go somewhere better."

"Leave?" Theresa said. "And go where? I can't go anywhere. My job is —"

"Theresa," Blac said, kneeling down in front of her. "I know I ain't always been what I was supposed to be, and I know I ain't always put you first like I should've. But I been through enough to tell you I'm done treatin' you like that. I want a better life, and I want you to be part of it." He took both her hands in his and said, "Come with me, trust me, and marry me, and I promise, everything gonna be just fine."

It looked like it caused her some pain, but Theresa smiled as wide as she could, leaned forward, and snatched Blac into the tightest hug he had ever received from her.

Inside the bedroom, Blac finished packing the duffel and pulled the draw ties on it.

His deadline had been extended till tomorrow at 8:00 p.m., but Blac didn't trust Cutty and his men, so he told Theresa it would be best if they stayed in a motel tonight.

He reached under the mattress and pulled out the gun he had taken off Steven Ballard. He ejected the magazine to see that it was still fully loaded. He raised the back of his T-shirt, slipped the weapon in the waist of his jeans while telling himself that one way or another, the senator was going to give him that money.

107

Eric saw that just the screen door to Theresa's house was closed. The big door stood open. He heard the TV going, then peered inside and saw the back of Theresa's head at the sofa.

He knocked softly on the wood frame of the door. "Hello? Blac home?" Eric called. He stepped away from the screen and waited till the door was answered.

When Theresa appeared, Eric was startled by how bad her face looked. She said, "It looks worse than it is." She managed a smile as she pushed open the door. "C'mon in."

Eric wanted to ask what happened, but something told him it had to do with the money Blac was trying to swindle from Senator Stevens, so he decided he didn't want to know.

"Blac is in the bedroom. First door on the left."

Eric walked down the hall and saw that

the bedroom door was halfway open. He stepped into the room without touching the door.

Blac looked to have been doing something with the back of his T-shirt then jumped at the sight of Eric.

"What the fuck you doing here?" Blac said, seeming to calm a little when he recognized it was his friend. He stepped toward Eric, his hand out, and gave Eric a soft shake and a half hug.

"What's goin' on with my brother and the senator?"

"Oh, so you know," Blac said with a sad smile. "I ain't no fag. I just —"

"I don't care about that. But you know you can't be doing this."

"I can't?" Blac said. "I'm assumin' my girl let you in. You see her face? I never told you this, but I owe some drug dealing fool 150K. I missed my first deadline and he did that to her. I miss the next, they gonna rape her, then go after my sister and nephew. That's why I can be doin' this and ain't nobody gonna stop me."

"I'm sorry about all that, but it don't have to go down like this, Blac. We can go to the police."

Blac laughed. "Look at your ass. Been living in the big house a little over a week and already forgot who you are. Nigga, how would that look? Me going to the police? That's not how I do things, and that ain't how you used to do 'em." Blac walked over toward the duffel and grabbed it off the dresser. "I think I'm good handlin' my business exactly the way I am."

"And what about us being boys?" Eric said. "Whatever happened to that?"

"Ain't shit happened to it. All the shit I did for you in the past, stepping up like I just did. If you in trouble, I would do anything for you, Eric. You know that," Blac said, staring directly in Eric's eyes. "I proved that. Now it's your turn. I need a hundred and fifty thousand dollars right now. You gonna give that to me? You gonna convince your brother to give it to me?"

"I don't know if he will, but I can try, Blac. I'll do that for you, 'cause I got your back, too."

"That's okay. Save that shit, Eric. I got it under control. Now I'm gonna need for you to leave, 'cause I have a very important meeting I have to make."

Eric stepped over toward the door, pushed it closed with his elbow, then said, "I'm sorry, Blac. But I can't let you do that."

108

Theresa sat in front of the TV, still smiling.

She pulled off the ring she always wore on her right hand and slid it onto the ring finger of her left. She held her hand out and imagined that ring to be the beautiful diamond engagement ring Blac would buy her.

She knew he wasn't perfect, but she also knew all he needed was a good woman to guide him, and she had always known she was that person. Blac needed someone or something to bring that to his attention, and that's why she pulled that stunt with Franklin.

Franklin had never been her boyfriend, but her best gay male friend, and it was actually he who thought up the scene they performed the other night.

"Wanna find out how much a man really loves you?" Franklin said. "Let another man come sniffin' around, talking about he wants to take you away. Your man will start openin' doors, buying you roses, and paintin' your toenails, girl," Franklin said, snapping three times.

Franklin was right, Theresa thought, the smile still on her face as she pulled the ring off and slid it back onto her right hand.

Theresa stood up from the sofa, feeling pain in her face. It was time for her to take another pain pill. But first she would see if Blac and his friend wanted something to eat.

As she made her way around the sofa, Theresa was jolted by what sounded like tussling in the bedroom.

She listened and asked herself, were they playing? Were they wrestling?

The noise became louder, the sound of a body being thrown against the wall, and she knew whatever was happening was not playing.

Theresa moved quickly toward the bedroom door, but was stopped by the deafening crack of a gunshot. She froze, then she heard the heavy thud of what she knew was a body hitting the floor.

"No!" she heard herself say. She ran to the bedroom door, threw it open to find Eric, the man that Blac had called his best friend, standing over Blac, a gun in his hand.

"What have you done!" Theresa cried, throwing herself down to Blac's body. Blood saturated the front of his shirt, still gushing from a large hole in his abdomen. She kneeled by his head, scooped it into her arms, and gently slapped his face. "Blac, wake up! Wake up, Blac! Please. Please!" she whined. But when she looked down into his open, blank, staring eyes, she saw that they were lifeless, and knew that he was gone.

She screamed, looked up at Eric. He froze, looking as though he had no idea of what he had done.

"I'm sorry," she heard him say, then watched as he turned and ran out the house.

109

Tyler and I were in the living room, when I heard Eric's car pull up outside.

A moment later, I heard the front door being unlocked, and I stood, filled with an immeasurable dread.

Again I prayed that everything had gone the way Eric planned, but seeing the look on his face when he walked in the room, I knew they had gone horribly wrong.

"What happened?" I asked, rushing over to my brother. Tyler was right behind me. He actually reached around me, grabbed Eric by the shoulder, and said, "What did he say? Is he still going through with it?"

Eric was in a daze. He stared past the both of us. "No. Because he's dead," Eric said, walking over to the sofa and sitting himself down. He reached behind him, pulled a huge gun from the waist of his jeans, and set it heavily on the coffee table.

Tyler looked at me as if at a loss for words,

then walked over to Eric, stood in front of him, and held out a hand. "I want to thank you."

Eric turned his stare on Tyler as if he had never seen him before. "For what?"

"For doing like I asked. For taking care of him."

Eric stared at Tyler a moment longer, then looked off and said, "Go away."

No, I thought to myself. Eric couldn't have done that. He wouldn't have.

Tyler walked back over to me, an expression of relief on his face. He took me by the elbow, led me out of what he figured was Eric's earshot. "He looks to be in a little shock," Tyler said. "But when he comes out of it, tell him how much I appreciate this. There's most likely going to be repercussions. Tell Eric I will support him in this." Tyler slapped me on the shoulder. "Whatever he needs."

"Hold it. Eric didn't do this. He didn't kill that man, and he definitely didn't do it because you needed it done."

Tyler smiled. "I know that. He did it because *you* needed it done. Like I said, let me know if there's anything I can do. Now I have to get home to the family."

Tyler left me standing there staring at my brother. Eric sat straight up on the sofa, his hands folded in his lap, staring, blank faced, out in front of him.

"Eric," I said, walking slowly over toward him. "You didn't do what Tyler thinks you did, did you?"

"No." He didn't look at me.

"Are you sure?"

His eyes landed on me this time. "I wouldn't let him blackmail you and the senator. I wouldn't let Blac leave to do it. He pulled a gun out of nowhere. It startled me. I reached for it. We fought and he was shot."

"Well, maybe he's not —"

"He's dead." Eric lowered his head and closed his eyes. "His girlfriend was there. I think she knows who I am. The police will be coming soon. They're going to take me back to prison. And Jess won't ever let me see my daughter again." A tear spilled down Eric's cheek. He looked at me again. "I'm sorry, Cobi. All you did to give me a better life. I guess having nothing and being in prison is the life I'm supposed to have."

"No!" I said, sitting down next to my brother. "This was an accident. Self-defense. I'm going to call Sissy so she can get down here. I'll represent you if the police come, and we're going to get through this."

Eric shook his head and smiled sadly. He

grabbed my hand. "It's not gonna work. I'm on parole. The minute they see I had contact with Blac, let alone killed him, I'll be going back in. There's nothing you can do."

I stood. "You're not going back to prison. You've been locked up your entire life. I'm not letting you go back. I'm not." I headed toward the stairs.

I raced up them, ran to Austen's door, and banged on it. When she opened the door, I said, "Eric is in the living room. He's in trouble. Please, go down there and be with him till I figure out what to do."

"Okay," Austen said, hurrying toward the stairs.

I headed to my father's study, pulled out my cell phone, and dialed Sissy's number.

When she picked up, I said, "Sissy, you need to get over here right now."

"What's going on? You sound terrible."

"It's an emergency. Something has gone wrong. I need you here now."

110

Whatever was happening, Sissy knew it was catastrophically bad. She had never heard Cobi sound so worried in her life.

She threw on the first pair of slacks and shirt she put her hands on, raced out to her car, and sped over. This would have something to do with that convict brother of his, Sissy knew. When she entered the gates that opened to the drive of the Winslow mansion, she knew things were much worse than she thought.

There were more than half a dozen police cars, parked out front, lights flashing, painting the house red and blue.

Sissy skidded her car to a slanted halt, threw the door open, and rushed out toward the house.

A young officer held out a hand, trying to stop her.

"Let me through!" Sissy demanded. "This is my house!"

She was allowed to pass.

As she stumbled toward the door, she had expected the worst. She didn't know exactly what that would be, but she knew it was coming.

Making her way inside, she ran down the hallway. In the living room, she saw that the situation was bad, but nothing that she hadn't expected.

There were four uniformed cops standing around, radios squawking on their hips, and three plainclothes detectives. On one side of the room, Sissy saw Eric in jeans and a bloody, torn T-shirt, his hands cuffed behind his back, a detective standing over him, looking as though he was about to read him his rights. On the other side of the room, she saw Austen and Cobi standing. They looked frightened. Sissy made her way to her brother to try to comfort him.

She gave Cobi a hug, but he did not hug her back. She understood, considering all that was going on.

"I told you it would end like this. I told you not to have anything to do with that criminal," she said, cutting a look across the room at Eric. "But he looks like he's getting what he deserves, so you can just relax and tell me what happened."

Cobi didn't speak, but Sissy heard her

name being called by Eric.

She looked around at him, then back to Cobi, and said, "Why is he calling me?"

Still Cobi didn't say a word.

The detective stood Eric up. Another detective took him by the other arm and started him toward the door.

"Sissy," Eric called again, more frantic this time. "It's me, Cobi."

Sissy turned to who she thought was Cobi, a bitter scowl on her face, then turned and rushed over to the man she now realized was her brother. The detectives stepped forward, as if to shield Cobi from her.

"I'm his sister. I need to speak to him. Please!"

The detectives stepped a few feet away, allowing Sissy to speak to her brother in private.

She looked at the man in front her, wearing those sagging jeans, that bloodstained shirt, and could not believe it was her brother. "Cobi?" she said, as though not sure.

"It's me, Sis."

"What the hell is going on? Why are you in cuffs? Why is he over there?"

"I told you," Cobi said. "Everything went wrong. I went to talk to Blac. He pulled a gun on me. We struggled, it went off, and I accidently killed him."

Sissy felt the room spin and thought she was about to faint but regained her balance. "No," she said. She looked back at Eric and Austen. Saw that they were hiding something, saw it in their faces that some deal had been struck, and what Cobi was telling her was nothing but a lie. "No!" Sissy said, trying to grab her brother by the arm. "You didn't do this. I know you didn't."

"Ma'am," one of the detectives said, rushing over, pulling Sissy off of Cobi. "He's already been read his rights. If you want to continue to speak to him, you'll have to come down to the station."

"Cobi," Sissy said, crying now. "I'm right behind you. Do you hear me? You have nothing to be afraid of. I'm right behind you."

To Sissy's surprise, Cobi looked calm. "I'm not afraid, Sis. Come down to the station, and we'll work it all out."

Sissy gave Cobi a quick, tight hug, then stormed back over to Eric and Austen.

"I don't know what the fuck is going on," Sissy said, stabbing a finger at Eric. "But I know this is all you. I know you had everything to do with it and somehow managed to convince my brother to take the blame.

I'm not going to let that happen. I'm going to find out what really went on, and I'm going to have your ass sent back to prison for killing that man. And it will be for life. Do you understand me?" Sissy screamed hysterically. "For life!"

111

Eric stood in the front doorway and watched as Sissy sped away.

Moments earlier, as the police walked Cobi out to their car, Sissy continued to curse and threaten Eric, looking over her shoulder as she hurried to her own car. She promised to devote her life to making sure Eric paid for what she was sure he had done, and by the look in her eyes, Eric knew he had reason to be concerned.

He thought back to half an hour earlier. He and Austen were downstairs on the sofa. She was near tears with worry, clutching his hands in hers. "Are you sure he's dead? Maybe he's just —"

"Austen, he's dead, okay?" Eric said. "I killed him, and I'm gonna have to 'fess up to this. His girlfriend saw me."

"Won't they put you back in prison?"

Eric believed her fearing the answer to that question was what caused the tears. He knew in the short time they saw each other, he had developed deep feelings for her, but he was surprised to know she might have felt the same for him.

"Yeah, they probably gonna send me back. There's no other way it can go."

"Maybe there is," Cobi said from the stairway. He descended the last couple of stairs and walked into the living room. "I've been thinking and I came up with something, but I'm going to have to tell you quickly. The police should be here soon. I called them and told them what happened."

Eric heard a gasp from Austen, felt her grip tighten on his hands. "Already? You called and told them? Couldn't you have —"

"Don't," Eric said. "He did the right thing."

"That's right," Cobi said. "It was self-defense. If that is truly what it was, then there is nothing to hide. We have to report what happened."

"But Eric won't stand a chance when —"

"Blac had photos that could do serious harm to my reputation, and he threatened to blackmail me with them," Cobi said, ignoring Austen, and then sitting down on the sofa opposite her and Eric. He focused very closely on the both of them. "When *I* went over there to confront him —"

"What?" Eric said, releasing Austen's hand and standing.

"I said, when *I* went over there to confront Blac about the blackmail, he pulled a gun on me. In my attempt to defend myself, we struggled, the gun went off, and he was killed."

Eric turned to look at Austen, then back to Cobi, not believing what he had just heard. "But Theresa saw me," he finally said.

"Theresa saw me." Cobi stood, an unsure smile on his face.

"You can't do this," Eric said.

"There is no other way."

"This can't work."

"Did you touch anything while you were there?"

"I don't . . ." Eric started, reviewing the steps he took leading up to the shooting. He knocked on the door, Theresa opened it for him. He didn't touch the door when he walked into the bedroom and pushed it closed with his elbow. He tussled with Blac, but once Eric put his hands on him, he didn't let go, until they were around Blac's hands as they held the gun. "Only thing I touched was the gun."

"And you brought that with you," Cobi said. "There are no fingerprints there. His girlfriend doesn't know it was you there and not me."

"But you'll go to jail for something I did," Eric said, worried.

"Will I? I'm Cobi Aiden Winslow," he said, extending his arms out to his sides. "State's attorney, member of the powerful Winslow family, and Blac is an ex-con who's been in and out of the system since he was a child."

"I'm sorry I didn't tell you," Eric said shamefully.

"No time for that now. I will tell the story and it will be believed. There will be an investigation, but considering what I just told you, would you convict me?"

Eric didn't think he would, but Cobi's experiences were on the right side of the courts. Having been a defendant, Eric knew unanticipated things could happen. "No, I wouldn't. But what if they do?"

Cobi forced a smile again. "Then I do the time, shoulder the weight. It's the least I can do, considering the hell you went through all your life for me."

"I ain't do it for you. I did it because I had to."

Cobi shook his head. "You did it for me. You just didn't know it till I found you. Now come on, the police will be here any moment."

"If you do this, everyone will know you're gay," Austen said, standing.

"I'm tired of hiding."

"And what about the arrangement?" Austen asked, taking Eric's hand.

Cobi glanced down at their interlaced fingers, then he looked back up at Austen. "We'll figure it out later. But now —" Cobi paused.

Eric heard police sirens in the distance.

"Take off your clothes," Cobi said to Eric.

"No. I can't let you do this. It's wrong."

"Do you hear the sirens?" Cobi said forcefully, pointing angrily toward the front room windows. "Do you want to go back to prison? Do you want never to see Austen again, never to see your daughter again? If not, shut up and take off your fucking clothes, Eric. Please!"

Eric continued to stare out of the front door of the mansion, wondering what would happen to him and what would happen to his brother.

Cobi told Eric he had nothing to worry about. He knew that Sissy would come after him. "This is my home, but till I come back, it's yours. Sissy can say what she wants, but she can do nothing to you," Cobi said, a reassuring hand on Eric's shoulder. "You and Austen are safe here."

They had switched clothes, and Eric stood staring at Cobi, as if looking into some weird 3-D mirror. Eric could've cried at that moment. He felt the tears ready to fall, but he pushed them back. No one, no one in the world had ever sacrificed a thing for him, but Cobi was risking his reputation, all that he'd worked for, even his freedom. Eric threw himself into his brother, wrapped his arms tightly around him, and said, "I love you for this, Cobi. And for everything you did." The tears started to fall, and he buried his face into his brother's shoulder.

Cobi hugged Eric back for a moment, then leaned away from him. "Everything is going to be all right, you hear me? All this will work out, and I'll come back home, and then we'll work on catching up on those thirty years we lost, okay?"

Eric wiped the tears from his face, smiled as best he could for his brother, then said, "Yeah, okay."

Eric felt an arm move around his waist, then felt Austen's body behind his. She kissed him on the back of his shoulder, lay her cheek there, then said, "Are we going to be all right?"

"I'm gonna do everything I can to make sure we are," Eric said, staring out into the distance before him. "And Cobi said we will be, so we will."

I thank God for blessing me with my son, and allowing him to be a part of my life for fifty-four years. He was a good child and I truly miss him. Written with his friend, RM Johnson, to whom I am forever grateful, this book was a departure for Lynn and also very dear to him. It could not have been published without divine guidance and the help of those around me who kept me encouraged, especially my granddaughter Roshaunda C. Rand.

I am very fortunate that Dermot Damian Givens, Esq., Karen Hises, Esq., and publishing attorney Lloyd Jassin were there to help me navigate the unfamiliar publishing waters, among other things. I am grateful to my lil' cousin Gail Burney for her important role in my life and the life of this book; and to Kerri Kolen, my son's editor, for her concern, patience and respect. To the bookstores, book clubs, students of E. Lynn Harris from U of A Fayetteville, up-and-coming authors he helped to get started and all the readers who have supported him from day one: Thank you and may God bless each and every one of you.

Discovered on his computer and cowritten with RM, this book, and also the other published and unpublished material my son left behind, are fragile gifts from God and reminders of his artful gifts, humor and courage.

— Etta Harris, 2011

ABOUT THE AUTHORS

E. Lynn Harris, a #1 national and *New York Times* bestselling author, wrote twelve acclaimed novels including *Basketball Jones, Just Too Good to Be True,* and *I Say a Little Prayer.* There are more than four million copies of his novels in print. He died in 2009 at the age of 54. Visit elynnharris.com.

RM Johnson is the author of nine novels, including bestsellers *The Harris Family* and *The Million Dollar Divorce.* He holds an MFA in Creative Writing from Chicago State University. He currently lives in Atlanta, Georgia.